Nothing but Drama

Antony Moussignac

iUniverse, Inc.
New York Bloomington

Nothing but Drama

Copyright © 2008 by Antony Moussignac

All rights reserved. No part of this book may be used or reproduced by any means, graphic, electronic, or mechanical, including photocopying, recording, taping or by any information storage retrieval system without the written permission of the publisher except in the case of brief quotations embodied in critical articles and reviews.

This is a work of fiction. All of the characters, names, incidents, organizations, and dialogue in this novel are either the products of the author's imagination or are used fictitiously.

iUniverse books may be ordered through booksellers or by contacting:

iUniverse
1663 Liberty Drive
Bloomington, IN 47403
www.iuniverse.com
1-800-Authors (1-800-288-4677)

Because of the dynamic nature of the Internet, any Web addresses or links contained in this book may have changed since publication and may no longer be valid. The views expressed in this work are solely those of the author and do not necessarily reflect the views of the publisher, and the publisher hereby disclaims any responsibility for them.

ISBN: 978-0-595-47738-8 (pbk)
ISBN: 978-1-4401-1119-8 (ebk)

Printed in the United States of America

iUniverse rev. date: 3/5/09

This book is dedicated to my mother Marie Carmelle Moussignac; the strongest woman I know. Thank you for believing in me and helping me to accomplish my dream of becoming a writer. You are my role model. I love you mom!

Their faces were close. She peeked towards her ex again and this time found him scowling. She bit her lip to keep from laughing out loud. It felt so good to have the power reverted back to her. Now it was time for the grand finale. She stared at Sean seductively.

"Kiss me," she ordered caressing his face.

He was taken aback. "Huh?"

"I said kiss me," she repeated huskily in his ear.

"Wait, are you serious?" he asked again cautiously.

"Yes!" she responded irritated this time. *What the hell was he waiting for?* She was afraid Michael would quickly lose interest in their scene.

"But—"

She didn't wait for him to finish. She held his face and kissed him hard. At first she didn't feel a response so she forced her tongue into his mouth. He finally relaxed as the kiss deepened. His tongue was soft yet strong. She sucked on it softly. She began to feel dizzy again. She felt her knees go weak but he held her tight. Her heart pounded loudly in her chest. She felt confused. She panicked. *What the hell am I doing??*

Prologue

▼

"Come on Monica, it's your thirtieth birthday. Not the end of the world."

Monica groaned loudly into her phone receiver. "Girl, don't remind me. I can't believe it. I'm thirty years old. I feel so old."

Her friend Tina sucked her teeth on the other line. "Girl will you stop whining? You'll feel better once we go out and have some fun. Let's go *clubbin'*. We need to celebrate."

Monica Stevens sat on her bed Indian style with a large bowl of chocolate chip ice cream on her lap. For the past hour, it was her best friend Tina Sommers who continued to console her over the phone. Monica felt she had reached the prime of her life and felt like crying her eyes out.

"Man, if you're acting like this at thirty, how are you going to take it at forty?" Tina asked again.

Monica sighed. "Tina you don't understand, my biological clock is ticking fast. I'm not a young woman anymore."

"Girl please, you're thirty not fifty. You're taking this way out of proportion. All you need is—"

"A man," Monica interrupted sarcastically as she placed another spoonful of ice cream into her mouth.

Tina laughed. "I wasn't going to say that."

Monica didn't laugh with her. "But it's true, right?" she asked after she swallowed quickly. "Look, do you remember that list I had in college?"

Tina sighed heavily over the phone. "*Aghhh*, how many times are you going to bring this up?"

"Do you remember?" Monica repeated ignoring her question.

"Yeah, the one that said that—"

"*I was going to be engaged by twenty-four, married at twenty-six and have at least one child before thirty,*" they stated in unison.

Tina chuckled. "Okay so you're a few years late. What's the big deal?"

"A few," Monica exclaimed. "How about eight years late. At the rate I'm going I might be forty by the time I have my first child."

"Again, you're blowing this way out of proportion," Tina argued. "You know you can't dictate your life on paper. Sometimes things just don't turn out the way you want it. Look at me. I'm not married."

"No, but at least you have Joshua," Monica pointed out.

Joshua is Tina's six-year old son. "Yeah but his father and I aren't together. Honey, every woman wants the whole package, not just you. Look, we were in college when you made that plan and didn't take into account the things that could go wrong."

Monica and Tina met freshman year in college. They ended up as roommates when their assigned roommates decided to attend other colleges. They were paired up by their resident advisor after orientation and remained best friends ever since. It was during their junior year at a basketball game when Tina first laid eyes on Joshua's father, Bryan Henderson. He was tall, with caramel skin and mysterious dark brown eyes. She was mesmerized by his athletic build. She followed his every move as he ran up and down the court.

"*Hey, who's that guy with the ball?*" Tina asked tugging at Monica's sleeve.

Monica giggled. "*Girl, that's Bryan Henderson, star player of the team. Haven't you been reading about him in the school newspaper? He's one of the top twenty picks for the NBA.*"

Tina shook her head. "*Now you know I'm not into sports but him,*" she paused as she watched him throw the ball directly into the net. "*I'm definitely into.*"

They laughed in unison. Suddenly everyone in the gym began to shout Bryan's name. He had just stolen the ball again from the other team. He began dribbling quickly towards the basket on the opposite side. Tina braced herself as she watched him jump up and dunk the ball into the basket in one swift move. The crowd went wild. Both she and Monica jumped from their seats and cheered. Right then was when she first fell in love.

Soon after, she began to drag Monica to every one of his games. She became jealous of the many girls, aka gold-diggers, that flocked behind him after each game. She fantasized about him daily and longed to be with him in more ways than one. Her fantasy finally became reality when he approached her after a game. They talked for a while, then to her surprise, he asked her out. She happily accepted while receiving dirty looks from the gold-diggers who impatiently waited for him by the locker room. After a couple of months of dating, the two became inseparable.

On their six month anniversary he told her he loved her. Towards the end of their senior year, he began receiving several offers from professional teams. He was ecstatic. She had never seen him happier, but unfortunately his dreams were quickly shattered a couple of months before graduation.

"What do you mean you're pregnant?" he asked unbelievably. He began to pace up and down his dorm room floor while she sat quietly on his bed. "Are you sure it was positive?"

Tina nodded silently. Her eyes were puffy from hours of crying. "I took the test three times. And I missed my period last month. I thought it was stress from finals but I guess I was wrong."

He groaned. "I can't deal with this right now. I have a state championship game coming up. I thought you said you were on the pill?"

She frowned at him. "Bryan, the pill is not one hundred percent effective. Look, do you think I want to deal with this right now? I'm not ready for any of this either but we have to figure out what we need to do."

He finally stopped pacing and sat down next to her. He took her hand. "Tina we're both too young to have a baby. We have only one choice."

She raised an eyebrow. "One choice," she repeated. "What choice is that?"

"Look I heard there's a clinic a couple of miles from—"

She wrenched her hand away. She stood up and glared at him. "Wait, you want me to have an abortion? Bryan you know I don't believe in that." She placed her hand on her stomach. "How can you even think of killing our baby?"

"Tina—"

"No," she interjected. "Why can't we just get an apartment together after graduation? You can find a job and—"

He rolled his eyes in frustration. "And what, get on welfare?" he interrupted. "Hell no, I refuse to have our lives messed up like that."

Tears began to well up in her eyes again. Part of her hoped he would be a little happy about the baby. "Look this baby is a part of you and me. How can you believe our lives will be messed up? Yes things will change, but we can make this work." She sat back down on his bed. She took one of his hands and placed it on her stomach. "A tiny life is growing inside me and it's ours."

They were quiet for a moment. He finally shook his head. "I don't know about this Tina," he told her still skeptical

She pulled him to look at her. "Bryan, do you love me?"

He didn't look towards her. He shook his head instead. "That has nothing to do—"he began.

She placed both her hands on his face. She forced him to look at her. "Do you love me?" she repeated more firmly.

He closed his eyes briefly. "Yes. Yes, I love you but what if things don't work out the way we want?"

She stroked his face. "I'd feel better knowing we at least tried. Baby, we'll take it one day at a time." She kissed him lightly on the lips and gave him a hug. He hugged her tightly in return. That night as they lay in each other's arms, Bryan's mind was still flooded with doubts.

"Aren't you scared?" he asked her.

She remained quiet for a moment. "Terrified," she admitted finally. "But having you by my side makes everything better." She snuggled closer to him and quickly fell asleep. He lay awake as she slept. His views were definitely different from hers. He had other plans for his future and having a baby was not a part of them. He kissed her softly on the forehead then tried to focus on sleeping. He just prayed that things would turn out for the best.

After graduation they ended up getting an apartment together as planned. He turned down all offers from professional basketball teams and began to look for a full-time job. Things slowly began to change when he could not find a job. Many rejections were due to lack of experience.

They began to argue constantly throughout her pregnancy and within two months got evicted from their apartment. They each ended up moving back home with their parents. Tina became very depressed. She lost weight and was put on bed rest for the remainder of her pregnancy. As time went on she began to see less of Bryan. He didn't return her calls and missed most of her doctor's appointments.

When Tina went into labor, it was Monica who was by her side in the delivery room. Joshua Steven Henderson was finally born after sixteen hours of labor. They both cried as his tiny naked body was placed into Tina's arms. Tina began sobbing afterwards. Monica felt helpless. The next morning she called Bryan and threatened his life if he didn't come by to see the baby. A couple hours later he showed up at the hospital with no apology. He reiterated that he was not ready for the responsibility of taking care of a child and thought it was best they went their separate ways.

Afterwards, Tina had a nervous breakdown. She wouldn't eat and had many sleepless nights. At times she didn't even want to touch Joshua because he reminded her so much of his father. Her parents fought her to seek counseling. She reluctantly agreed. She even found a support group for single moms and went once a week. She began to feel better when she saw other women in her situation.

"Trust me Monica," she continued. "I love Joshua with all my heart. I would do anything for him but if I could go back, I would do some things differently. I put up with a lot of shit from that man. I thank God everyday for giving me the strength to make it through," she paused. "Wait hold up, when did this conversation turn on me?"

Monica laughed. "I guess you have some things on your mind too?"

Tina snorted. "Yeah, like what I ever saw in that man in the first place."

"Admit it Tina, you still love him."

"We are not talking about me right now," Tina reminded her. "Anyway, all I care about is making sure my child support check is in the mail *on time*."

A couple of years after Joshua's birth, Bryan returned to school and obtained his graduate degree in Finance. He became a successful stockbroker. It was then Monica convinced Tina to put him on child support. Out of anger, he demanded a paternity test. When the results came back positive, his anger quickly diminished. He finally realized he had to be a father to his son. Now along with making child support payments, he picks up Joshua every other weekend for some father/son time. Tina didn't like it at first, but after seeing them together she knew she couldn't bear to tear them apart. Not only did Joshua need his mother, he needed his father as well.

"You're so mean," Monica giggled. "Well, at least he's come to his senses now."

Tina sucked her teeth again. "*Anyway*, back to the subject at hand. Honey, you have a great life. You're smart, beautiful, independent, and have a wonderful job. What more can you ask for?"

Monica was quiet for a moment. Her friend was right. What more could she ask for? As an Accountant Executive at Meyer and Jacob Associates, she made a pretty decent salary. She owned a beautiful town home and just purchased a brand new car. She had everything she needed to be happy yet something was still missing...*a man*.

"Will you stop feeling sorry for yourself?" Tina snapped, interrupting her thoughts. "This conversation is starting to make me feel old."

Monica giggled. "Wait, you are older than me, aren't you?"

Tina laughed. "Only by a couple of months, if you want to get technical, but forget all that; right now I want you to go to your closet and put on that cute black dress you brought from Shauna's job last week. We can go to the Moonlight. I'll call Shauna and tell her to get ready."

Shauna Knowles completed the trio of best friends. They met at a night club several years ago. Shauna was passing through the dancing crowd after she had just brought herself a drink when some random guy brushed passed her and squeezed her ass. She yelled at the guy then threw her drink in his face. Some of her drink ended up on Monica and Tina while they were dancing. She quickly apologized but they weren't angry. They were amazed to see a woman at her height be able to stick up for herself. Shauna's five foot four frame was nothing compared to the guy who was over six feet tall, but she stood her ground. After that night, the three became best of friends.

Monica sat up quickly. "The Moonlight, hold on that's Michael's spot."

Michael Edison was Monica's ex-boyfriend. Dark and sexy, was the only way to describe him; from his broad shoulders to his rippled chest. She thought he was absolutely FOINE! They were together for a year. The sex was phenomenal. He satisfied her sexually in so many ways. He was a freak just like her. From handcuffs, blindfolds, whips; they had fun learning each other's desires. She fell in love quick and hard.

Two weeks after their one year anniversary, he gave her the *'I just need some time to find myself'* speech, aka *'I want to sleep with skanks one last time before I really commit to you'* speech. She was crushed, yet she didn't give him the satisfaction of seeing her break into pieces. Instead she told him she felt the same way.

"And," Tina scoffed. "Michael doesn't own the club."

"Tina, it's only been a month since our breakup," she stated miserably. "I don't feel like seeing him yet. What if he's out there with some *hoochie*?"

"So what, I bet you she won't look as good as you do?"

"That's not the point," Monica disagreed.

"No, the point is, it's your birthday and I'm not going to let you spend it alone because you don't want to bump into your ex. Do you know how many fine men will be out there tonight?"

Monica thought for a moment. She placed her bowl of ice cream on her nightstand next to a framed picture of her and Michael. She picked it up and stared at it for a moment. After their breakup, she packed all his belongings into a large box then threw the box in the back of her closet. For some reason she couldn't let go of their picture though. "I don't know. I'm really not up to it tonight," she finally replied.

"*Girl*, don't make me hurt you," Tina finally threatened with a little edge in her voice.

Monica sighed then placed the frame back on her nightstand. She slid off her bed. The truth was she really didn't want to stay home. Sulking with a pint of ice cream was definitely not something she was looking forward to do on her birthday. "All right, all right, I'm already heading for my closet."

Tina squealed in delight from the other end. "Good, now while you're in there, bring me that black halter top I like."

Monica snorted. "You might as well keep it. You wear it more than me."

Tina ignored her comment. She was too busy deciding which black pumps she was going to wear with her friend's top. "Just hurry up and get dressed. You know tonight is ladies night. Ladies free before midnight."

"I know the routine. I'll be there in an hour."

Chapter One

▼

The Moonlight Lounge was already in action as they pulled into the parking garage located across the street. Loud sounds of hip hop music filled the air. The club had just opened up in the outskirts of L.A. It was three stories high and considered the hottest new club in the city. Many stars were spotted lounging in the V.I.P. area, yet only once they caught a glimpse of LL Cool J's sexy lips and Michael Jordan's chocolate smooth head. By the time they got to the front of the line, the end of the line was around the corner.

As they walked into the club, Monica could feel eyes on them. She smiled to herself. She had to admit, she looked damn good in her short strapless dress. Her shoulder length hair was pulled to the side with a shiny silver barrette. Already she was starting to feel much better. *Maybe this night won't be so bad after all*, she thought. They spotted empty bar stools as they made their way towards a bar near the back of the club. They faced the dance floor once they sat down and bobbed their heads when the DJ switched the music to the latest tune of Mary J Blige.

"Can I get you ladies anything?" the bartender yelled loudly behind them.

Monica didn't turn around. She immediately began to scan the room for Michael. "Hey Monica, what do you want to drink?" asked Shauna.

"Long Island Ice Tea," she answered, "Easy on the ice please."

"Hey, make sure you make it real good too," she heard Tina say. "Today is my girl's thirtieth birthday."

Monica frowned at her friend. "Damn Tina, you don't have to tell the whole world."

Tina grinned. "Well, I could ask the DJ to make an announcement."

Monica widened her eyes in alarm. "Girl, if you do, I'll never speak to you again," she threatened with a smile. "And if—"

"Happy Birthday," a deep male voice interrupted.

Monica's heart beat wildly in her chest. His sexy voice sent shivers down her spine. She could recognize it in a crowded room. She turned to find her ex, looking fine as ever in a black dress shirt which outlined his broad shoulders perfectly. His face was clean shaven without an imperfection in sight. *Damn why he has to look so delicious,* she thought miserably. She watched in slow motion as he licked his lips then sized her up and down. Tina quickly bumped shoulders with Monica to get her out of his trance.

He glanced at her friends. "Hello ladies," he smiled then turned his attention back to Monica. "So beautiful, how you've been?"

She refused to look at him again. "I've been just fine. And you?"

Through her peripheral vision, she could see his eyes trail down towards her chest. "Good, good. Nice dress."

She stood up and twirled around purposely, "This old thing?"

"Well, you certainly can make something old look real good," he replied still watching her hungrily.

She didn't respond to his compliment. She wanted to remind him of what he was missing. She sat back down, picked up her drink and took a long slow sip. She sat up straight and made sure her breasts stood up the way they were supposed to.

He came close. "So, can I give you a birthday dance?" he murmured into her ear.

She shook her head then placed her drink on the counter. "Maybe later, right now I'd rather dance with my *gurls*." She quickly grabbed her friends' hands and pulled them onto the dance floor. They all cackled as they began to dance to the music.

"You're so bad," Shauna laughed giving her friend a high five.

Monica laughed in return. "He must not know who he's *messin'* with. Can you believe him? Chile please, if he wants to play games, so can I."

"That's my girl," said Tina. "I was getting worried back there for a second."

Monica winked at her friend. "Don't worry. I got this." After dancing to at least two songs, Monica began to grow impatient. "Hey is he still over there?" she asked Shauna as her friend danced in front of her.

Shauna hastily looked behind her friend. "Oh hell yeah, and watching you hard too. Girl he's looking like a lost puppy."

Monica smiled in satisfaction. Suddenly the music changed and the DJ announced he was changing to a slow jam. "*Aw shit,*" she groaned as soft sounds of music filled the air.

"What?" her friends asked in unison.

"This is our jam. Look, you can't leave me if he comes over to—"

"Are you ready for that dance?" Michael's voice interrupted behind her. His breath was warm on her neck. It sent chills throughout her body. "He's playing our song."

She looked towards her friends for help but two fine men had already approached them for a dance. "Monica, we'll check you later," yelled Tina as they were led away.

Monica gave them a look of desperation but it didn't work. *Shit!* She finally turned towards her ex and glared at him. "This song is no longer ours," she stated firmly.

He held out his hands. "Come on, just one dance for old time sake?" he bargained with a grin.

She rolled her eyes then walked into his arms cautiously. She placed his hands on her back then raised an eyebrow. "Don't get too comfortable," she warned.

"Damn girl, can't I get a dance without restrictions?"

"You lost that privilege."

He pulled her close. "Still hot-headed I see."

She pulled back. "And you still think you're all that."

He chuckled. "Well if you don't think I'm all that, why are you dancing with me?"

She shrugged nonchalant. "I feel sorry for you," she stated bluntly. "I mean you practically begged me to dance with you."

"Oh, so that's how it is?"

"Yep, that's how it is."

For a moment their eyes locked. As they began to dance, his hands gradually roamed towards her backside. "You know you look real sexy when you're angry," he told her huskily.

She broke the gaze and put his hands back where they belonged. "Sexy huh, well that's not how you felt a month ago. You said you needed your space remember? What happened, Michael? Tired of being a *playa*?"

He nodded. "Okay, my bad. Can a brotha be wrong sometimes?"

She sucked her teeth. "Whatever."

His nose brushed up against her neck. "You smell so good," he whispered a moment later. His mouth tugged at her earlobe. He knew her neck and ears were her most sensitive spots. She closed her eyes. She tried to pull away again but he held her tight.

"Um hmm, it's the perfume you brought me for—" she began.

"Valentine's Day," he finished.

"Wow, I'm surprised you remembered," she mumbled groggily unable to move from their position.

"Of course I remember," he answered. "I also remember a lot of other things. Like the way you like your coffee in the morning, the way you like for me to hold you in my arms after a whole night of love making and the way you like to make love again in the shower the next morning." He now began to suck her on her neck softly. She stood frozen enjoying the way he was making her feel. "I miss you baby."

Her mouth went dry as it opened slightly. "M-Michael this is what you w-wanted."

"I know and it was the biggest mistake of my life," he admitted. "I want you back baby. No I need you... tonight."

She felt him grow hard against her. His mouth moved away from her neck to her lips. He kissed her softly. She found herself kissing him back. Her anger melted away quickly. "Oh baby, I miss you too," she finally confessed as they pulled away. "Maybe we can—"

"*Michael,* I've been looking for you everywhere," a whiny girl's voice interrupted her.

Monica turned to find a pretty young girl in almost the exact same black dress she was wearing. Only the girl's chest was bigger than hers. *Definitely a boob job,* she thought disgustedly. "I have our drinks we just need to find a table," the girl informed him with a hint of jealously in her voice. She sized Monica up and down. "Is this *your cousin* you've been looking for?"

Monica crossed her arms against her chest. She shot her ex a poison dart look. The look on his face was priceless. "Monica—" he began.

She didn't wait for him to finish. She turned towards the girl. "I'm Monica, his ex-girlfriend *not* his cousin. Um, can I see one of those for a moment?" Without waiting for an answer, she took one of the drinks from the girl's hand. She turned swiftly and threw the drink in Michael's face.

She walked away abruptly. *What an asshole,* she thought disgustedly as she headed back towards the bar. She couldn't believe she fell for his weak lines again. She needed a drink fast. Not many people were lounging around the bar. They were on the dance floor where she was supposed to be. She sat at an empty stool and faced the floor. For some reason her eyes seemed to search for Michael again. "A shot of tequila please," she ordered behind her.

"Coming up," a male voice stated loudly. "There you go," he announced a moment later.

She gulped it quickly. It burned while going down but she began to feel better. When she turned back around, she spotted her ex immediately. He was now dancing with her clone. She was on him like glue. Monica's blood began to boil. She took some money out her purse and slammed some bills onto the bar table. Angrily ordered a second shot. She coughed as she swallowed it down quickly. "Another one please," she demanded hoarsely.

"Long night?" the bartender asked.

She turned with a frown. "Excuse me?"

He placed another drink in front of her. "I said it looks like you're having a bad night."

She gulped her last drink then sized him up. He was a very good-looking man. His light-brown eyes that stared back at her were hypnotic. The bottom half of his face revealed a perfectly trimmed goatee. His lips were definitely kissable. He smiled as she admired him. *Hmmm...and a nice smile too*, she thought approvingly. "And what makes you think I'm having a bad night?" she asked defensively.

"Well, you look really pissed and you're not dancing. Isn't it your birthday?"

She wondered how he knew it was her birthday, but then remembered how Tina had announced it earlier on. She rolled her eyes and twirled her finger in the air. "Whoop dee do."

"Let me guess, your friends dragged you out here to celebrate?"

She nodded. "I just wanted to stay home, eat my favorite ice cream and maybe watch my favorite movie, but nooo."

"I'm sure they thought you didn't want to be alone."

She raised an eyebrow. "Who said I was going to be alone?"

He held his hands up in front of him. "My bad, I must be crazy to think that a fine sista like you would be single."

She felt her cheeks heat up. *Damn it's hot in here*, she thought. "Can I have a cup of ice please?" He placed a cup full of ice in front of her. She placed a piece of ice in her mouth. She took another careful look at him and realized that he also looked really young. "How old are you?"

"Why do you ask?"

"Well my friend told you my age, so it's only fair I know yours."

He began to wipe off the counter. "Good point. I'm twenty-two," he answered finally.

She almost choked on her ice. "Are you okay?" he asked concerned.

"D-did you s-say twenty-two?" she asked when she was finally able to catch her breath.

"Yeah, is that a problem?"

She suddenly felt uncomfortable. "Um, you're young."

He winked at her. "And legal if that makes it any better."

She broke into a smile, "And got jokes too."

He chuckled. "You know I have other fine qualities I wouldn't mind showing you either."

She laughed. "Didn't your mama ever tell you to respect your elders?"

He leaned over the counter and took her hand. He pulled her to stand. "First of all, you're definitely not an elder she was referring to, second she always taught me to treat a woman with respect, which I happen do all the time and third…" he paused then gazed into her eyes.

She couldn't do anything but stare back into his bedroom eyes. They were the type that could get a woman naked in minutes. She was able to break his gaze when someone bumped her from behind. She pulled her hand away and sat back down. "And third?" she prompted anxiously waiting for his answer.

He grinned sexily. "I can't remember. You're beauty has me intrigued."

Damn! The brotha had it together. Speaking proper and shit. Monica shook her head and laughed. She liked his flirting but her thoughts also kept wandering towards Michael as well. "Hey, can I get two shots of whiskey?" someone asked interrupting their conversation. While he got the drinks, she faced the floor again. Michael was now in a corner with his date. They were making out heavily. She wanted to scream. She was supposed to make him jealous tonight not the other way around.

"Hey," said the bartender behind her.

She turned around and decided then to give him her full attention. "*Hay* is for horses," she informed him.

He gave her a sly grin. "You're right. I apologize. So does a name come with that beautiful face of yours?"

She was getting used to his comments. "Monica," she answered starting to feel like a school girl with a crush. She liked the way he was making her feel, like she was the only woman in the room.

"Nice to meet you, Monica," he nodded then raised an eyebrow. "Wait that's not a fake name is it?"

She decided it was her turn to flirt. She leaned in close making sure her breasts stood out. "Trust me, nothing about me is fake."

His eyes traveled over them. "I can see that."

Customers had interrupted them again. He began to mix drinks for them quickly. "So what's your name?" she asked after he handled the last customer.

"Sean."

She held out her hand, "Nice to meet you, Sean."

He took her hand and kissed it on top. "The pleasure is all mine," he winked. She was surprised by his gesture. The mere act showed he was very romantic. She began to feel hot again. She couldn't tell if it was the alcohol or him turning her on. Whatever it was, it was helping her forget about Michael real quick. Suddenly, Sean took off his apron. He told the bartender on the other side he was taking a break. He came around and stood in front of her. "Hey, would you like to dance with a young, funny brother?" he asked her.

She hesitated, but then remembered Michael having his fun. She smiled. "Don't mind if I do."

She stood up then unsteadily sat back down again. She felt dizzy. "Hey, you okay?" he asked trying to hold her steady. His strong arms felt good around her.

"Yeah, I'm okay," she laughed embarrassed. "I keep forgetting I don't do well with alcohol."

"You want to sit for a minute?"

She shook her head. "No, no. I'm fine. Let's do this."

She took his hand and led him towards the floor. Sounds of reggae music filled the air. On the dance floor she immediately began to rotate her hips against him. She smiled as his torso matched her every move. Her body responded to him instantly. At that moment it seemed like nothing else mattered. "You've got some nice moves," she commented.

"You're not so bad yourself," he murmured with a smile. *He's twenty-two!* Her mind continued to remind her body but it wasn't listening. When she had a chance, she searched the floor for Michael. She found him watching them hard from across the room. Instantly she placed her arms around Sean's neck and began to concentrate on their dancing again. Their faces were close. She peeked towards her ex again and this time found him scowling. She bit her lip to keep from laughing out loud. It felt so good to have the power reverted back to her. Now it was time for the grand finale. She stared at Sean seductively. "Kiss me," she ordered caressing his face.

He was taken aback. "Huh?"

"I said kiss me," she repeated huskily in his ear.

"Wait, are you serious?" he asked again cautiously.

"Yes!" she responded irritated this time. *What the hell was he waiting for?* She was afraid Michael would quickly lose interest in their scene.

"But—"

She didn't wait for him to finish. She held his face and kissed him hard. At first she didn't feel a response so she forced her tongue into his mouth. He finally relaxed as the kiss deepened. His tongue was soft yet strong. She sucked on it softly. She began to feel dizzy again. She felt her knees go weak but he held her tight. She ran her hands through his soft hair. Her heart pounded loudly in her chest. She felt confused. She panicked. *What the hell am I doing??* Before she could end the kiss, someone grabbed her arm and began to drag her away. It was Tina.

"Girl, what the hell are you doing?" she asked appalled.

"Monica, wait," Sean yelled behind them.

She couldn't turn to answer him. She held her head which was pounding furiously. "What? We were just dancing," Monica winced.

"And kissing," Shauna supplied coming up next to them. "I know he's fine but damn girl."

Monica closed her eyes for a moment. She began to feel lightheaded. "I-I was... j-just," she stuttered. "Aw damn, is it just me or is the room moving?" she groaned.

"Monica, you're drunk," Shauna confirmed. "Now you know you can't hold your liquor. You get tipsy off wine coolers. I knew we shouldn't have left you alone."

They headed towards the front entrance. "I'm not drunk," Monica argued. "Maybe a little bit tipsy, wait...we're not leaving are we? I was just starting to have fun."

"Yes, we are," Tina answered. "If we don't get your ass out of here, you will continue to make a fool out of yourself."

Monica pouted. "But it's my birthday. You're such a party pooper," she giggled uncontrollably. Before they walked out the door she took a last glimpse from behind. From afar she could see Michael shaking his head angrily. Sean on the other hand looked confused and disappointed. She felt bad that she used him to get Michael jealous but didn't have any more time to think about it. As soon as her friends helped her into her car, she threw up all over the front passenger seat.

Chapter Two

Tina looked at her watch when she heard her doorbell ring. "I'll get it," yelled Joshua jumping up from the kitchen table.

She pulled him back down. "No, you sit here and finish your breakfast. I'll get the door."

"Aw okay," he sulked.

Tina opened her door to find her son's father on her doorstep. "You're late," she snapped.

Bryan glared at her. "Well good morning to you too."

"You were supposed to be here at ten."

"I'm only five minutes late. Where's Joshua?"

She moved back to let him in. "He's finishing up his breakfast."

Moments later, Joshua came running into the living room with a huge smile on his face. He ran straight into his father's arms, "Hey daddy."

Bryan picked up his son and gave him a big bear hug. When they pulled apart they did their secret handshake. Tina smiled as she watched them together. She was thankful Bryan had come to his senses about being a part of Joshua's life. There were some things a mother could not teach her son. Having a male figure in his life was a good thing.

"Hey little man, are you ready to go to the amusement park?" he asked.

Joshua nodded enthusiastically. "Yep, I can't wait to ride that monster roller coaster."

Tina gave Bryan a nervous look. "Don't worry he'll be fine," he assured her.

He grabbed his son's jacket from the coat rack. "Mommy, aren't you coming with us?" Joshua asked as his father placed his jacket on him.

She looked towards Bryan who avoided eye contact. It would have been nice if they could go as a family, but that wish couldn't come true. He was seeing someone so she was totally out of the picture. She knelt down in front of her son. "Not today honey."

"Why not?"

She held his face gently. "Well, today you're going to spend time with daddy. You two can ride roller coasters all day and tomorrow I promise we can spend the whole day doing anything you want."

His face brightened, "Anything?"

She rubbed noses with him. "Anything, you want. Now, you go have a great time today, okay?" She gave him a hug. "I love you, baby."

"I love you too."

She let him go then walked them to the front door. Bryan paused for a moment and told his son to wait by the car. "Tina, thank you for what you did back there," he told her as their son walked away.

She crossed her arms against her chest. "I didn't do it for you."

He rolled his eyes. "I know, but thanks anyway."

She shook off his gratitude with a shrug. "By the way, I haven't received a child support check this month," she informed him changing the subject.

He frowned. "Is that all you think about?"

"Look, I'm just making sure you're taking care of my son."

"He's *our* son and I am taking care of him. The check is in the mail."

She smirked. "And let me guess, it probably got lost right?"

"What? You don't believe me? Look, I could go get my checkbook out the car and write you a check right now if you want. No, as a matter of fact…" He paused to take his wallet out of his pocket. "How about I give you cash?"

She glared at him. "I'm not desperate for money. I just want to make sure you remember we have an agreement. "

He rolled his eyes and put his wallet back in his back pocket. "Damn woman, can't we be civilized for once? You put me through this every time I pick up Joshua. Aren't you tired?"

"I will never get tired of making sure my son is taken care of. And why shouldn't I trip? You're the one who left me alone to take care of him the first couple of years of his life. Where were you when he took his first step? Where were you when he got his first tooth? Where were—"

He interrupted her with a groan. "Here we go again. Tina why won't you just let it go? That same crying game is running dry."

"The truth hurts doesn't it?"

"Look, how many times do you want me to apologize? It seems like that's all I do when I'm around you. I'm in Josh's life now and I plan to be there from now on."

She shrugged. "That's fine and dandy but what about your girlfriend Sheila? How does she feel about that?"

"Her name is Sharon."

She suppressed a snicker, "Oops, my bad."

He ignored her. "Look, she knows my son means the world to me. He comes first in everything I do."

"Well, I've heard different from Josh. He thinks she doesn't like him."

"What? Where did you—"

"Daddy, come on," Joshua whined from outside.

He turned to look at his son. "I'm coming little man. Just wait by the car."

He turned back to Tina. "We'll finish this conversation later. I'm going to find out what's really going on. I hope you're not doing this to get between Sharon and me."

She gave him a disgusted look. "Oh, please, get over yourself. I have better things to do with my time."

He shook his head and stormed out the door. She watched them get into the car and waved as her son waved back at her frantically. She watched them drive off until they were out of sight. She frowned as she closed the front door. *How dare he think she would do something to sabotage his relationship*, she thought angrily. Even though she never really stopped loving him, she always made sure to keep her true feelings hidden. She was really worried about her son though. The conversation they had the other night at bedtime was very disturbing.

"Alright Joshua, say your prayers," she murmured softly tucking him into bed.

She watched him close his eyes and entwine his hands together. "Thank you God for everything you have given me, God bless mommy and daddy, Auntie Monica and Auntie Shauna, grandma and grandpa, and…oh yeah, my fish Goldie. Amen."

Tina smiled then gathered his covers over him. She planted a kiss on his forehead. "Now get some sleep."

"Mommy is daddy ever coming to live with us?" he asked suddenly.

She stroked his cheek. "Honey, I already told you the answer to that and I thought you said you understood."

"I do, but when I'm with daddy, I miss you and when I'm with you, I miss daddy. If we we're all together, I wouldn't miss anyone at all."

Tina felt like crying. He was hurting and she couldn't do anything about it.

"Honey, I can't promise you that your daddy and I will be together again but I want you to remember that we both love you very much."

He smiled. "I know that," he paused. "Can I ask you another question?"

"Of course, baby, but that'll be it for tonight."

"Okay... um, what does the word marry mean?"

She raised an eyebrow. "Where did you hear that word from?"

"I heard daddy say it to Sharon."

She paused then pulled him onto her lap. She couldn't believe how Bryan had put her in such a predicament. And how dare he even talk about marriage to Sharon? They've only been together for six months. "Joshua, when you want to marry someone, it means that you love that person very much and want to be with that person forever."

His eyes grew large. "Wow, that's a long time."

She laughed. "Yes it is."

"So how come daddy didn't ask you to marry him."

She shook her head. "I don't know honey," she answered honestly.

"I really wish he would. I don't want daddy to be with Sharon. I don't think she likes me."

She raised an eyebrow. "Why do you say that?"

He shrugged. "I don't know? She looks at me funny. And one time she yelled at me to pick up my toys."

Oh no she didn't! "It's okay honey, maybe she was having a bad day. The next time she makes a funny face at you, you make one like this." She made a funny face and he giggled. "Okay, now it's really time for bed." She tucked him into bed again and smiled. "Sleep tight."

He grinned. "Don't let the bed bugs bite."

Suddenly the phone rang interrupting her from her thoughts. She ran into the kitchen to answer it. "Hello?"

"Is Bryan there?" a woman's voice asked rudely.

"Who's speaking?"

"Sharon, *his gurlfriend*," she drawled making sure the last two words were stressed.

Tina ignored her so-called title. "First of all, this isn't Bryan's house so he's not here. Second, it would be nice for you to learn some manners when calling someone's home."

Sharon sucked her teeth loudly. "*Whateva*, look the only reason why I'm calling your house is because he's not answering his cell."

Tina snorted. "Hmph and I wonder why. He probably realized you have no class."

"Wait, hold up honey, you don't know me. You're just mad because you ain't got a man. You think I don't know you still want him? He told me all the shit you put him through since he and I got together. And you talk about me having no class? Chile please, he's with me because he now knows what it means to be with a real woman. All you are to him is baby momma drama."

Tina wanted to explode but maintained control. "Now you listen to me you ghetto ass *heifer*," she seethed. "Don't you *ever* call my house and disrespect me. You're just jealous Bryan pays more attention to me than you. FYI, if I wanted him, I definitely wouldn't have a problem getting him back. And if you ever yell at my son again, you will have to deal with my ass personally."

She laughed loudly in Tina's ear. "I ain't scared of you, bitch! What goes on with your son at his daddy's house is my business so get over it. Oh yeah, if *my man* calls, tell him I'll be waiting for him in *his* bed tonight."

Before Tina could say another word, she was cut off by a dial tone.

Monica groaned as she awoke to the sound of ringing in her ears. Her eyes fluttered open. She looked around then frowned. She was in her bed but couldn't remember when and how she got there. The ringing continued until she finally realized that it was her phone. She sat up quickly and groaned. Her head was pounding. She picked up her receiver unsteadily. "H-Hello?" she mumbled.

"About time, I thought were never going to answer your phone."

"Tina?" she asked groggily.

"Yeah, wake up. It's almost six o'clock."

Monica held her head. She had a piercing headache. "In the morning?" she asked.

"Oh Lord, girl it's 6 p.m."

Monica looked at her alarm clock beside her. It confirmed the time precisely. "Aw damn, I can't believe I slept the whole day," she moaned snuggling back under her covers. "What the hell happened last night?"

Tina laughed on the other end. "Hmph, I should be asking *you* that question."

Monica ran her fingers through her hair. "I don't know. All I remember is Michael pissing me the hell off and then I remember throwing a drink in his face."

Tina laughed. "*What!!* Wait, I missed all that?"

Monica smiled to herself. "Girl, it was hysterical."

"Okay so... you mean to tell me that you don't remember kissing that sexy bartender."

Monica sat up quickly then moaned holding her head again. "Please tell me you're joking."

Tina snorted on the other end. "Wish I were. Anyway we'll talk more about it later. Look, I'm picking you up in an hour so we can go meet Shauna at The Blues."

"Ugh please don't talk about food."

"Sorry honey, you can't back out of this one. You know we're supposed to discuss Shauna's wedding plans tonight."

"Aw man, I totally forgot. Can't you make up some excuse for me?"

"No, I can't. This is important to her. You have to be there, hangover or not. Keith is going to be there and I'm not going by myself, so get off your butt and get ready. You should've known better anyway."

"Oh, be quiet. None of this would've happened if I was home in my bed sulking like I planned."

Tina sucked her teeth on the other line. "Girl, stop *trippin'* and get dressed. I have to tell you about a phone call I got."

Monica perked up a little. "What happened?"

"I need to tell Shauna too. Hurry up and get dressed."

"Alright I'm going, I'm going."

"Good. Oh yeah and you had better get your car cleaned. You left yourself a surprise in the front seat."

Monica groaned again. Slowly the scene of her throwing up in her car came flooding back to her. "Aw man, now I'm going to be late for work tomorrow morning. I can't ride around with that smell in my car."

"Well, you better wake up really early then. Hey, I'm out. I'll pick you up in a few."

Monica sighed as she placed her portable phone on the nightstand. She moaned and pulled the covers over her head. A few minutes later she dragged herself out of bed and headed to her bathroom for a hot shower. Slowly the events of last night came back to her as she lathered herself.

She couldn't believe she made such a fool of herself over Michael. *Sean probably thought I was such a slut. My God, an old slut*, she thought in embarrassment. She touched her lips lightly then smiled. *Man that was some kiss though. Too bad he was so young.* She sighed as she rinsed herself off. She shook her head as she vowed never to step foot in that club again.

About two hours later, she and Tina headed out to meet Shauna. The restaurant was very exquisite, expensive and packed wall to wall with high class individuals. The food was exceptional. The chefs were considered the finest in the area.

"Thank God you guys made it," said Shauna as she saw her friends approach her table. "I feel like I'm the only black person in here."

Tina quickly scanned the room before sitting down. "Damn, I think we are. Who picked this place anyway?"

Shauna rolled her eyes. "Keith, of course," she stated. "This is his favorite restaurant. I mean the food is great but I just feel so uncomfortable in here. I could always feel the cold stares," she shuddered.

Monica took a seat next to Tina. "So, stare back," Monica retorted. "We have just as much right to be here as everyone else. Besides, Keith is paying so I have no problem."

"Don't mind her. She's trying to get over of her hangover," Tina informed Shauna with a snicker.

"Tina, don't you start," Monica warned.

"Man, last night was something, huh?" said Shauna unfolding her napkin.

Monica shook her head. "I don't want to talk about it. Where's Keith?"

Shauna rolled her eyes. "Where do you think? He had an emergency surgery so he's going to be late. You know, I'm getting tired of him neglecting me. I hardly see him anymore. By the time he gets home from work I'm fast asleep. I might as well be living alone again."

Shauna and Keith met two years ago, when Shauna got into a terrible car accident. She had to have major surgery. Keith was her surgeon. He saved her life and fell in love with her under the knife. When Shauna moved into his home six months ago, a proposal came soon after on Valentine's Day. He surprised her with a delivery of five-dozen roses to her job that morning. That night he flew her to his private beach house in the Bahamas for a candlelit dinner. The next morning Shauna awoke and found a three carat diamond ring placed on her finger.

Monica shook her head. "Girl please, you're a very lucky woman. Do you know how many women would love to be in your place?"

"Yeah, like me," Tina agreed. "Last time I was in the hospital, I got a tetanus shot and you snagged a doctor."

Shauna smiled yet shook her head. "Ladies trust me. It's not all what it's cracked up to be."

Tina snorted. "You think you have problems, how about a bitch from hell?"

"Bitch from hell?" Shauna repeated confused.

Tina nodded. "Yeah, aka Bryan's girlfriend; how about that heifer had the nerve to call *my* house looking for him."

Monica gasped. "Hold up, she called your house?"

"Not only did she call my house," Tina continued. "She called me baby momma drama at that. Can you believe her?"

"What did you say?" asked Shauna.

"She hung up the phone before I could tell her where to put herself."

Monica laughed. "So Bryan's dating a ghetto chick, go figure."

Tina scowled at her. "It's not funny. I don't understand men, what do they see in these types of women?"

"I know exactly how you feel," said Monica empathetically. "Michael was with some hoochie last night too. I'm sure they had a lot in common. She probably doesn't even have a degree." The words left her mouth before she could stop them. She looked at Shauna apologetically remembering too late her friend didn't attend college. "Hey, I didn't mean," she began.

Shauna shook her head. "It's okay," she answered feeling a little embarrassed.

Tina frowned at Monica and gave her an *'I can't believe you said that'* look. Monica returned a helpless look. Tina quickly changed the subject at that point. "Well, since you're bringing up last night, what's up between you and that sexy bartender?"

Monica shook her head. "Nothing's going on, we started talking and he asked me to dance that's it."

Shauna raised her eyebrow. "He looked kind of young. How old is he?"

Monica didn't respond. She took a big gulp of her water then cleared her throat. "He wasn't that young," she disagreed.

"Twenty-six?" Tina guessed suddenly.

"Twenty-four?" followed Shauna when Monica didn't answer.

Monica picked up her menu. "This is so ridiculous. Can we just order please?" she begged ignoring their guesses.

Tina took the menu out of her friend's hand. "Please tell me he's at least old enough to buy you a drink."

"Duh, of course he is," she answered finally tired of their guessing game. "He's twenty-two," she exclaimed throwing her hands into the air. "There I said it."

Her friends' mouths hung open. "Damn girl, I didn't know you liked them that young," Shauna giggled. "Look at Stella trying to get her groove back."

Monica shifted in her seat embarrassed. "Now you know me better than that. I'm not interested in men that young."

"Well you kissed him didn't you?" Tina pressed.

"Okay look, I only did it to make Michael jealous," she confessed.

Shauna shook her head disapprovingly. "Monica I can't believe you. That was low."

"Yeah," Tina agreed. "That boy has a crush on you and you used him for your scheming plans."

"He's not a boy and he doesn't have a crush me. Besides, I feel bad enough already. I acted like a jealous ex-girlfriend. Look, can we just change the subject please. Let's just order some appetizers while we're waiting for Keith."

She took back her menu and motioned them to pick up theirs. They reluctantly did and scanned their menus in silence. All of a sudden Tina put down her menu. "I'm sorry, but I have to ask. Was the kiss at least any good?"

Shauna snickered as Monica put down her menu and rolled her eyes. "I'm not going to answer that," she said stubbornly.

"Just admit you liked it and we'll let it go," bargained Tina.

She blushed nervously. "Even if I liked it a *little* bit…" she began.

Tina and Shauna both burst out laughing hysterically and gave each other a high five. "*Go Stella, go Stella,*" they chanted in unison.

Monica looked around embarrassed. People were beginning to stare. "Shhh, will you two keep your voices down. You know I'm not looking for a relationship with a twenty-two year old," she declared in a hush tone.

Shauna shook her head. "Who said anything about a relationship?"

"Yeah," Tina agreed. "I think booty call sounds a lot better."

They cackled again while Monica took another mouthful of her drink. She crossed her arms against her chest while trying to ignore their laughter. She didn't like being the brunt of their jokes. "It's not like I'm going to see him again anyway," she continued once their laughter died. They looked at her skeptically. "I'm serious. I'm not going to step foot in that club again," she stated more firmly.

"I hope you ladies haven't been waiting long," a male voice interrupted them.

Keith showed up just in the nick of time. He smiled as he approached their table. He was a tall man; half Italian, half African-American with a suave smile. He always wore the finest Italian suits showing off his high-quality taste. His green eyes were what always caught women's attention. His head full of dark curls were shimmering tonight showing proof of a recent shower.

He gave Tina and Monica each a kiss on the cheek then Shauna a light kiss on the lips. He placed a red long stemmed rose on her plate then sat himself down. She smiled then pulled him close for another kiss. "It's nice to see you ladies again," he smiled opening up his napkin and placing it on his lap.

"Same here," Tina and Monica murmured in unison.

"Did I miss anything?" he asked opening his menu.

"No," Monica quickly answered. "We're just going over your wedding plans. Shauna have you decided what color you want us to wear?"

"I was thinking baby blue," she answered. "The style I'm designing would really look good with that color."

"Honey, are you sure you won't change your mind about designing those dresses. What about those designers from Paris my mother suggested," persuaded Keith.

Shauna frowned. "Keith, we went over this before. This is what I love to do. Putting these dresses together will be a piece of cake."

"Okay, then what about your wedding dress?" he pressed. "I'm sure you're going to need help with that."

She began to get irritated. "No I won't. Look can we not talk about this right now."

"Keith, everything is going to turn out beautiful," said Tina trying to stray them away from a heated argument.

"Yeah," Monica nodded. "She's so talented."

"Oh, I know that," he boasted pulling Shauna close. "I just don't want her to get too stressed."

"I'll be fine," Shauna stated pulling away. She didn't like the way he tried to make her look small in front of her friends. A waiter finally appeared and everyone placed their orders.

"Hey, we were thinking about having a small get together in the next couple of weeks for the wedding party," Keith announced as the waiter walked away. "You all can get to know each other better and you can bring someone if you like."

"Hey Monica, isn't there someone you'd like to invite?" asked Tina raising an eyebrow with a smile.

Monica gave her a dirty look. "No, I'll be fine by myself."

"Monica I've been meaning to talk to you. I'm sorry you and Michael didn't work out," Keith murmured remorsefully. He had introduced the two. He and Michael were fraternity brothers at Morehouse College and best friends. "I really thought you two were great together."

Monica shrugged indifferently. "It's okay. I guess it wasn't meant to be."

"And I just want to warn you in advance," he added. "I've asked him to be my best man."

"I figured that," Monica returned. "I'm a grown woman Keith. I know how to act when I'm around an ex-boyfriend."

Tina snickered and Monica kicked her under the table. "Yeah," Tina agreed clearing her throat. "She's not the type to make a fool out of herself over some man."

"Um, yeah," Shauna chimed in. "I mean, if he came with another woman, she wouldn't care one bit."

Monica rolled her eyes. They were just making things worse. "Where is the food," she groaned covering her face.

Keith looked confused. "Did I miss something?"

The girls burst out laughing and for the remainder of the evening Monica was no longer the topic of conversation. Her mind kept drifting elsewhere from time to time though. She found herself thinking about Sean. She couldn't get that kiss off of her mind. But he was so young. She couldn't really be interested in him, right?

Chapter Three

Shauna bit her lip as she scanned her college application for the third time. *Going back to college was something you've always wanted to do, so why are you so nervous,* she asked herself. At eighteen she was thrown into adulthood after her parents died in a car accident. It was the summer before she was supposed to start Feldman University. She wanted to major in fashion design, but as the eldest of three, she was left alone to take care of her little brother and sister.

Her youngest sibling, Ciara, took it the hardest. She was twelve years old and daddy's little girl. She and her father were inseparable. After the funeral her sister's outgoing attitude changed completely. After school she'd stay in her room and wouldn't speak to anyone. Her brother, Andre, at fifteen was completely the opposite. He would just act out in school every day and get into fights. There was no way she could go off to college knowing that her siblings needed her. She got a full-time job and decided to put off college for later; now that her siblings were on their own, she was now able to go back for her degree.

"Shauna, are you home?" yelled Keith from their living room.

Startled, she quickly threw her application into the nearest drawer. She hadn't spoken to Keith yet about returning to school and finally decided to bring up the subject at dinner. "I'm in the kitchen," she yelled in return.

She grabbed a plate from the cupboard and began piling some vegetables onto it. Keith hugged her from behind. "Mmm, something smells good," he whispered into her ear.

"You're late," she responded bluntly.

He planted a kiss on her cheek. "I know. I'm sorry. I was beeped on the way out. There was a major accident on the expressway. I had to help out with some surgeries."

She sighed and turned to face him. "You do this all the time Keith. When are you going to have time for us?"

He went to the kitchen sink to wash his hands. "Shauna, we had this talk already. You know being a surgeon is demanding. I have no control over my schedule at the hospital."

She laid his plate on the table and went back to get hers. "I don't want to fight. I just want one quiet dinner with my fiancé."

He walked towards the table and sat down. "I have no problem with that. Let's just relax and eat."

She came back to the table with her plate of food, "Fine."

After a few minutes of dining, he finally spoke. "So, how was work today?"

She shrugged. "Tiring, the boutique was packed today." She took a deep breath. She decided to bring up the subject about returning to school quickly before she chickened out. "Listen, I wanted to talk to you about—"

His cell phone interrupted her. She shook her head and went back to her food. He answered the phone then went into the other room. He came back a moment later. "I have to go back to the hospital."

She dropped her fork onto her plate with a frown. "Are kidding me? You just got here!"

He sighed. "Look, Dr. Hutchinson is sick with the flu. They're short staffed."

She shrugged. "So?"

"So, I'm on call this week. I have no choice."

"But you do have a choice Keith. Tell them you have an emergency. Tell them whatever. I really need to talk to you."

He was already wrapping up his plate of food to put in the fridge. "We can talk when I get back. It shouldn't take long. They only want me cover one patient."

She glared at him. She was pissed at the way he was brushing her off. "I want to talk now. You've been blowing me off for a while and I'm sick of it."

"Blowing you off?" he scoffed. "What are you talking about? I'm working for the both of us, to keep up with this kind of lifestyle."

"Look, I didn't move in with you for this lifestyle. I want to spend some time with you, not some fancy house."

He snorted. "I don't hear you complaining while shopping."

She got up from the table. She threw the rest of her food into the garbage then faced him. "Whatever Keith. Say what you want. We both know this is not about money. All I want is your time. Is that so hard?"

He came towards her and hugged her waist. "No, it's not and I'm sorry."

Her voice became soft. "When you asked me to move in with you, I thought things would change. I've only seen things get worse."

"And they will change," he assured her. "You just have to be patient. Look, I'll try to be back as soon as I can."

"Keith—"

His beeper cut her off. He sighed and turned it off. "I have to go." He tried to kiss her but she pulled away and went back to clearing off the table. When she heard the front door close, she dropped the dishes loudly into the sink. She never felt so alone in her life. She felt like screaming. Since he didn't seem to think their talk was important, she decided to go ahead and fill out the application without his advice. She grabbed her car keys, her application from the drawer and headed out the door.

She stopped at Mimi's Café, her favorite coffee shop located in the city. They served the best coffee and pastries in the area. She ordered a cappuccino then sat in a booth closest to a window. She began filling out the application nervously. She didn't want to make any mistakes. She paused as she began to feel tense. She closed her eyes and let her mind wander elsewhere. Finally she sighed then looked out her window. *Are you ready for this,* she asked her herself.

"Excuse me, have we met before?" a male voice asked interrupting her thoughts.

Shauna turned towards the voice annoyed. She was not in the mood for any hook up lines. Her eyes fell on a sexy man with dreads. He wore a black tank top that showed off his muscles nicely. A book bag hung on his left shoulder. His mysterious dark brown eyes gazed at her. She didn't recognize him at all. She went back to her writing. "No, I don't believe so. Look I'm really busy right now so if you don't mind."

"Shauna Knowles is that you?"

She looked up again. This time he smiled. Suddenly something about him felt familiar. *Those dimples.* Her eyes grew large. "Pete?" she inquired finally. He nodded. She stared him down again. "Wow, you've changed," she told him incredulously.

He smiled proudly, "For the better."

She could not believe her eyes. This was not her senior prom date from over ten years ago. He used to be overweight, wore thick glasses yet had a baby face. But this gorgeous man who stood in front of her now was someone totally different. His weight was now replaced with muscles. He no longer wore glasses. She was now able to see his chocolate brown eyes. She moved her application aside and motioned for him to sit down. He placed his coffee cup on the table and sat down. "Man, I can't believe it's you. I would have never recognized you," she laughed.

"I guess I have changed a little, but so have you. I see you've grown your hair out."

She had always worn her hair short but after she met Keith, he pleaded her to grow it long. To please him, she kept it at least shoulder length. "I'm surprised you recognized me."

"I would recognize that beautiful face anywhere."

She blushed. "Still polite, I see."

"That part of me hasn't changed," he smiled. "I'm still good ole Pete from high school." He paused then stared deeply into her eyes. "Man, it's so good to see you." His seductive voice sent chills throughout her body. "I was hoping to see you at our class reunion. I was disappointed when you didn't show."

Shauna bit her lip. She didn't go to her reunion because she didn't want everyone to find out that she hadn't gone to college. Hearing about everyone's accomplishments would make her feel out of place. "I was out of town that weekend," she lied.

"That's too bad. I thought maybe we could reminisce about old times. Maybe even about prom night."

Her mouth formed a smile as she remembered her senior prom. It brought back so many memories for her. When Pete asked her to prom, he caught her off guard. He was considered an outcast while she was popular. Going to prom with him would have been a disaster in the making. She remembered that day like it was yesterday. She was sitting with her friends at lunch. Her friends Monique and Gina had just finished telling her that they had heard her crush, Chris Montana, was going to ask her to the prom.

"Shauna, I'm telling you he's going to ask you to prom today. I overheard him telling Travis at his locker," said Gina excitedly.

Shauna squealed excitedly but then raised an eyebrow. "Are you sure you heard my name."

Gina held up her right hand. "I swear, if I'm lying, I'll throw away my make-up bag right now."

"Now you know she ain't lying Shauna," laughed Monique. "She doesn't go anywhere without that bag."

They cackled in unison.

"Um, Shauna?" said a male voice interrupting their laughter.

Shauna turned to see Pete standing before her.

She smiled, "Oh, hey."

She knew Pete from art classes they had together. He was a great artist. She was always fascinated by his drawings. The colors and textures he used always complimented his work. They often worked on several projects together. He also had a great sense of humor. He made her laugh all the time. She had to admit she always had a fun time when they were together. "Hey, I-I hate to bother you at lunch and all…" he paused.

Her friends snickered around her. She gave them a dirty look. "You're not bothering me, what's up?" she asked turning back to him.

He shifted uncomfortably. "I was j-just wondering if anyone has asked you to prom yet."

She paused for a moment. For the past month, several guys had asked her but she was waiting for Chris to get his act together and ask her. "Yes, but nothing is definite, why?"

He shifted in place. "Well I was wondering…maybe we could go to prom together."

Her friends broke into laughter. Shauna didn't know what to say, but knew exactly how he was feeling right then. She herself was also picked on in middle school. She used to be overweight and was teased daily. Luckily she lost the weight before entering high school. There was no way she was going to go through four more years of pure hell.

The thing was she really liked Pete. He had a great personality and she loved being around him. She didn't care about his weight. She poked Gina in the ribs who laughed hysterically next to her. Being overweight was hard enough for him but then to have a girl turn him down in front of everyone was harsh. With a look of embarrassment, he turned to walk away. "You know what forget it," he told her suddenly.

Shauna bit her lip. "Sure, I'll go with you Pete," she finally blurted.

He turned back to look at her. "What did you say?"

"I said, I'll go with you." she repeated. He quickly broke into a grin exposing a dimple on each cheek. It was first time she had ever seen him so happy other than working on art. It made her smile.

"A-Alright, I'll check with you later," he told her backing away. He bumped into two chairs and a wall along the way. People began to laugh but he didn't care.

When he was out of sight, she turned back towards her friends. They looked at her as if she was crazy. She gave them an innocent look. "What?" she asked dumbfounded.

Gina groaned next to her. "Shauna, are you insane? I just told you that Chris was going to ask you to prom and you said yes to Peter Morris? Have you lost your mind? Do you want everyone laughing at you too?"

Shauna shrugged and popped her last French fry into her mouth. "Pete's cool. I don't know why people hassle him all the time."

Monique sucked her teeth. "They hassle him because he's a loser. Did you see those jeans he was wearing? He's probably had those since the eighth grade," she snickered. Shauna rolled her eyes and Gina frowned. "Oh please, stop trying to act like you've never laughed at him before," she told her.

It was true. She did say a couple of mean things behind his back when she was with her friends but she never felt right about the whole thing. "I know, but that was before I got to know him," she answered defensively. She picked up her lunch tray and took it over to the nearest trash bin. "Look, can we talk about something else before we go to class?" she asked once she got back.

Monique shrugged. "Alright then, it's your funeral."

"Yeah, that was some night," Shauna told him taking another sip of her drink. And it truly was for her.

When Pete picked her up on prom night, he had shocked her completely. He looked like a totally different person. He wore a black tuxedo and had a new haircut. The smile he gave her melted all her nervousness away. Although Pete wore a smile on his face, he was trembling and sweating profusely. It took him a while to pin on her corsage. Shauna decided to relieve his discomfort by pinning her corsage on herself. "Let me help you with that," she laughed.

"I'm sorry," he told her. "You just look so beautiful."

"Thank you," she smiled. She knew she had made the right choice by designing her own dress. She fell in love with a satin red dress she had seen in a magazine. Soon she began sewing a similar design right away. "You know you don't look so bad either," she commented adjusting his tie.

He blushed then held out his arm. "Thanks. Are you ready to go?"

She nodded. "Ready when you are."

When they walked into prom, all eyes were on them, but she wasn't nervous at all. She held his arm proudly but she could feel him tensing up as they passed through the crowd. "Relax," she murmured. "Remember we're here to have fun."

He gave her a small smile. "Ready to dance?" he asked. She nodded as they stepped out onto the dance floor.

He was a perfect gentleman throughout the night. Opening doors and pulling out her chair. He only had a couple of mishaps in the beginning. On the dance floor he stepped on her feet twice and spilled his drink only once but his clumsiness attracted her somehow. Towards the end of the night his awkwardness disappeared and they began to have fun. It was one of the best dates she ever had. It was then she began to realize that she had true feelings for him.

After prom, they decided to go to the beach and hang out. "I had a good time," he told her as they sat down listening to waves crashing against the shore. His jacket covered her shoulders to keep her warm.

She took off her shoes and grinned, "Me too."

He chuckled nervously. "Look, thanks for doing this. I know this was a pity date. I mean, I'm not usually the type of dude you date and—"

She interrupted him with a kiss on the lips. When she pulled away, she looked him straight in the eye. "Now… do you still think this is a pity date?"

"You know, you haven't changed one bit," Pete continued to tell her.

"Come on, not at all?"

He looked her over for a moment then smiled. "Hmm, come to think of it you have put on some weight."

Her mouth flew open embarrassed. "Oh, thanks."

He chuckled then winked. "Don't get me wrong, they fell in all in all the right places."

She blushed. "So, um…what's been going on with you? Are you married? Do you have any children?"

He shook his head. "No children but I did get married."

She tried not to look too disappointed. "Oh really? Congratulations."

"Thanks but it didn't work out. I've been divorced for four years now."

She winced. "Wow, I'm sorry."

"Yeah, it was a lesson well learned."

"So you haven't met anyone else since then?"

"No. I mean I've gone on dates but nothing serious. What about you?" he asked eying the engagement ring on her finger. "Are you married?"

She placed her right hand on her lap so that her ring was no longer visible. "Oh no…um, just engaged." Suddenly she felt embarrassed about the word *engaged*.

"Congratulations."

She smiled faintly. "Thanks."

"If you don't mind me saying, you don't sound too happy."

She brightened up a little. She couldn't believe her expressions were giving her away. "Oh, I am. Just a little nervous, I guess."

"Well, take it from someone who's been through it. It takes two to make a marriage work. And no matter what you think, you can't change your partner."

Was I trying to change Keith, she wondered. "I know what you mean," she concurred finally. "So… are you still into art?"

He nodded. "I think that's the only thing that hasn't changed in my life. I'm an art teacher at Sheldon Middle School a couple of miles from here. I also teach art classes Saturday nights at Brown's Community College downtown."

She smiled. "I see you're still doing your thing."

He took a sip of his drink then nodded. "You know art is my passion and showing my students how to see art in different ways is what I love to do. Man, some of their work blows me away sometimes. My kids are so talented."

She quickly became jealous. "I'm happy to hear you're doing what you love to do. I wish I could say the same."

He raised an eyebrow. "Don't tell me the fashion diva isn't designing clothes for the elite these days."

"I wish," she sulked. "My parents died the summer before I was supposed to start college. I had to make sure my little brother and sister were taken care of."

His voice became soft. "I heard about that. I wanted to call you but I didn't think..." his voice trailed.

She wished he had call. I would've been great to hear his voice. "It's okay, I understand. Anyway, with a full time job and taking care of my siblings, I didn't have a chance to go to college or work on my designs."

He pointed to her application. "And, I see you're ready to go back."

She picked up her application then laid it back down on the table. She groaned. "Do you think I'm crazy?"

He shook his head. "No. As a matter of fact, it's a smart decision. It's never too late to go back to school. I'm very proud of you."

She smiled shyly. Those were the exact words she wanted to hear from Keith. "Thanks. I am so nervous. I want this so bad yet I'm so afraid of failing too."

He placed his hand on top of hers. "Don't be. You have the drive, you can do this."

Her heart fluttered. Slowly she slid her hand away. His touch sent electricity down her spine. He was making her nervous. She couldn't believe he still had an effect on her. She took another sip from her drink and could feel him staring at her. "You know you always know what to say to make me feel better. I really miss talking to you," she confessed while looking out her window instead of him. "I'm glad I decided to have a cappuccino today."

He reached over and pulled at her chin to look at him. Their eyes locked. "I've missed you too."

She gave him a half-hearted laugh. "I'm really shocked to hear that. Especially the way I messed things up." It was the worst decision she ever made.

At the beach they talked and joked about various things. She couldn't believe they had so much in common. "I can't wait to start design school," *she told him excitedly.* "You know I designed this dress myself."

He looked at her impressed. "Damn girl, you've got skills."

She beamed and raised her arm. "Thanks and my bracelet makes it so perfect."

He tugged at the charms on her bracelet. "You love these things don't you? Every time I see you, you're wearing a different one."

She nodded. "I love charm bracelets. My dad travels with his company around the world and brings me back a different charm each time."

He began to play with some sand next to him. "That's cool. So are you a little nervous about college?"

She nodded. "Yeah, but I can't wait to work with designers in the industry. I just wanna get noticed you know."

He sighed. "I feel you. I would love to see my art work in museums or magazines but I can't help thinking, what if I don't make it? What if they don't like my stuff?"

"Pete your art is all that. Don't let anyone tell you different."

He smiled. "I guess you're right. You just better listen to your own advice. Your style is unique too, you know."

She bit her lip worriedly. "You think?"

He shook his head. "No I don't think, I know. You're going to be something big one day."

She smiled feeling more confident. "Thanks. You know you're the only person who's seen my designs."

He frowned, "Really, why?"

She shrugged. "I don't know, I guess popularity goes well with shopping not sewing clothes."

His face turned sour. "And my opinion wouldn't matter anyway right?"

"That's not what I meant. I showed it to you because I knew you'd understand me. It's weird. I feel so connected to you."

He rolled his eyes and looked away. "Of course it's weird. Like I said before I know you said yes to prom out of pity, a girl as fine as you could never really be into me."

She pulled his face to look at her. "It's weird because I've known you for a short time. I've never felt like this before. Look you need to stop putting yourself down. I'm not into dudes who always feel sorry for themselves."

At last he grinned revealing his dimples. Suddenly to her surprise, he leaned towards her and kissed her lightly on the lips. As they pulled away, he began to apologize. "Shauna I'm sorry, I didn't mean—" He was cut off by another kiss from her.

She didn't know what came over her. Something about him was so sweet and innocent. It intrigued her. She's had a couple of heavy make-out sessions with a couple of boys but never ended up having sex. She knew all they wanted was to gloat on who took her virginity first. "Pete, are you a virgin?" she asked him between kisses.

He paused for a moment then blushed. "Yeah, is that a problem?"

"No, as a matter of fact it's perfect," she assured him. She began to unbutton his shirt but he stopped her uncomfortably. She held his face. "Don't be embarrassed. It's only me and you."

He finally nodded slowly. Her tongue sought his mouth with urgency while she undressed him. He began to undress her when they pulled apart. His eyes held hers until she was fully naked. He stared at her body in awe. She blushed. "What?" she asked. "Is something wrong?"

"You look like an angel," he whispered.

She smiled and pulled him for another kiss. His hands explored her entire body. When he placed his mouth on her breasts, she moaned with delight. His tongue played with her nipples causing her to want him even more. She pulled away from him and fixated her eyes on his. "Pete, I want you to make love to me," she whispered.

"A-Are you sure this is what you want" he asked. "That should be shared with someone—"

She cut him off by placing a finger to his lips. "I'm sure," she replied. "I've always dreamed my first time would be like this. This is what I want."

That night they made love for the first time under the stars. He was careful not to hurt her when he entered her. For her it was painful yet exciting at the same time. Each of her thrusts matched his. When she was about to climax, all she could do is hold on to him for dear life. He on the other hand called her name and told her he loved her.

At that point she didn't know what to do. She knew she had fallen for him too, but all she could think of was what would everyone think. She didn't want to relive those horrible episodes of middle school again. The reminder of being taunted again scared her, so she just remained quiet in his arms. All she knew was that it was a night she would never forget.

"Look, about the way I left things…," she began

He held his hand up. "All is forgotten."

But all wasn't forgotten for her.

Pete walked into school Monday morning feeling like a totally different person. He was in love. He never felt like this about anyone in his life. He had fallen for Shauna the first time she walked into his art class. He never dreamed they would end up making love. He wanted to do something special for her so he purchased tickets to a Janet Jackson concert for that weekend. He also brought her a long stemmed rose. He hid the rose behind his back as he spotted her at her locker. He took a deep breath and headed towards her.

"Hey Shauna," he called out.

Shauna froze in place. She was not ready to confront him just yet. She thought about him all weekend. She had decided to tell him what they did was a mistake. She couldn't bear anyone laughing at her again. She turned around slowly.

"Hey Pete, what's up?" she asked forcing a smile.

There was a moment of uncomfortable silence. They continued to gaze at each other for what seemed like an eternity. She wished he would just take her into his arms and everyone would disappear around them. She broke the gaze first. She decided it would be safe to look towards the ground instead. "Look um—"

"Hey… listen before you say anything I want you to know that the other night was very special to me."

"It was to me too," she agreed. "It's just that…"

He could feel something was wrong by the sound of her voice. "What's wrong?"

She couldn't find any words. "Nothing…um, I think—"

"Do you want to go out Friday night?" he blurted before she could finish. "I have tickets—"

"Yo Shauna, can we talk?" a male voice interrupted loudly behind them.

They both turned to see Chris Montana heading towards them. He was tall with smooth chocolate skin. His dark brown eyes shined as he smiled. He got upset when he finally asked her to prom and found out he was too late. She thought that would be the last time he would talk to her.

Frantically, she searched for her compact in her locker. "Hold up a minute Pete," she told him as she applied some lip gloss. Pete rolled his eyes and took a step back.

"What's up, Chris?" she murmured shyly as he jumped in front of Pete.

Chris stood close and ran his finger up and down her shoulder sending electricity down her spine. She blushed. "Look I want you to know that you looked damn good at prom," he acclaimed. "Where have you been hiding that sexy body of yours?"

Pete felt his blood boil but remained silent.

She giggled. "Um, it's been right here."

"Yeah, so you wanna hang out Friday?" he asked continuing to eye her like a piece of meat.

She didn't even hesitate, "Yeah, sure."

He grinned. "Cool, talk to you later, okay."

She grinned in return. "Okay," she replied then watched him walk away. She wanted to burst. She had a date with Chris. Her friends were going to flip. It was a moment later when she realized that Pete had asked her out first. She turned around quickly. He stood there looking smug. "Oh shoot Pete, listen I—"

He backed away shaking his head. "No, it's okay. I guess I was wrong. You're not who I thought you were." He dropped the rose on the floor then walked away abruptly.

She picked up the rose and her heart sank. "Pete wait," she called after him but he didn't turn around. It was the last time he ever spoke to her.

"But what I did was so mean," she pointed out.

He nodded. "Yes it was," he admitted. "And I was hurt. But that was high school and we've grown up. I'm not the type to hold grudges. As a matter of fact, I want to thank you."

She shook her head confused. "Thank me, for what?"

"For that night; thank you for sharing that with me."

She shifted in her seat. "You don't have to thank me. That night meant a lot to me too."

He looked skeptical. "Are you sure, because I kind of got the feeling you were into someone else."

"Everything was just so complicated at that time."

"You don't have to explain a thing. What you did motivated me to change things I was unhappy with in my life, like my weight. So I started going to the gym every day and changed my diet. The rest is history."

"And you look great." *Or should I say fine as hell.*

"Thanks."

She reached over and touched one of his locks. "And when did you start growing this?"

He grinned. "Almost three years ago. You like it?"

Oh hell yeah. She nodded. "I love it."

They continued to talk and laugh for a while. They ordered more drinks while he filled her in on who came to their reunion. Suddenly an ambulance passed by with its sirens blaring loudly. Immediately she thought of Keith heading home as they spoke. She didn't want to leave. She hesitantly looked at her watch. "Wow, it's getting late."

Reluctantly, he did the same. "I guess it's true what they say, time sure flies when you're having fun. Hey…," he paused. "I want to see you again."

She swallowed hard. "Um…again?"

He sensed her hesitation. "As friends," he quickly added.

She felt a little relieved and disappointed at the same time. "Okay," she agreed as they both scooted themselves out the booth. They stood in front of each other awkwardly.

Finally he held out his arms. "Is it okay if get a hug?" he asked.

"S-sure," she stammered embarrassed, "Of course it's okay." She embraced him uneasily. His strong arms held her tight. She closed her eyes. His aroma overwhelmed her. Her heart raced. She pulled away quickly then smiled shyly. "I guess I'll see you around."

He smiled then took a card out of his wallet and handed it to her. "Call me."

Chapter Four

▼

Monica sighed as she headed towards Mr. Dykes door. She was not in the mood to listen to another thirty minute history of how and why he made it to the top of the company. Before she could step foot into her office that morning, his secretary had informed her that she was to report to his office right away. Since he was the head of her department, she had no choice but to haul her ass straight there.

She was tired of not getting recognized for her hard work. A numerous of amount times, he got the recognition for accounts she stayed late working on. He received bonuses while she got a pat on the shoulder. She vowed one day to move up the ladder and take his position. She wanted to be on top too. She took a deep breath as she plastered a smile on her face. She knocked on his door softly.

"Come in," he yelled from behind the door.

She opened the door and peeked in. "Mr. Dykes. You wanted to see me?"

"Yes, Ms. Stevens. Come in. Come in. How's that Hutchinson project going?" he asked as he leaned back into his large leather chair.

She walked in and closed the door softly behind her. His office was at least three sizes bigger than hers. It had a nice view of the skyline, modern furniture was displayed throughout the room and then there was his chair. She imagined herself numerous times spinning around in his oversized leather chair laughing hysterically.

She saw someone's head in one of the seats in front of his desk but could not make out a face. *Probably a new prospective client*, she thought wearily. New clients meant more work for her. "The project is coming along great," she informed him. "I'm almost done with most of the calculations. Do you want to see what I've done so far?"

"Um no, not right now, just keep up the good work. I'm glad you're on our team."

Team my ass! She put on a fake smile. "Thank you Mr. Dykes, I'm glad to be part of it."

"Now the reason why I called you into my office today is to introduce you to our new intern. Ms. Stevens, I would like you to meet Mr. Sean Madison."

She walked up to the chair and held out her hand. She was taken aback once she saw who stood up from the seat. It was Sean from the club. He definitely wasn't looking like a bartender that morning. He was wearing a dress shirt and tie. He looked so professional and so delicious. He shook her hand. "It's nice to meet you Ms. Stevens."

She nodded and swallowed hard. "S-same here Mr. Madison."

"Sean will be graduating from California University in a couple of months with a double Bachelor's in accounting and business administration," Mr. Dykes continued. "He's in the top five percent of his class and thinking about coming aboard with us after graduation. I trust you will show him the ropes around here for the next couple of days."

She nodded again still in a state of shock. Mr. Dykes came from around from his desk. He patted Sean on the back. "Trust me son, you're in good hands."

Sean looked back at Monica and smiled. "Thank you Mr. Dykes, I trust your judgment."

She blushed furiously and headed for the door. "Well, I guess we should get started then."

He came quickly in front of her and held it open for her. "Thanks," she mumbled.

"I'll check on you two later," said Mr. Dykes behind them.

The silent walk to her office was too long. She told Sean to close the door behind him as she walked into her office and sat herself down. Nervously, she began to fiddle with some papers on her desk. She didn't know where to start. She could feel him watching her. "I guess I should make an agenda on what we're going to do today," she told him not looking up.

He sat down in front of her. "That's fine. Anything you want."

She sighed and finally looked up at him. "Out of all the accounting firms in all of L.A., you had to pick mine to do your internship."

He raised an eyebrow. "So this is your firm?"

"Very funny that's not what I meant...oh forget it."

"I take it you're not happy to see me."

She shook her head. "I didn't say that."

"Oh so you're happy to see me then?"

She shook her head again. "I didn't say that either."

"Okay look I didn't know you worked here. I picked this firm because I heard it has a good reputation. If you don't want this arrangement to continue, I can tell Mr. Dykes to put me with someone else."

"That's not necessary. I'm just surprised to see you."

"Okay then. So…."

"So?" she repeated.

"What happened to you the other night? You left without saying goodbye."

"I don't think that is an appropriate topic to talk about at work."

He held his hand up. "All right, my bad."

She stood up abruptly and walked around her desk. "Come I'll introduce you to the other workers."

He walked behind her. "Lead the way."

When she walked out of her office, she found several female co-workers running away from her door. She rolled her eyes. They all looked like they were pretending to do something. They must've heard the news of the new young male intern. "Well, since most of our staff seems to be hanging all out here. Let me introduce you," she told him.

She clapped her hands together. "Everyone if I can have your attention. I would like to introduce you to our new intern Mr. Madison. He will be interning here for the next couple of months. I'm sure you all will make him feel welcome."

He smiled and waved as if he was a superstar, "Nice to meet you all."

Some women giggled, waved back, while others came up to him and introduced themselves personally. They were acting like he was Denzel Washington. "Come on," she ordered pulling him along. "Let me introduce you to our Senior Vice President."

The Senior Vice President, Paula Jackson was not in her office. They found her bent behind a male worker's chair. She was whispering something in his ear as he typed on his computer. She was wearing a short tight skirt which clearly revealed her long slim legs. There was a rumor that she slept her way up to the top and Monica believed it. There were too many private meetings in her office to not believe it. Monica looked at Sean who couldn't seem to look away.

She cleared her throat quickly, "Um, Ms. Jackson?"

Startled, Paula turned around with a frown but her frown quickly replaced with a smile once her eyes set on Sean. She pulled on her shirt to make her breasts look fuller. "May I help you Monica?" she asked still eying Sean hungrily.

Monica tried to hide her look of disgust. "I just wanted to introduce you to our new intern Sean Madison," she muttered.

Sean held out his hand. She shook it but lingered a little. "Well, it is very nice to meet you Mr. Madison."

"Call me Sean," he told her as she released his hand.

She flipped her hair off her shoulder. "And you can certainly call me Paula. Monica, make sure you bring this young man by my office later. I'd like to go over some things he needs to know about our company."

He smiled. "That'll be great. I'm sure you can show me a lot."

"Yeah right," Monica mumbled under her breath.

"You said something Monica?" Paula asked her with a threatening tone.

"Uh no," Monica answered. She didn't retaliate for a reason. No one in the company wanted to be on Paula's bad side. She had most of management wrapped around her finger which meant if she wanted to get rid of someone it would be done very quickly. Monica began to lead Sean away again. "Well, we better get going. We have lots more offices to stop by."

When they were a few feet away she pulled him aside. "You know you don't have to go by her office," she informed him with a hint of jealousy in her voice.

"Well she says she wants to go over some stats," he interjected with a grin.

"Hmph, now you know stats are the last thing on her mind."

He raised an eyebrow. "Are you jealous?"

She blushed furiously. "No, I'm just warning you that she's the company *ho*!" she disclosed discreetly.

He chuckled. "Don't worry, I'm a big boy, I can take care of myself."

She shrugged. "I'm sure you can. So all that flirting back there didn't faze you?"

"I don't mean to sound conceited but I get hit on all the time at the club. I don't let that stuff go to my head. I'm here to learn, not to get a piece of ass."

She was impressed by his response. "I'm glad to know that you have your priorities straight."

"I didn't know you cared."

"I don't."

He smiled. "If you say so."

They spent the remainder of the morning in her office. She showed him some accounts she had completed within the last couple of months. He seemed very impressed with her work. At one point his hand brushed hers as they reached for a pen at the same time. She flinched as if he had burned her. She couldn't believe the way she was acting. *Control yourself Monica!* She looked at her watch relieved to see it was lunchtime. "Hey, it's lunchtime. You want to go get something to eat then meet me back here in an hour?"

He got up and stretched. She began to imagine how he looked with his shirt off. "Sounds good but I have an even better idea. How about I treat you to lunch?"

She shook her head. "I don't think—"

She was interrupted by a knock at her door. It was Mr. Dykes. "So Mr. Madison, how is everything going so far? I hope Monica is not overwhelming you."

Sean stared at Monica. "No Mr. Dykes, she's been great. She's been going over the history of the company and showed me several accounts she's completed. She's doing an amazing job."

She turned to look at her boss. "I was just sending him out to lunch."

Mr. Dykes frowned. "Alone?"

"Uh, yes," she paused. "I was—"

"Surely you can't let him eat alone on his first day," he interrupted. "Why don't you take him to that nice bistro off on Madison Street? They serve the best BLT sandwiches."

Sean nodded in agreement. "A BLT sounds great."

She no longer felt like arguing. She grabbed her purse and stood up. "Okay, I'll drive."

The bistro was packed inside, so they decided to eat lunch outside in the patio area. It was a nice day out, not too hot but Monica was sweating profusely. Sean was looking better and better by the minute. She became mesmerized by his features as the sun shined slightly onto his face. It showed off a glimmer in his eyes.

As the day went on she became more and more confused about him. He held doors open for her and even pulled out her chair when they were placed at a table. Courtesy was not a trait she thought boys his age actually portrayed. Finally, a cute waitress popped up at their table. Her eyes traveled over Sean oblivious that Monica was sitting across from him.

"So, are you ready to order?" she asked staring at him intently.

Monica cleared her throat loudly. The waitress turned and gave Monica an impatient look. "Yes," Monica stated firmly. "I would like the grill chicken salad with ranch dressing on the side and some ice tea."

The waitress scribbled the order down quickly then turned to Sean. "And you, honey?"

Honey? Monica rolled her eyes while he hid a smile at her response. "I'd like to try that famous BLT you guys have and a Coke," he answered.

She gave him a quick wink, "Coming right up, sweetie."

When the waitress left there was an uncomfortable silence. Monica kept her eyes occupied everywhere else but at him. "You seem far away," he observed finally speaking up.

She shifted in her seat. She didn't realize she was making herself look so obvious. "Huh? Um no, I was just thinking about some things I need to get done before the end of the week," she lied.

He smiled. "You love your work don't you?"

She shrugged. "I guess you can say that. Sometimes I feel it consumes all of my time but its how I make a living, you know?"

He nodded. "I can understand that but right now we're outside. It's a nice day out and we have an hour to enjoy this. So relax." He loosened his tie. She began to imagine what he would look like with his shirt off.

She wrenched her eyes away and let out a deep breath. She couldn't find anything else to concentrate on. The waitress finally came with their drinks. She gulped a good amount. "So, how do you like the company so far?" she asked pouring extra sugar into her drink.

"What can I say? The stats are phenomenal," he answered. "I'm just glad Mr. Dykes chose me to intern here. I heard I was picked from one hundred applicants. I wouldn't mind working here when I graduate."

I wouldn't mind either, she thought as she watched him lick his lips. She cleared her throat. "I guess we should keep our fingers crossed. Oh and I also want to congratulate you on being top five percent of your class. Your parents must be very proud of you."

"She is," he informed her. "All my hard work is for my mother. My father left us when I was ten. She struggled while taking care of me and my four brothers on her own so I want to make her proud."

She became enthralled. His maturity made him even more attractive. "She's lucky to have a son like you." She took another sip of her drink. "So where are you from?"

"Jersey."

"I've been there a couple of times during the winter. The snow is beautiful over there."

He took a sip of his drink, "Yeah it is, but I'll take the heat over snow anytime."

She began to get curious. There was no way a fine man like him didn't have a girlfriend. "So…how do you have time for your girlfriend with school and work?"

He smiled shyly. "It wouldn't be hard if I had a girlfriend."

She looked surprised. "A nice young man like you without a girlfriend, what's up with that?"

"I guess my schedule doesn't meet certain needs. My last girlfriend complained that I didn't have time for her, so it didn't last too long. One night she broke a date with me and said she had too much studying to do. So I went out with my friends to some night club that had just opened up. I caught her there with some other dude. I ended it that night."

She winced. "Sorry to hear that."

He shook his head. "Don't be. It wasn't serious. Don't get me wrong, I know being in a relationship means spending time together, but she wasn't on my level. I need someone who understands that an education is important too. My mom didn't have enough money to send me to college, so I had to get scholarships and work to cover other expenses. I can't afford to get low grades."

"Yes, an education is important. So I guess bartending helps out a lot huh?"

He nodded. "Yeah, the tips are real good."

"And the half naked girls throwing themselves at you is a bonus huh?"

He laughed. "It's all good."

She didn't laugh in return. "I see."

He stopped laughing once he realized she wasn't happy with his statement. "I'm just kidding," he assured her. He leaned in closer to the table. "So…is it still a bad time to talk about Saturday night?"

"S-Saturday night?" she repeated.

"Yeah, you left so suddenly."

She looked around for their waitress. *Where in the hell was the food?* "Um my friends had to leave," she answered when she turned back to him. Before he could respond, their food had finally arrived. Relieved, she pulled out her fork from her napkin. "This looks great. I'm starving. Can you pass me the grated cheese, please?"

He handed it to her but lingered by holding her hand. She drew back. "Don't do that."

"Do what?"

She picked up her fork. "You know what I'm talking about."

"Why are you so tense? Am I making you uncomfortable?"

She put her fork down and laughed nervously. "Are you serious?"

"Yeah, I am."

She stared at him flabbergasted. "Well, you're not."

"Then why is your left hand shaking."

She looked down and realized her hand was doing exactly that. She quickly placed it under the table. "Can we just talk about something else please?"

"Okay then. How about that kiss we shared."

"Anything but that."

"Why, was it that bad?"

"No...it's just that I didn't know what I was doing. I had a lot to drink. I don't even remember how I got home that night."

He nodded disappointedly. "Oh."

She bit her lip. She decided just to tell the truth. "The truth is, I saw my ex watching us while we were dancing. I kissed you to make him jealous."

He leaned back into his chair dumbfounded. "Wow. So it was all just an act?"

"Sean, I don't usually act like that. It was childish. I'm sorry." He was quiet for moment but it seemed like an eternity. She never felt so guilty in her life.

"So the truth is you felt nothing?" he finally asked again.

"I'm sorry, but I didn't," she lied.

He nodded and remained quiet. He looked disappointed while she felt lower than dirt. "Sean, if I could take that whole night back, I would," she continued.

He didn't respond. Instead he grabbed his sandwich and took a big bite. He chewed slowly then broke into a smile. "Damn this sandwich is good. I need to thank Mr. Dykes for recommending this place."

She watched him eat for a couple of minutes. "So we're okay now?" she asked before she could finish her food. She wanted to make sure their work relationship wasn't ruined.

He nodded indifferently. "Oh yeah, everything's good. Eat up so we can get back to work."

She ate the remainder of her food in silence. She never felt so awkward in her entire life. When they got back to work, he excused himself to the men's restroom. When he didn't show up in her office after twenty minutes, she began to get worried. She walked out of her office and looked around. "Jackie, have you seen Mr. Madison?" she asked the office secretary.

She smirked. "Oh, he's in with Ms. Jackson. She saw him walking from the men's room and grabbed him up."

Monica raised an eyebrow. "Oh, really?"

Jackie smacked on her gum loudly. "Uh huh, I guess another one bites the dust," she cackled.

Monica didn't laugh with her. From afar, she could see Paula's door closed and wondered what was going on in there. *Could he really say no to her if she threw herself at him,* she wondered. "Jackie, hold all my calls. I'll be in my office for the rest of the day."

"Yes ma'am," she smiled as if knowing something Monica didn't know.

Angrily Monica walked back into her office in a huff. She let out a sigh as she sat in her chair and gathered her thoughts. *What are you so mad about? He's not your man. And you don't have any feelings for him, right?* For the rest of the day she tried concentrating on her project but couldn't stop looking at her watch every hour. At fifteen minutes to five, there was a knock at her door.

"Come in," she answered.

Sean's head peeked through. "I just wanted to say good-night."

She looked up for a moment checking for any signs of guilt his face but didn't find any. She looked back down. "Leaving early?"

"Yeah, Ms. Jackson said it was okay. She didn't want to show me too much."

She gathered all her paperwork into her briefcase. *What, too much cleavage for you?* "Oh I'm sure she didn't," she mumbled instead.

He frowned. He came in and closed the door behind him. "What's that supposed to mean?"

She continued to pack. "Take it however you want."

"I told you that's not what I'm here for."

"And I told you she has a reputation. She doesn't take no for an answer yet you still spent the rest of the day in her office. I hope you learned a lot."

"Wait, are you mad at me?"

She looked up again. "Why should I be mad at you? Did you do something for me to be mad about?"

He looked at her confused. "I don't get you? One minute you tell me you don't care and the next minute your acting like a jealous girlfriend."

She grabbed her purse and briefcase then stood up. "Whatever. Believe what you want. I don't have time for this. Have a good-night."

She tried to walk past him but he caught her arm. "No, I want to settle this before we leave. Why are you so angry?"

He was so close. He smelled so good. She took a step back. "I-I told you I'm not angry," she stammered suddenly feeling weak.

He took another step towards her and she began to tremble. He stroked her cheek. "You can't even stand close to me without trembling," he observed.

Her breathing increased rapidly as she began to feel moist between her legs. "Sean this is inappropriate. We're at work."

He looked at his watch. "It's five o'clock. Work is over." He took her briefcase out of her hand and placed it on her desk. He backed her against the wall.

"What are you doing?" she hissed frantically. She could hear some of her co-workers start to say their good-byes. She froze. She couldn't breathe.

His eyes locked with hers. His finger ran up and down her arm. "Do you know how beautiful you are when you're angry?" he asked huskily.

She closed her eyes trying to control her beating heart. "Please don't do this," she pleaded softly.

His face leaned towards hers. "If you want me to stop," he paused as he rubbed his forehead softly against hers. "Then stop me." Before she could answer, his lips were on hers. His kiss sent heat throughout her body. She felt herself go weak but his strong arms held her up once more.

His tongue plunged into her mouth without any notice. Her hand slowly loosened on her purse. It dropped to the floor. She began to kiss him back with such fervor she even surprised herself. Her hands willingly began to roam all over him. Through his shirt, she was finally able to feel his rippled chest. His abs were perfect.

A moan escaped from her lips as he began sucking on her neck. She could feel him grow hard against her. His hand cradled her breast. *Oh Lord forgive me for robbing this cradle*, she thought. She didn't want the moment to stop. Suddenly there was a knock at her door. She quickly snapped back to reality.

"Monica, are you still here?" she heard Mr. Dykes ask.

She pushed him away roughly. They began to fix their composures quickly. She ran back to her desk again then scowled at him. She couldn't believe she let him get to her. "Come in Mr. Dykes," she yelled moments later.

He looked at Monica disappointedly. "Now Monica when I told you to show him the ropes, I didn't mean for you to keep the boy working after five. You two need to be heading home."

"We were uh, just getting ready to do that," she told him. She grabbed her briefcase again. She held out her hand to Sean. "Mr. Madison, see you tomorrow?"

He shook it and smiled. His breathing was still a little heavy, "D-Definitely."

"Sean do you mind walking Monica to her car?" asked Mr. Dykes. "I hate seeing a woman walk to her car alone. It's already dark."

Nooo! She shook her head. "I'll be fine."

Mr. Dykes gave her a firm look. "No need to be modest Monica. These streets are not safe anymore."

Yeah , but who will keep me safe from him, she asked him silently.

"I really don't mind," Sean insisted. She finally nodded and wished Mr. Dykes a good-night. Once out of the building, she began walking rapidly to her car. "Slow down Monica. Why are you rushing?" he huffed coming up next to her.

"I'm tired. I just want to go home."

He pulled her to slow down. "Can you wait a minute? I thought maybe we could go get a cup of coffee."

She shook her head and pulled away. "No thanks." She continued to walk at a quick pace. She sighed in relief as she reached her car. "You know you didn't have to walk me," she told him as she tried to unlock her car door. She couldn't get her key into the keyhole. She was still shaken from their one minute make-out session.

"I wanted to," he murmured. "I wasn't going to let you walk alone."

"I've been walking to my car alone for the past four years and I've been fine," she snapped. She paused for a moment then sighed. *This is not his fault. You're the one who let everything get out of hand.* "Listen, what happened up there can't ever happen again."

"I don't understand, why not?"

"Sean this is my job and I won't do anything to jeopardize it."

"You're right, I'm sorry," he apologized. "I hope I didn't offend you. Everything just happened so fast. It's just that I feel this vibe between us. I know you felt it too."

She didn't respond and finally unlocked her door. He pulled her to look at him. "What are you so afraid of?"

She sighed. "Sean you're twenty-two and I'm thirty."

"So what, what matters is how we feel. Age doesn't make a difference."

She placed herself in the driver's seat. "Well it may not to you but it does to me." She closed her door then turned her key in the ignition. She could feel him still staring at her. He knocked on her window. She rolled it down impatiently. "Sean I have to go."

"Let me take you out to dinner," he suggested with a smile.

She suppressed a giggle. "Dinner...boy didn't you just hear what I said?"

He ignored her comment. "I just want to get to know you better even if it's just as friends. Just go out with me once. And if you still feel the same way, I'll leave you alone. I promise to make this simple."

Her mind was telling her no but her body was telling her yes. "I-I can't."

"Why not?"

"Look, I just can't okay. I have to go. I'll see you tomorrow."

She drove off quickly leaving him on the side of the road. *A date...was he crazy?* There was no way she could be alone with him again. What would've happened if Mr. Dukes hadn't come in? They would've probably had wild sex on the floor. She couldn't wait to take a cold shower when she got home.

"Okay Monica. What's going on? You sounded like you were having a panic attack on my answering machine," said Tina closing Monica's front door behind her. "And it had better be good because I'm missing my favorite TV show for you."

"Yeah girl what's going on?" Shauna inquired while settling on Monica's plush sofa. She had just walked in a couple of minutes before Tina.

Monica had left them both messages to come over as soon as they got home from work. She needed them to help her find a way to deal with Sean. She was pacing up and down in her living room literally leaving a mark on her carpet. She was biting her nails furiously.

"Uh oh, Tina, she's biting her nails. This must be serious." Shauna pulled her friend to sit next to her. "Honey, you need to relax. Just tell us what happened."

Monica let out a sigh. "I saw Sean today," she announced finally.

"Who?" Tina asked.

"Sean, the bartender who works at the Moonlight," Monica reminded her.

"Where?" Shauna questioned again.

"At my job," she answered.

"Your job?" Tina repeated confused. "Wait, you're not making sense. He followed you to your job?"

She took another deep breath and exhaled. "No, he's our new intern. He's graduating from Cal-U in a couple of months."

Tina leaned back into the sofa and burst out laughing. Shauna held her hand over her mouth to keep from doing the same.

"It's not funny," Monica told them seriously.

"But I thought you said you're not into him," said Tina between laughs.

Monica hit her with a sofa cushion and got up from the couch. "I'm not, but things sort of changed today?"

Shauna finally looked serious. "Changed?" she asked.

Monica stood up and began walking back and forth again. "Yeah, we kind of... sort of ... kissed again."

Tina got up quickly and pointed her finger at her friend. "Ah ha, I knew it. I knew you wanted him."

Monica shook her head and groaned. "No, you don't understand."

Shauna waved Tina to be quiet. "Damn Tina, let the girl finish."

"Okay look," Monica began. "We were in my office and he had me cornered. He was so close. He began caressing my face. I knew he was going to kiss me and I wanted him to. He just looked *so* good today." She covered her face with her hands and sat down again. "I don't know what came over me. I liked the way he made me feel and didn't want him to stop. If my boss hadn't knocked on my door, I don't know what would've happened. He made me feel so alive. What am I going to do? I can't have him cornering me like that again. I mean I told him I kissed him at the club to make Michael jealous so what's my excuse now?"

Tina's eyes grew large. "You told him what you did? Man you got balls."

"I mean I had to. I couldn't let him think I was into him."

"Girl you are a mess," Shauna laughed finally.

"I know, I am," Monica admitted somewhat embarrassed.

"Honey, why are you making such a big deal out of this?" asked Shauna. "Just go out with him. Older women go out with younger men all the time. It's how we keep ourselves young."

Monica grabbed one of the sofa cushions and held it tight. "Now I really feel like a dirty old woman."

"Monica you just can't ignore how you feel," Tina consoled her. "You're attracted to him and it's okay."

"Okay?" Monica repeated. "Hell no it's not okay. He's almost ten years younger than me."

"Well, maybe that's a good thing," Tina smiled and winked at her. "Maybe you could show him a few things."

Monica gave her a dirty look. "Can you be serious please? I'm really stuck on this. He asked me to have dinner with him."

Tina came next to her and rubbed her shoulder. "Okay, what did you say?"

Monica bit her lip. "I told him it wasn't a good idea."

Shauna shook her head. "You can't keep lying to yourself. Just go out with him and have some fun."

Monica looked astounded. "Girl, are you crazy?! I can't go out with him. Besides we don't have anything in common."

"Well, let's see," Tina analyzed. "You both work in the same field, you both like to dance, have great chemistry and *love* kissing each other. What else could you want?"

Monica rolled her eyes, "How about a man my age?"

"Okay, okay. Now, let's think this through," Shauna offered. "Well, you already turned down his offer. Maybe he'll back off."

"I doubt it," said Monica pessimistically.

"Wait, I have an idea. Just go out with him," suggested Tina again.

Monica got irritated quick. "Tina—" she began.

Tina cut her off. "Just listen for a moment. All through dinner you can do things to turn him off. You know, to make yourself unattractive."

Monica shook her head. "I can't do that."

It was now Tina's turn to frown, "Why not?"

"I-I don't think I-I can handle being alone with him a-again," she sputtered nervously.

"Damn Monica, this man has got you sprung already," Shauna observed.

"I'm not *sprung*," she argued then closed her eyes. "It's just that he's just so damn sexy. I've never been with a man who makes my toes curl with just a kiss. And the way he held me against the wall and took control, I wanted to tear him apart. It's like he knew my every desire. Just being near him makes me want to—"

Their laughter interrupted her. She opened her eyes and found them fanning themselves. Monica joined in the laughter. "Damn, can I borrow him for a few minutes," Tina giggled. "I want my toes to curl too."

"So what are you going to do?" Shauna asked as their laughter died down. "You can't avoid him forever. He may end up working for the company when he graduates."

Monica looked worried. "I know but trust me I can't go out with him. What if people stare?"

"So stare back" Shauna answered. "Tell them to mind their own business."

Monica shook her head. "You guys, I can't be alone with him," she repeated.

"Damn are his kisses that good?" Tina questioned again.

Monica smiled weakly. "Oh hell yeah, I mean look what his kiss has done to me and he hasn't gotten me into bed yet."

Tina went into the kitchen and took out three wine glasses from her friend's cupboard.

"Yet? Are you saying you might sleep with him?"

Monica blushed furiously. "No!! I was just saying…oh hell I don't know what I'm saying anymore."

Tina laughed. "Who would've thought you'd fall for a twenty year old?"

"Twenty-two," Monica corrected. "And I'm not falling for him. I'm just a little attracted that's all."

"Yeah right," Tina snorted. She found a chilled bottle of wine in Monica's refrigerator and poured some into each glass.

Shauna laughed. "I'd be attracted too. The brotha is fine."

Monica looked at her surprised. "Hey, aren't you getting married."

Shauna sucked her teeth. "Hell, I can look. I just can't touch."

Monica giggled then pouted. "You should see the girls at work. They're all over him. Why couldn't he be my age? I would feel so much better."

Tina came over with the glasses and handed each of them one. Shauna set her glass on the table. "Well, he's not," she reminded her. "The best thing you can do right now is to keep saying no. Once he finally gets the picture he'll leave you alone. A man hates it when you hurt his ego."

"Yeah," Tina agreed. "He'll lose interest after a while."

Monica shrugged. "Maybe you're right." She raised her glass in the air and they did the same. "Let the *dissin'* begin."

Chapter Five

"Hey, how about we have lunch today," Shauna suggested to Keith as she sat in front of her dresser mirror brushing her hair.

He massaged her shoulders from behind. "That sounds like a great idea. Maybe can even have dessert in one of the operating rooms."

Shauna giggled. "Didn't you have enough last **night**?"

The night before, he surprised her with a **romantic** candle lit dinner. After spoon feeding her, he carried her into their bedroom and gave her massage. He made love to her all night long. She **prayed** their marriage would always be like this.

"I can never get enough of you," he murmured into her ear.

She turned to kiss him lightly on the lips. He responded by picking her up from the chair and carrying her towards their bed. He placed her carefully on her back. "You're so bad," she giggled as he took off her shoes slowly. "We're going to be late for work."

He began to plant butterfly kisses on her right leg while slowly moving upwards. "They can wait," he murmured briefly. She smiled. In minutes they were on the bed savoring each other. Just when he was about to unbutton the last button on her blouse, his beeper went off. He groaned.

"Ignore it," she pleaded softly.

He pulled off her. "I can't. It may be an emergency." He looked at the number on his beeper then went to his cell phone. "I'll be right there," he told the person on the other end then hung up. Shauna rolled her eyes and began to button up her blouse again.

"I'm sorry," he told her as she reluctantly put her shoes back on. "Maybe we can finish this at lunch?"

"Sure," she mumbled.

He grabbed her by her waist then pulled her around to face him. He hugged her tight. "I love you, you know that?" he told her. She nodded. He kissed her on the forehead, grabbed his briefcase then headed out their bedroom. When she got to work, she was confronted with a store full of customers.

"Hey Shauna, both Cindy and Ann called in today so it's just you and me for the rest of the day," her manager Lisa told her once she got in. "We may have to skip lunch today."

"Are you kidding me?" Shauna responded annoyed. "I have a lunch date with Keith."

Lisa gave her a look of desperation. "Sorry, not today honey. I need you here. You know today is our rummage sale. I can't do this by myself," she told her ringing up the next customer.

Shauna nodded and opened up her register. When she was finally able to take a fifteen minute break, she called Keith. "Two people called in today," she told him. "She's only able to give me breaks."

"Man, I was really looking forward to lunch," he said disappointedly.

"I know but don't worry, we'll finish things later. What are you going to do for lunch?"

"I'll probably work through lunch myself. That'll give me a chance to come home early."

She giggled. "Down boy, I'll see you later."

He chuckled. "Alright honey, I love you."

"Love you too."

Shauna sighed happily as she hung up her phone. She began to feel the same way she felt when they first began dating. They talked on the phone for hours and couldn't wait to do it all over again the next day. Around lunch time, customers began to die down. "Hey Shauna, you did great today," complimented Lisa.

"Thanks," she answered glumly.

"Go to lunch."

Shauna's face brightened up quickly. "What? But I thought you said—"

Lisa raised her hand. "You better go before I change my mind."

Shauna squealed and grabbed her purse from under the counter. "Thanks Lisa."

"Just be back on time," she yelled behind her.

Before heading to the hospital, she stopped by his favorite restaurant and picked up some lunch. In the lobby she brushed by several nurses until she spotted a familiar face. "Hey Naomi, is Dr. Anderson in surgery?" she asked the head nurse who stood in front of the nurse's station.

"Oh hi Shauna, how are you doing honey?"

Shauna showed her the take out bag. "I'm fine, just here to surprise Keith for lunch."

She smiled. "Oh, that's nice. I get so jealous of you two lovebirds all the time. I can't think of the last time my husband and I spent lunch together." She took a quick look at her clipboard. "He's not scheduled for surgery for another hour. I thought I saw him heading for the cafeteria earlier. You'll probably find him there. It was nice seeing you again."

"Thanks, it was nice seeing you too," she returned as Naomi turned to walk away. She rolled her eyes in disappointment. *I thought he wasn't going to take lunch.*

She was expecting to have a private lunch. Reluctantly she headed towards the cafeteria in a quick pace. As she walked down the busy hallway, she could feel cold stares on her back. She looked behind her and found two young women in scrubs staring her down hard. She turned back around with a frown. *Am I seeing things?* That thought quickly disappeared once she approached her destination. She stood at the door and scanned the big room filled with employees. She finally spotted her fiancé, but he wasn't alone.

He was sitting with another woman. Her heart dropped. She also had a white coat on and a stethoscope around her neck. She was white. They were sitting across from each other, holding hands and having what seemed like an intimate conversation. She knew most of Keith's co-workers but didn't recognize this woman at all. The way she looked at Keith angered her. It was a look of lust. Suddenly she felt sick to her stomach. Furiously she threw his food in the nearest trash can and headed out the door.

On her way back to work, she sat in her car impatiently waiting for the traffic light to turn green. She held her steering wheel tight. The scenario at the hospital continued to play over and over in her head. The more she thought about the situation, the angrier she got. *There's no way in hell he's was cheating on me. He's not the type to have a fling at work. He loves his job too much…but…he loves sex even more. Ugh, your mind is playing tricks on you Shauna. Just relax. You'll find out what's going on soon enough.*

When she got home after work she expected to see Keith but he wasn't there. She was glad though. She was already worn out and was not ready to confront him just yet. She decided a hot shower would help her relax. She quickly disrobed then placed herself under the running water. The hot water felt good against her back. She closed her eyes and took a deep breath. She exhaled slowly.

Suddenly she felt strong arms embrace her from behind. Her anger began to diminish slowly. *Maybe I was overreacting*, she thought. She didn't turn around; instead she placed his hands gently over her breasts. He played with her nipples gently. She moaned and closed her eyes. Slowly he began to plant kisses up and down her neck. His kisses were soft, so loving and so familiar.

"You're so beautiful," he whispered huskily into her ear.

She smiled to herself then turned to return his kisses. Her mouth searched his with urgency. His tongue was soft yet demanding. His hands massaged her back then slowly roamed down to gently squeeze her behind. She giggled against his lips then went to run her fingers through his head full of curls but felt something else instead. *Dreads!*

Her eyes flew open. She gasped when she saw it was Pete who stood before her. He smiled unaffected by her response. She moved away from him and tried to cover herself as much as possible. She tried to say something but nothing would come out. Once more he continued to smile at her as he lathered himself gradually.

She couldn't tear her eyes off of him. He was perfectly sculptured from his broad shoulders to his thick legs. He moved under the shower head. He let the water run over his body. She watched him for what seemed like an eternity. In slow motion water slowly dripped down from his dreads unto his broad shoulders then down to his long thick muscular legs. He was certainly not the same boy who took her virginity.

He finally reached out for her but she shook her head terrified. He smiled. "Don't be afraid," he told her. "I just want to love you…let me taste you from head to toe." Her heart beat rapidly yearning for his touch. She headed towards him cautiously. His eyes had fire in them. She closed her eyes anticipation ready for him to make her scream yet nothing happened.

Her eyes flew open to find no one there. The shower was still running, but he was gone. It was like he disappeared into thin air. *Was it a dream? It seemed so real.* Immediately she began to feel guilty about the whole ordeal. She lathered and rinsed off quickly. She threw on her robe and did a quick look around her bathroom. She groaned and rolled eyes. *What am I doing? I'm an engaged woman looking for a naked man in my bathroom.* She dismissed all thoughts of Pete and headed downstairs for her favorite pint of ice cream. She found Keith laying the sofa engrossed in the sports channel.

"When did you get home?" she asked coming up behind the sofa.

His eyes didn't move from television. "Hey honey, almost an hour ago. Man you were in that shower for a long time."

She blushed and tightened her robe around her. "I had a long day. I guess I lost track of time. Look we need to talk."

"Now?"

"Yes now," she snapped.

He reluctantly turned off the television and came in front of her. He held her by the waist. "You smell good, ready to continue our workout from this morning?"

She pulled from his embrace and hugged her shoulders. "What's wrong?" he asked.

"I went by your job today to surprise you with lunch," she informed him.

He frowned. "You did? Why didn't you have someone page me?"

"They didn't have to. I was told you were in the cafeteria."

"And?" he prompted. "Why didn't you come find me?"

"I did but you looked pretty occupied."

He looked at her confused. "Occupied?"

She glared at him. "Don't play dumb Keith. Who was that woman you were all intimate with?"

"Intimate with? Honey, what are you talking about?"

"It's funny how you seem to forget. You were sitting all cozy with her in the cafeteria."

"Wait, are you talking about Marilyn?"

"Whatever her name is, I don't care. Who is she Keith? And why haven't I met her before."

"She's an old colleague of mine," he explained. "She just moved here from Washington last week. We went to medical school together."

"Oh, so you too just had to get acquainted again, huh?"

He pulled her to sit down on the couch. "We were just having lunch. She was on break and asked me to join her."

"But we were supposed to have lunch together."

"I know, but you called me and said you couldn't get out of work."

"So she just happened to take my place, just like that?"

"Are you kidding me? You're taking this way out of proportion."

She stood up from the couch. "Oh am I? How would you feel if you found me having lunch with some man you didn't—" She caught herself in mid sentence. She was doing the exact same thing with Pete weeks ago. *But it's not the same thing,* she thought to herself.

He groaned. "You can't be serious about this."

"I saw you two holding hands."

"She just went through a bad divorce and lost everything. She even lost custody of her daughter. She just moved here two weeks ago with nothing. I was just consoling her."

"Oh," she continued more calmly. "Well, I'm sorry if you feel that I'm blowing this out of proportion but when I saw you two together…" her voice trailed as an image of the two flooded back into her mind.

"Shauna trust me, it was nothing."

She nodded slowly. "Okay, I believe you but I want to meet her. As a matter of fact, why don't you invite her to dinner?" She waited to see his response, any reaction that would find him guilty, but he didn't flinch.

"Sounds like a good idea. She told me she can't wait to meet you. How about we do it Saturday night?"

A twinge of guilt hit her. Here she was accusing him of having an affair while she just had a sexual dream about Pete in the shower. She decided it would be best to have Pete meet Keith and fast. Hopefully after meeting some the guilt would go away. "That's fine. And I also have someone I want you to meet."

He raised an eyebrow, "Oh, really?"

"Yeah, I bumped into an old friend of mine from high school the other day. Wait," she paused then broke into a smile. "I have an even better idea. How about we make it a dinner party like we planned? We could have it early instead of waiting for a couple of months."

He smiled in return. "Brains and beauty, it's a great idea honey."

She yawned then got up from the couch. "Thank you and I'm glad we got this settled. I feel so much better. I'm going to bed." She headed for the stairs in a fast pace.

"Hey, I thought we could continue where we left off," he protested disappointedly.

She turned around and winced. "Aw, honey I'm really tired. I just want to get to bed okay," she told him tiredly continuing up the stairs. There was no way she could make love to Keith. She couldn't get Pete off her mind. She could still feel his hands on her. *Lord please help me get this man out my head*, she prayed with a sigh.

*   *   *

When Monica arrived to work the next morning, she found a bouquet of red roses on her desk. She sighed as she laid her briefcase down next to the vase. *This is going to be harder than I thought.* She began to take in the aroma then smiled. She had to admit the perk of being admired by someone was nice.

"Nice flowers," interrupted a male voice.

She looked up and saw Sean at her door. She took off her jacket and sat down. *Let the dissin' begin.* "Yes they are, but don't you think it's a bit much?"

He walked into her office. "A bit much?" he repeated.

"Yeah, sending me flowers is not going to change my mind about going out with you."

"Um, those aren't from me."

She looked at him confused. "What?"

"Maybe you should read the card."

She pulled the card from the bouquet and read it to herself. *Thinking of you, Michael.* She looked up in embarrassment, "I'm sorry. I thought…" her voice trailed.

"It's okay. So… you have an admirer."

She shook her head. "An ex is not an admirer."

"The same guy at the club?"

She nodded.

"So I guess the kiss worked," he continued.

She shrugged. "I guess."

"So are you going to call him?"

She moved her flowers to another location. "I don't think that's any of your business."

"You're right. It's not," he concurred.

She motioned him to sit down. He closed the door behind him and took a seat. "Look about what happened yesterday," she began. "I really feel uncomfortable about the whole thing. It was unprofessional."

"I agree."

"You agree?" she repeated.

He stood up and adjusted his suit. "It was my fault and I apologize."

"Okay, um—"

"And I also think that maybe I should have someone else show me the ropes from now on," he interjected.

She frowned. *What the hell?* "Sean that's not what I meant."

"No, you're right. This is for the best. I hear you loud and clear."

She looked helpless. "O-okay, I guess I'll let Mr. Dykes know."

"No need. I spoke to him this morning. I told him I didn't want to take up all of your time. He agreed to have your co-worker Simone Hopkins, show me around from now on."

"Oh really?" Not only was Simone, beautiful and young. She was unfortunately very available.

He looked at his watch. "Yeah, it's all set."

"So this transition was done this morning?"

"Yes."

Monica couldn't believe what was happening. Her plan was working a little too well, "Before our talk?"

"Yes."

He began walking towards her door. "I better go. I told Simone I would only be a minute." Monica sat there speechless. She didn't think he would give up so easily? "Hey," he murmured softly. "I guess I'll see you around."

She put on a fake smile. "Yeah, see you around." Her smile faded as her door closed. She wanted him to stop asking her out but not to stop working with him completely.

"Monica, you have a call on line one," interrupted Jackie on her speakerphone.

"Who is it?" she asked a little annoyed. She was not in the mood to speak to anyone.

"He wouldn't say. He insisted I put him through."

Monica sighed. "Put it through."

She heard the line click over. "This is Ms. Stevens, how can I help you?"

"Did you get the flowers," a deep voice answered.

Michael...Damn. She leaned back into her chair and rolled her eyes. She took the card from the roses again. Her plan had worked but at that moment, he was the last thing on her mind. "Yes I did. What's the occasion?"

"No occasion, just missed you that's all."

She sucked her teeth. "Missed me? I'm sure my clone kept you too occupied to miss me."

"Come on Monica, you know me better than that. That girl meant nothing to me. There's no one else but you."

She rolled her eyes. "Look I have a lot of work to do, what do you want?"

"You."

She began to look at her nails already bored with their conversation. "Me? Um, I don't think so."

"Don't tell me that *kid* has occupied all of your time."

"Kid?"

"Yeah, the one you were kissing on at the club."

She smiled to herself. "What's the matter, afraid of a little competition?"

"From what I saw, I wouldn't call him competition."

She laughed half heartedly. "So you we're watching us that hard? Tsk tsk sounds like jealousy to me."

"I'm always watching you," he admitted huskily. "But I thought the eighteen and under club was down the street," he added sarcastically.

She grew hot. "Ha ha, very funny, he's more of a man than you will ever be."

"There is no way he can satisfy you the way I do."

"And who told you, *you* satisfied me."

"Trust me. A man knows when he is doing something right."

She cleared her throat. He indeed was the best lover she ever had by far. "Look, I have to go."

"Listen, I wanted to tell you…" he paused.

"Tell me what?"

"I didn't mean for things to turn out the way they did. I acted like an ass. I want us to be together again."

She laughed sarcastically. "So let me get this straight. You broke up with me to date chicken heads and now that you've had your fun, you now want to be together. Wow, I'm so flattered."

He sighed. "Monica I made a mistake."

"You've made too many."

"Come on Monica we can do this."

"Sorry, it's too late."

"It's never too late."

"I'm hanging up the phone."

"I'm not giving up on you."

"Bye, Michael."

She hung up the receiver with a smile. She had him right where she wanted him, begging for mercy. For the remainder of the morning, her thoughts continued to wander towards Sean. At lunchtime she called Tina and told her she was treating her to lunch. As she walked outside, she found him and Simone at one of the picnic tables outside the employee break room. They were chattering and laughing as if they were old friends. She tried her hardest not to look their way.

"Hey, Monica," yelled Simone waving for her to come over.

Monica put on her brightest smile as she approached their table, "Hey you two, how's it going?"

Simone smiled. "Great, what's up?" She had beautiful teeth.

Monica shook her head, "Nothing much just ready for some lunch."

"Well you can join us if you like. Sean was just telling me some crazy stories from his bartending job at night." They both looked at each other and snickered. He didn't even look Monica's way. He was acting like she wasn't even there.

Monica pursed her lips and felt a twinge of jealousy. "Um, no thanks, I'm meeting a friend for lunch and I'm already late. Maybe next time, okay?"

She walked away before Simone could say another word. *Why are you making such a big deal every time he's with another woman? You wanted him to stop asking you out and he did so get over it,* she scolded herself.

Tina was already pissed when Monica picked her up for lunch. She and Bryan had a conference scheduled with Joshua's teacher the next morning. He was acting out in class.

"I don't know what's going on," she rambled while cutting up her steak. "Joshua never acts out in class. I'm telling you that heifer has something to do with it. I hope she's not threatening my baby. I'll stick my foot so far up her ass—"

"Tina you don't know if she has been doing anything," Monica interjected

"Of course I do. I don't trust that woman. She has my baby scared stiff and I'm not going to put up with it."

"What are you going to do? Beat her up right in front of her house?"

Tina began to butter her roll. "Girl don't tempt me. You know I can get ghetto when I need to."

Monica laughed. "Hmph, is this about Joshua or Bryan?"

Tina put down her knife. "Bryan? Please don't go there."

"I don't know," Monica continued playfully. "You sound a little jealous to me."

Tina glared at her. "Oh, so now you got jokes."

Monica shrugged with a giggle. "I'm just saying."

"I know you're not talking. I'm not the only one who's not over her ex."

"I am over him." Monica disagreed.

"Yeah right, I'm not going to even argue with you. Anyway, did Sean ask you out again?"

"Nope, it's over girl." Monica filled her in on this morning's events including the call from Michael. "He's already given up and I'm glad because now I don't have to think about him anymore."

Tina raised an eyebrow. She could tell her friend was lying right through her teeth. "It could all be a front you know."

"Even so, it's for the best."

Suddenly Tina took her knife and pointed it at her friend. "Don't tell me you're going to start seeing Michael again?"

Monica rolled her eyes. "No...no, and will you put the knife down. Geez, like I said, I'm just *playin'* him a little longer."

Tina shook her head. "You need to stop playing games and let him go."

Monica frowned. "He started it. He needs to suffer."

"This is not about suffering. You still love him."

"Okay maybe I do a little," she admitted. "It's just going to take time for me to get over this hump. Wait hold on. Look who's talking about playing games. You're the queen of playing games."

Tina wiped her mouth with her napkin. "You're just mad because my game is *tighter* than yours."

Monica's jaw dropped. She threw her napkin at her friend then they both burst out laughing. Just then their cute waiter walked by and gave them a sexy smile. "You ladies need anything else? Some desert maybe?"

Tina gave him one of her famous smiles. She eyed him up and down. "Are you on the dessert menu?"

He grinned then scoped her in return. "No, but maybe that can be arranged," he chuckled.

Monica smiled. Her friend's game *was* tight but she had to cut lunch short. She didn't want to be late getting back to work. "Thanks Alex but we're done for now. Can we have the check please?"

He nodded and continued on his way. "Damn he's fine. Did you see that ass?" asked Tina watching him walk away. "If he walks by our table one more time, I might be tempted to grab it."

Monica giggled. "You are off the chain." She then sighed. "So you think he still loves me?"

Tina sucked her teeth then took out her compact and lipstick from her purse. "Who Michael? Oh please, the only person he loves is himself."

"I know, I know, but when I'm around him," she paused. "I don't think before I act."

"Hmph, you've been doing that around Sean too," Tina pointed out.

Monica shook her head. "Sean is not an option anymore."

Tina quickly applied some fresh lipstick. "That's what you think," she told her friend as she snapped her compact shut. "I'm telling you he's still into you."

"Tina, Simone has him under her wing now. She's closer to his age and beautiful. There's no way he'll be after me again."

"And what are you, the ugly duckling? Trust me, he's just trying to get you jealous."

Monica looked hopeful. "You think?"

"Of course, so what are you going to do about it?"

Monica crossed her arms against her chest. "Nothing, I'm not into playing games."

Tina raised an eyebrow. "Oh so, when you used Sean to make Michael jealous, you weren't playing games?"

"That was different."

"Different? How is that?"

Monica grinned. "That was revenge."

Tina laughed. "Revenge or not, if you want something you should go after it. It's all about power."

"Power, huh?"

"Power," Tina repeated firmly. "Watch this."

She fixed her composure quickly. She waved Alex back over who was watching them intently. He placed their check on the table. "Can I help you ladies with anything else?" he asked.

"Um yes, Alex we were just wondering if this restaurant provides valet parking?"

He shook his head. "No, unfortunately we don't."

Tina pouted then pulled her legs out from under the table. "Oh that's too bad. It's just that my legs are so sore from working out all morning and the car is so far," she told him as she ran her hands up and down her slim legs.

Alex licked his lips voraciously. "Well, I have a break in the next five minutes. If you can tell me where the car is, I'll pull it around for you."

Monica pressed her lips together to keep from laughing, *poor guy*. He looked like a dog in heat. Tina placed her legs back under the table and smiled. "That would be very nice of you," she purred handing him Monica's car keys. "But I don't want you to go out of your way."

"It's no problem," he assured her. "I don't mind helping two beautiful ladies in need. I'll be right back."

"Tina you better pray that boy brings my car to the front," Monica told her after Alex was safely away. "What if he decides to go joy riding in my car?"

Tina rolled her eyes. "Relax, he's ain't crazy. Now back to what I was saying. Women will always have something men want."

Monica pretended to act dumb. "And that is?"

Tina danced in her seat. "The kitty cat power, of course, but it's up to how we choose to give it up."

Monica shook her head and smiled. "You're no good, you know that?"

Tina winked at her. "Don't worry he'll get a nice tip."

Monica laughed as she placed some bills on top of their check. They walked outside and found Monica's car parked in front of the restaurant. Monica let out a sigh of relief. Alex held the car door open for Tina then anxiously asked her for her number. "How about you give me yours?" she persuaded as she closed her door.

He smiled. "As long as you use it, sexy," he responded. She handed him a pen and a piece of paper. He scribbled a number down quickly. "Make sure you call me now," he reminded her as he handed back her pen and paper.

"I can't believe you. You're probably won't even call him," Monica scolded her while driving off.

"Hey, you don't know that. He might come in handy," Tina replied putting the number into her purse.

Monica giggled. "Poor guy, he doesn't know what he's getting into."

Tina rolled her eyes. "Anyway, now back to you. What are you going to do about Sean?"

"Nothing, what do you want me to do? Loosen the buttons off my blouse and throw myself at him? Hell no. I'm not *pimpin'* myself to get him back."

"I didn't say all that. Just let him know two can play that game."

Monica sighed. "I'll think about it."

Tina shrugged. "It's up to you. Don't come crying to me when you're invited to their wedding."

Chapter Six

"I don't understand this, Ms. Johnson. Joshua has never been disruptive in class before," Tina informed her son's teacher for the second time. She and Bryan spent the last fifteen minutes listening to Ms. Johnson describe their son's behavior. Joshua sat in the corner of the classroom with headphones on playing on the class computer.

Ms. Johnson shook her head. "I don't know what to tell you. I was surprised myself. Lately he just hasn't been himself. Yesterday when art time was over, I told him to put away his art supplies and he ignored me. When I repeated myself firmly, he began throwing his markers all over the floor. I told him he needed to sit on the bench at recess for fifteen minutes because of his behavior and he told me he didn't care."

"I can't believe this," said Bryan speaking up. "My son is never that rude."

"He's right," Tina chimed in. "Something must be really wrong."

"Mr. and Mrs. Henderson—," Ms. Johnson began.

"We're not married," Tina interrupted.

"Oh, I'm sorry," she apologized.

"That's beside the point," said Bryan a little irritated at Tina's correction. "Ms. Johnson, do you have any idea why he's acting this way?"

She nodded. "I think I have an idea." She took out some drawings from her desk and handed it to them. "This week we worked on family portraits. I asked the students to draw a picture of their family and this is what he drew."

In the picture were four people. There was a couple on one side holding hands and a woman standing alone on the other side. She was crying. In the middle was a little boy with a sad face. Tears began to well up in Tina's eyes. The picture hit her hard. Her son was hurting. "When I saw this picture, I decided to call you both," Ms. Johnson concluded. "Is there something going on at—"

"He's just dealing with some things that we have no control over," Tina interrupted again. She was not ready for any accusations. She had tried her best to make sure they didn't fight in front of their son, but now she began to worry. What if he was watching without them knowing?

Ms. Johnson shook her head. "Look, I'm not here to throw blame. This is about Joshua and how he's feeling right now."

Tears rolled down Tina's cheek. She wiped them away quickly. A moment later she felt Bryan caressing her back softly. "Ms. Johnson we understand what you're saying," he stated. "We will talk to Joshua about it. He may be having a hard time dealing with the fact that his mom and I are not together."

"That's understandable but he can't continue to be disruptive in class. So I am suggesting that maybe you three should spend some quality family time together or maybe even seek counseling so he can cope with this. Just to let him know that even though you two are not together you could still spend time together as a family."

Tina finally looked at Bryan. "We will do anything to help out our son," she declared.

Bryan nodded in agreement. "His mother and I will work this out."

His teacher stood up and went around her desk. "Good. I'm going to get Joshua."

As soon as she walked away Bryan sighed and leaned back in his chair.

"Look, I know what you're going to say," Tina began.

He raised his eyebrow. "Do you really?"

"Yes. You're going to say you don't agree with us spending time together."

He shook his head. "Not at all, I think it would do us all some good."

She looked at him stunned and relieved at the same time. "Wow, I think this is the first time in a long time we've agreed with one another."

He smiled. "You know, you're right. If we keep this up we could actually have a normal conversation."

She smiled in return. "Whatever."

That afternoon, they had a long talk with Joshua. Together they chose two days out of the week to have family dinner. They also decided to do an activity twice a month together as a family. Joshua was so excited. He couldn't stop talking about the places he wanted to go. He finally settled down when they tucked him in at bedtime.

"He's like a different kid," Tina told Bryan as they left his room. "I've never seen him so happy."

He chuckled. "Yeah, I think he should be okay now."

They both became silent as they walked into the kitchen awkwardly. Without the arguing, it was hard for them to have a conversation. Tina headed towards the stove as she heard her tea kettle whistle. She turned off the burner then pulled open her cupboard. "Do you want some tea?" she asked grabbing for a tea cup.

"No thanks, I better head home. Sharon has been calling me all day."

"Oh really," she paused placing a tea cup on the counter. "Speaking of Sharon, I got a call from her the other day. Would you kindly tell her never to call my house again?"

"She told me about the conversation. She said you were giving her a hard time."

Tina turned around with a frown. "Me? That woman called me baby momma drama. Have you been complaining about me?"

He frowned in return. "No."

"Well she seems to think that I've been giving you hell since you two got together. I wonder who gave her that idea."

"Tina I'm not in the mood to argue with you."

She ignored his comment. "Have you had a chance to ask Joshua how he feels about her?"

"Yes and he doesn't exactly adore her but I told him that he needs to get to know her. She's a good woman Tina."

Good woman my ass, she thought. She began pouring some hot water into her cup, "So good that you'd want to marry her?"

He was silent for a moment. "Maybe," he answered finally.

Her hand trembled at his response. It caused some of the hot water to splash on her hand. Instantly she dropped her cup into the sink. "Ow! Shoot."

Immediately he was by her side. "Are you okay?"

She nodded as her hand continued to throb. "Yeah, I'm okay." He took her hand and examined it closely. Her heart fluttered. She pulled her hand back hastily. "I'm fine."

He pulled it back. "You need to run some warm water on that," he ordered softly.

He turned on the faucet and held her hand under the running water. He was so close she couldn't breathe. "Thank you," she muttered. "For doing this for Joshua, this is exactly what he needs."

"You don't have to thank me. I would do anything for him." He turned off the water. He took a towel from the counter and wrapped it around her hand. A moment later she began to laugh. "What?" he asked.

"Nothing," she answered trying to contain her laughter.

"No really, what?"

She smiled. "Déjà vu."

"What?"

"Déjà vu," she repeated. "This just reminds me of something that happened in college. Remember when I tried to make that nice candlelit dinner for two for our first date."

His mouth formed a smile. "Oh yeah, that was some night. I didn't know you're supposed to bake pork chops for over five hours."

She pouted. "I was just making sure that it was tender."

"Yeah, but it caught on fire instead. And then you tried to take it out the oven with no gloves."

She laughed. "I was so nervous. I just wanted that night to be perfect."

He chuckled. "Yeah, but it turned out great. We shared our first burnt dinner together."

"And our first kiss," she supplied a moment later.

"Yeah, I remember," he said softly. "You know Tina, I never meant to hurt you."

She looked away and remained quiet. Tears stung in her eyes without her consent.

"We just didn't want the same thing at that time," he continued.

"And now?"

He pulled her chin to look at him. "And now we have a great son. I wouldn't trade that for anything in the world."

She nodded and finally gave into her tears. He brushed them away then embraced her. She melted in his arms. It felt good being in his arms again. It was where she belonged. "I'm happy you're now apart of his life," she muffled against his chest.

He pulled her away from his chest then gazed into her eyes. Then to her surprise, he began kissing the tears that wouldn't stop falling. Her heart pounded loudly in her chest as his warm lips stroked her face. His lips were now close to hers. Slowly their faces leaned towards each other but before they could meet, his cell phone rang. He paused before letting her go. He walked a few feet away to answer his phone. She could hear Sharon yelling on the other end.

"I have to go," he told her a moment later as he snapped his cell phone shut.

She nodded a little hurt. "You never jumped like that when we were together," she remarked.

He put his jacket on slowly. "It's not what you think. She says she's not feeling well."

"Yeah right," she mumbled under her breath.

"Excuse me?"

She shook her head. "Nothing, just do what you have to do."

"Look about what just happened," he paused.

She glared at him. "Let me guess, forget it ever happened?"

"That was not what I was going to say."

Her voice softened a little. "Okay then, what?"

"It's just that Joshua is my main priority. I don't want to confuse him."

She frowned. "But it's okay to confuse me?"

"No it's not, look today has gone so well. Let's just leave it at that okay?"

She turned away heatedly without a response. A moment later she heard his footsteps head towards the door. "Do you love her?" she blurted when she heard her door open.

"Do you really want to know the answer to that?"

"It's a simple question."

"This is crazy. I really don't feel like getting into this right now. Is it okay that I pick up Joshua from school tomorrow?"

She glanced back at him. "Sure."

*   *   *

Monica thought about what Tina said on the ride back to work. Just as she pulled into the parking garage, she spotted Sean on his cell phone by the entrance. A moment later he headed towards the elevator. *Maybe one little button won't hurt,* she thought as she loosened the top button on her blouse. She did a quick check in her rearview mirror and quickly got out of her car. She got to the elevator just as it opened. He gave her a nod and let her on first.

Once the doors closed, he pressed the button for their floor and stood quietly on the other side of the elevator. There was an uncomfortable silence. Through peripheral vision she could see him continue to look straight ahead. She cleared her throat loudly but he didn't flinch. His nonchalant attitude was driving her crazy.

"Okay that's it," she exclaimed out loud. She pressed the emergency button on the elevator and it came to a halt.

He frowned. "Whoa, what are you doing?"

She stood in front of him. "Why are you acting like this?"

He gave her a blank look. "Acting like what?"

"Like I don't exist."

He frowned. "I don't know what you're talking about. Look I don't think stopping the emergency button is safe." He pressed the release button and they began to move once more.

She turned around and pressed the emergency button again. The elevator came to a halt. She glared at him. "Look when I turned you down for dinner, I didn't think you'd take it personally."

"Didn't think I would take it personally?" he repeated. "Of course I took it personally. You take me as a joke so how did you expect me to react?"

"Maybe like an adult," she answered irritated. *Why did he have to make things so complicated?*

He laughed at her response. "I can't believe this. You're the one who stopped this elevator complaining that I'm not paying attention to you. Who's the adult now?"

He was right. The argument was becoming a little juvenile. She closed her eyes for a moment. "Look, I just don't want things to be awkward between us."

"Why should it matter? You don't feel anything right? Monica you can't have your cake and eat it too. I know you're attracted to me but you're too stubborn to admit it. I've never met someone so spoiled in my life."

Her eyes grew large. She couldn't believe he was snapping at her. "I am not spoiled. I just want..."

"Want what?" he asked impatiently.

"I-I just want us to be friends."

"Friends," he mocked angrily this time. "So you loosened the top button of your blouse to be friends? You're so pathetic."

Instantly, she raised her hand to slap him but he grabbed it instead. He pulled her close. *"Let me go!"* she yelled angrily trying to pry away from him.

He continued to hold her tight. "Why don't you just admit that you want me?"

She rolled her eyes and struggled harder. "You're so full of yourself. I can't stand you," she seethed.

"Oh really, you can't stand me yet you still want to be friends?"

"Y-you self-centered s-son of..," she stammered. She stared back into his light brown eyes that were now piercing. *Why did he have to be so damn sexy?*

"Do you really want me to let you go?"

She struggled for an answer. "Yes...no...just."

He began to rub the tip of his nose lightly on her neck. She trembled. He gazed into her eyes once more, "Just what?"

She responded by kissing him hard. He was caught off guard but then he returned her kiss fervently. Her tongue eagerly searched for his. He picked her up and leaned her against the elevator wall. Instantly she wrapped her legs around his body. She sucked his bottom lip playfully. Her body ached for his painfully.

She stopped suddenly and stared at him intensely still breathing heavily. It was as if someone had taken over her body. She roughly pushed her body towards his until they both fell onto the floor. He moaned as she quickly opened his shirt and began kissing his chest. With one free hand, she massaged his groin below. She could feel him grow beneath her hand. *Damn he's big*, she thought. The thought of him inside her made her even more restless.

In one swoop he pulled himself from under her and placed himself on top. He unbuttoned the rest of the buttons on her blouse then pulled her bra to the side. She cried with pleasure as his mouth met her breasts. His teeth tugged at each nipple softly. She moaned with pleasure.

His hand moved downward to pull her legs apart. His hand ran over her black lace panties. She began to get moist quickly. With one finger he pulled her panties to the side. His finger anxiously dug into her moistness. She couldn't stop trembling. She whimpered as he made circular motions around her clit.

He took hold of her mouth again as his motions became rapid. She couldn't breathe. "Ohhhh Sean," she sighed as their kiss ceased. Slowly he inserted his finger inside her. His mouth moved back to her breasts. She closed her eyes. Her body screamed with ecstasy. "P-Please, you're driving me insane," she begged. She could feel herself ready to cum.

"Come on baby," he told her. "Tell me you want me."

Damn why did he have to speak? She froze and lost her nerve once more. Yes, she wanted him, but showing it and saying it were two different things. Her eyes fluttered open. "Sean, stop."

"Huh?"

She pushed him away and closed her legs. She began to button up her blouse. "I can't do this."

He gave her a cynical look. "You've got to be kidding me."

She stood up then leaned on the wall for support. Her legs were weak. She pulled up her underwear. "Unfortunately I'm not."

He watched her as she smoothed out the wrinkles on her blouse. He stood up disappointedly and began to button his own shirt. Finally she pushed the emergency button to restart the elevator. "I'm sorry," she told him finally. "I can't believe I let things get out of hand again."

He adjusted his tie and gave her a dirty look. "This is exactly what you wanted."

She came towards him. "No, really. I wanted to fix things. I wanted—"

He took a step back. "To what, humiliate me again?" he interrupted.

"You know what I can't deal with your multiple personalities anymore. Just stay away from me."

The thought of not being close to him again scared her. She shook her head. "I-I can't do that."

"And why not?"

She bit her bottom lip. "Because I do want you," she confessed finally. "But not like this."

"Monica I'm not in the mood for anymore games."

She picked her purse off the floor. "I'm not playing games. I'm just nervous. I've never been with a younger man before. This attraction is all new to me. We can still have dinner if you still want to but if you've changed your mind, I understand."

His expression changed a little. "I haven't. I just want to make sure that this is what you want. I don't want you to change your mind later on."

She shook her head. "I just want to get to know you better before things get out of hand again. I'm just so focused on the age difference."

He broke into a grin. "By the time I'm done dining you. Age will be the last thing on your mind. How does tomorrow night sound?"

She gave him a warm smile. "Sounds good."

He took her hand and brought it to his lips. "Trust me. You won't regret this."

She nodded. Just then the elevators opened. She pulled her hand away quickly and cleared her throat. There were a couple of people waiting impatiently. She looked straight ahead then headed towards her office quickly. She could feel cold stares on her back. She never wanted to be the topic of gossip at work but that was certainly out of the question now.

"Um, Monica," called Jackie from behind her desk.

"Not now Jackie," she exclaimed hurriedly in a hush tone. "I'll get my messages later."

"But—"

She waved her off and walked into her office in a fast pace. She closed the door behind her then closed her eyes and exhaled in relief. Her heart pounded loudly in her chest.

"You sound like you could use a massage?"

She jumped. The deep male voice sounded all too familiar. She looked up as her chair swiveled around to reveal her ex staring at her. Her eyes grew large. "What the hell do you think you're doing?" she asked angrily heading towards her desk.

He chuckled. "Calm down baby, I came here for a delivery."

"Michael if my boss finds you here I could get in a lot of trouble. I can't believe Jackie let you in here," she told him furiously.

"I told her I was a client and that you'd be expecting me."

She headed towards her phone. "Get out or I'm calling security." She picked up her receiver and began dialing.

"So I guess you don't want this then?"

He placed a long velvet box on the desk in front of her. She paused on the last number. "What's this?"

He rubbed his hands together and smiled proudly, "Just a little token of my affection."

"A token of your affection?" she repeated placing her receiver back in its place.

He laid the box in her hand. "It's your birthday gift. Open it."

She rolled her eyes and opened it slowly. "Michael if you think this..."

She gasped as her eyes set on a diamond tennis bracelet. *DAMN!!!* She remembered seeing the same bracelet in a jewelry store months ago during a lunch date with him one afternoon. She never thought he would actually buy it. The cost was three thousand dollars.

"My God Michael... is this is the same bracelet..." Her voice trailed as he nodded. He took it out of the box then came in front of her. He fastened it on her wrist. She admired it for a moment. "I don't know what to say."

"I remember how much you wanted it. You could never just pass that store without looking at it"

She was actually touched that he remembered. "I can't believe you remembered that."

"How could I forget?" he smiled taking her hand. "You dropped hints about the thing for two solid weeks." Then without warning he pulled the palm of her hand to his lips. She closed her eyes. It didn't matter what he did, her body responded to him immediately.

Suddenly the images of him at the club with his hoochie mama popped into her mind. She yanked her hand away and began to unfasten the bracelet. "I can't accept this." She placed it back in the box and handed the box back to him. "Thanks, but no thanks."

He refused the box. She grabbed his hand and wrenched it open. She placed the box in it. "Monica, I'm just trying to be real," he told her sincerely.

She gave him a stern look. "Oh really, were you trying to be *real* at the club too? Michael, I've moved on, I'm through playing games with you."

"Look, I apologized about that. If you want me to shout it to the world, I will. I'll do anything to be with you again. We're a match. It just took me a while to realize that. I can be a good man for you again. Just give me a chance to show you. " He handed her the box again. "Please, take it."

She crossed and arms against her chest and looked away. He laid the box back on the table. "You deserve the best and that's what I plan to give you."

"Michael I'm not—"

He placed his finger to her mouth to silence her. "I'll talk to you soon."

He planted a kiss on her forehead and headed out the door. Once her door closed behind him, she walked back to her desk and sat down. She stared at the velvet box for a while. She finally opened it up and took out the bracelet again. She placed it on her wrist and smiled. *I do deserve this. After all, it was my birthday.*

"Ms. Stevens. Mr. Dukes is on line one," interrupted Jackie.

Monica straightened quickly. "Put him through Jackie." She hoped it get through to him that Michael had dropped by. It was policy that employees were not allowed to have visitors while on the clock.

"Monica did you finish the Hutchinson account as of yet?" he asked.

She shuffled through some papers off her desk. Her desk was never this messy. Her head was definitely not in the right place. "Almost," she answered. "I'm trying to finish up some last minute numbers right now," she lied finally finding the paperwork. She wasn't even half way through with the calculations.

"Good, I just spoke to Mr. Hutchinson himself and he asked if we could have the paperwork done by Friday morning."

"F-Friday morning?" she repeated.

"Is that a problem?"

"No, no. It's not a problem I'll have it for you first thing."

"Good. I knew I could count on you. Well, I'll let you get back to work."

She groaned when the line went dead. *Two days? Two days to finish two week's worth of work? Damn.* Her date with Sean was definitely out of the question now. She would have to work straight through the night and tomorrow night. For the rest of the day she stayed in her office and worked on the account.

"Monica, can I come in?" Sean's voice muffled through her door later that day.

She looked at her watch and realized it was thirty minutes after five. She had completely forgotten she needed to cancel their date. "Come in," she called out.

"Working late?" he asked as he stepped in.

She did not look up from her computer. "Yeah, I was just informed the Hutchinson deadline was moved up. I have so much work to do."

"Is there anything I can do to help?"

She finally looked up from what she was doing and sighed. She held her head frustrated. "No, not really. I have everything under control. Uh look Sean, about tomorrow night—"

"I've been thinking about it all day," he interrupted excitedly. "I called La Mira and made reservations for eight o'clock."

"La Mira?"

"Yeah, have you been there before?"

She shook her head. "No, I've always wanted to go there but never had the chance to check it out. I heard it's hard to get reservations."

He headed towards her desk and beamed. "I got a few connections. I guess it's a good thing I came along then, huh?"

She bit her lip. "Sean, you're making this really hard."

"What's wrong?" he asked confused.

"I can't go."

He frowned. "You can't go, why not?"

She leaned back in her chair disappointedly. "I lied and told Mr. Dykes I was almost done with the account but I'm not even halfway through it. How about we go out Friday night?"

"I'm working."

"Oh."

"I'm sorry Sean, for the next two days, I'll be a prisoner here and at home," she told him helplessly.

"I get it," he assured her unhappily. "I was just really looking forward to this."

She smiled sadly. "Can I get a rain check?"

"Of course."

She came from around her desk and stood in front of him. "If it makes you feel any better, I was really looking forward to being with you too."

He smiled a little. "It does, but I hate that I have to cancel those reservations. I'd better call them back. " He turned to head towards the door. She caught his arm gently.

"Wait since I'm going to be cooped up in my house," she murmured sexily playing with his shirt collar. "I won't have time to cook tomorrow night. It'll be nice if a sexy man were to stop by and surprise me with some dinner."

He grinned then wrapped his arms around her waist. "Is that an invitation?"

She smiled at him tenderly. "I guess we'll see what happens tomorrow night."

"Just make sure you're appetite is ready, for food and me."

She caressed his cheek lightly. "Hmm, I like that combination."

He spotted Michael's gift on her arm. "Hey, is that new?"

"Um yeah, uh I just put it on. It's a birthday gift from an old friend of mine."

He raised an eyebrow. "Wow, you must be a *good* friend to get diamonds."

She laughed nervously. "I deserve the best right."

He smiled. "Yeah, you do. Don't forget I still owe you a gift."

"Sean, you don't have to."

He shook his head. "I don't need you telling me what I don't have to do. Let me be the one in charge for once."

He slowly leaned towards her for a kiss. His kiss made her moist again. She loved it when he took charge. When he left, she went back to her desk and sat down. She giggled to herself as she remembered the scene in the elevator. She felt like a different woman around him. Hiding her feelings was getting too hard. She was happy that she finally confessed. She was anxious to see him again outside of work. She felt guilty for not telling him about Michael's gift though. He wouldn't understand that it was only a gift and didn't mean a thing.

She stayed a couple more hours at work and was exhausted by the time she shut the Hutchinson file. She gathered her things quickly to head home for a relaxing bubble bath. When she closed her office door behind her, she began to search for her car keys in her purse. All of a sudden she heard muffled voices coming from down the hall. She didn't think anyone else was working so late. She got curious and wondered if someone was having an office affair just like her. She walked towards the voices and ended up in front of Simone's office.

Her blinds were partially closed. She bent down to peek through them cautiously. She could see Simone but she was not alone. There was a man with her. They were holding each other close. He was stroking her hair. She could not see his face but somehow he looked familiar. She gasped as the couple pulled apart. Her heart dropped. It was Sean.

Chapter Seven

The next time Monica awoke, it was to the sound of ringing in her ears. She groaned. She had overslept and was late for work. She quickly grabbed her robe and headed for the shower. When she got to work, she was called into Mr. Dykes's office. He reminded her of their deadline again.

"Monica, I'm really counting on you to get this done. This is a real big account and we have a lot of money riding on this. Now if you can pull this off by tomorrow, then you can definitely see a promotion in the near future. But if you can't do this then—"

She quickly cut him off. "I can do it. I'll have the papers on your desk first thing Friday morning."

He gave her an appreciative smile. "Now that's the Monica I know, strong-willed and determined."

"Thank you Mr. Dykes, I promise I won't let you down." She hurriedly headed back to her office to continue working on the account. She had already informed Jackie she wasn't accepting any visitors or calls especially from Sean.

A promotion would be the highlight of her career. She was not going to let any man ruin that for her. She skipped lunch again that afternoon. While she was in the middle of calculating numbers, Sean walked in. She frowned. He didn't even knock. Jackie came in running behind him. "I told him you didn't want to be disturbed but he wouldn't take no for an answer" she protested.

"It's okay Jackie," Monica assured her.

Jackie gave Sean a dirty look then left. He closed the door behind him and leaned against it. Monica ignored him and continued working on her calculations. She could feel him staring at her. She pretended to be engrossed in her work but couldn't think in his presence. He walked around her desk. He bent down next to her. "Want me to take your mind off work for a little while?" he murmured.

She rolled her eyes impatiently. "Look I have a deadline," she declared heatedly. "I don't have time to fool around."

"Okay, okay, my bad. Listen about tonight, I was thinking—"

"Didn't you hear what I said or don't you know what priorities mean?" she interjected. "I have a deadline to meet. I don't have time to procrastinate. Maybe when you have a career you'll be able to understand what I am talking about."

He was taken aback. "Whoa, what's up with you?"

She shot him a poison dart look. "I told you I was busy and you're just not getting it."

"Do you have to be rude about it?"

"Look I don't have time for this. Why don't you just leave?"

He looked puzzled. "Where is all this coming from? Monica you really need to relax."

"Relax?" she repeated angrily. *Oh no he didn't just tell me to relax!* "Because I fooled around with you, I'm behind in my work. It's going take me forever to finish this account."

"Well how is that my fault? Sounds like you're the one that doesn't have *your* priorities straight," he retaliated.

Her face grew hot. She glared at him. "I want you to leave now."

He pursed his lips tightly then headed towards her door. "You don't have to tell me twice. Call me when you're able to put me on your priority list."

"Don't count on it," she mumbled under her breath. He paused at the door hoping she would stop him but she didn't. She began typing on her computer again. She forced herself not to look towards the door. A moment later her door closed with a slam. Her eyes began to water but she fought them back. *Girl you've come too far to jeopardize your career now. He is not worth your time*, she scolded herself sternly. *But why did it have to hurt so much*, her heart asked her. She pushed herself to keep working with him out of her mind for the rest of the day.

The day went fast. By five o'clock, she could hear co-workers shuffling to leave the office. She had hoped Sean would come by again but he didn't. Two hours later she shuffled her way out to her car. When she reached home she checked her messages hoping once more that he had called but there was only one message from Shauna inviting her to a dinner party for next Saturday night. She placed a frozen dinner unhappily in the microwave. She continued to work while she ate.

Within an hour, her living room had turned into something from a wasteland. Documents were scattered everywhere. She was a mess. Her mind was somewhere else. She groaned and closed her eyes. *Get a hold of yourself Monica. You're a grown woman. You can't let him get to you*, she scolded herself again. The phone rang interrupting her from her thoughts. Relieved she picked up the receiver.

"Hello?"

"Girl, where have you been?" asked Tina from the other end. "I've been trying to reach you at work all day. Jackie said you weren't accepting any calls, what's up with that?"

"I have this deadline to meet tomorrow. I can't do anything until I have this account done. I've been procrastinating all week."

"Hmm, and I wonder with who?"

"Yes and I've been punishing myself for the past two days because of it. And guess who had the nerve to stop by my office unannounced."

"Don't tell me, Michael?"

"Yes he did."

Tina laughed on the other line. "And you didn't call me? You better give me all the details and don't you dare leave out anything."

She hollered at the other end when Monica told her about her birthday gift. "I can't believe it. He went all out this time."

Monica tugged at the bracelet around her arm. "I've never seen him like this before. Maybe I should start taking him seriously now."

Tina sucked her teeth on the other line. "Girl, all Michael wants is some *booty*, besides what about Sean? I thought you were really into him."

Monica sadly informed her of the scene she saw the other night and their little argument. Tina became sympathetic. "Wow, I'm sorry. I thought he was really into you."

"So did I. How could I have been so stupid? I should've known he just wanted to hook up. I cancelled dinner so he found the next booty to take my place. I can't believe I was falling for him."

"You can't blame yourself for that. You didn't know this was going to happen. Are you sure you saw them together? It was probably something innocent."

"Eyes don't lie Tina. He was with Simone and they were in each other's arms. There was nothing innocent in the way he was holding her. It keeps running through my mind over and over. The thought of them together…" her voice trailed.

Tina was sympathetic. "I'm sorry honey. I can't believe it. I thought he was different."

"He's not, so this *thing* we had is over. I don't care if—"

Before Monica could finish there was a beep on her line indicating another call was coming through. "Hold on, Tina. I have someone on my line." She clicked over quickly. "Hello?"

"Hey, did you get my message?" asked Shauna from the other end.

"Yeah I'll be there," Monica told her a little bothered. Talking about Sean had gotten her worked up.

Her friend sensed her frustration. "What's wrong? Did I catch you at a bad time?"

"No. Hey, Tina's on the other line. Let me call you back so we can all talk on three-way."

Soon they were all on the phone chattering away. Monica knew she had to get back to work but her mind was elsewhere so there was no point.

"I'm a little nervous about the wedding," Shauna blurted suddenly in mid conversation.

Tina laughed. "Where did that come from?"

"I don't know, as the day gets closer…" she paused.

"That's normal honey," Monica told her. "Marriage is a big deal. Keith is the man you're going to be spending the rest of your life with. Having cold feet is normal. Just be happy that you've found a man who loves you and wants to marry you. You love him, don't you?"

Shauna sighed. "Of course I love him. I'm just afraid things will change once were married. What if he turns into a completely different person?"

"I doubt it," Tina disagreed. "He has three things most black men can't offer black women these days. He's educated, has a career, and most of all, he has money. That's definitely a plus in my book."

They all cackled. "*And* he's not a player," Monica added. "A dog, a gangsta, a thug, shall I continue?"

"So he says," said Shauna finally. She told them about Keith's lunch date.

"Having lunch with a co-worker does not constitute cheating," Monica told her.

"Yeah," Tina agreed. "Don't make a big deal out of nothing. Your man is the real deal. You don't want to lose him over assumptions."

"I know. That's why I told him to invite her to the party. I want a chance to check her out up front. What if she has other intentions? I'm not going to give her a chance to steal my man? Plus there's something else."

"Something else?" Tina repeated. "Oh Lord. Shauna what did you do?"

"Nothing," she protested. "I just met someone. I-I mean I didn't meet someone. I've known him since high school."

"And now you don't want to marry Keith?" asked Monica confused.

"No, no. Of course I want to marry Keith," Shauna stated quickly. "There's no doubt about that."

"So what's going on?" Tina inquired again.

"Um… I'm just…I mean I think I'm a little attracted to him. His name is Pete. He was my prom date." She neglected to tell them that he was her first. She knew it would make things look worse than it already is.

"Prom date," Monica persisted. "When did you run into him?"

"A couple of weeks ago," she answered. "It's just that he's changed a lot from the last time I saw him. He looked great. Oh hell, the man looked amazing." She proceeded to give details of her day dream. "I don't know what to make of it," she proceeded. "I can't stop thinking about the dream. It felt so real."

"But it wasn't," Monica reminded her. "Dreams don't necessarily mean anything."

"She's right," said Tina. "You said the man is hot so of course something like that might happen. But damn, I wish I would have dreams like that, maybe I'd sleep happier at night."

They laughed together once more.

"Okay maybe you're right," said Shauna feeling reassured. "I was getting worried over nothing. So are you two going to help me with the dinner party?"

"Like we have a choice," Tina answered sarcastically.

"Do you want me to invite Bryan?" Shauna continued ignoring her sarcasm.

"You can invite whomever you want?" Tina responded nastily. "It's not like we'll be there as a couple."

"Damn Tina, what's up with you?" asked Monica. "You're starting to sound like a bitter old woman."

Tina sighed heavily over the phone. "Alright, alright. I guess I should tell you that Bryan and I had a moment too," she confessed. "We almost kissed."

Both Monica and Shauna squealed into the receiver but she calmed them down quick. "Calm down. Calm down. I said we *almost* kissed," she reiterated loudly. Her voice came back to normal as she remembered the way he caressed her. "It was so nice. We talked about old times, we laughed, we were so close, and then he gets a call from Sharon and poof the moment went away. It's like she has voodoo on him or something. I know he still has feelings for me."

"Well now can you admit you still have feelings for him?" persuaded Monica.

Tina groaned. "I hate to admit it but I do. I tried to get over him, but it's been so hard. I can't believe it, after all he's done I still love the man. Aw man, what's wrong with me?"

Shauna laughed. "Nothing, you can't help who you love. So do you want to try to work things out again?"

"How can I with that woman in the way? I mean he's great with Joshua. You should see them together. He loves his daddy. We've all been spending more time together and it's been great. It's how I wanted my life to be like. It's not fair this *woman* is taking that away from me."

"So what are you going to do?" asked Monica.

"Nothing," Tina answered. "It's up to Bryan. I can't force him to leave her. He has to find out for himself that I'm the better woman for him."

"And he will," Monica told her confidently. "Look you need to—" Her doorbell caught her in mid-sentence. "Hey, my doorbell just rang," she told them.

"You think it could be Sean?" asked Tina.

"If it is, he's going to see the door in his face real quick."

"Wait I thought you liked him?" asked Shauna confused.

The doorbell rang again. "Tina, fill her in for me. I'll talk to you guys later."

She hung up the phone and opened her door in a huff. "Sean, you got a lot of nerve—" she began but stopped in mid-sentence.

"Sorry to disappoint you," Michael announced with a hint of jealousy in his voice.

She walked away from him. "What are you doing here?"

He walked in behind her and closed her door, "Trouble in paradise?" he speculated.

"I asked you what you're doing here?" she repeated turning to look back at him. "And I don't remember letting you in."

"I just wanted to stop by to see how you were doing."

"I'm fine, now bye," she muttered gathering all of her papers together on the floor. "I have a lot of work to do."

"But you have time for *Sean*?"

She gave him a poison-dart look. "Don't even start."

He sat on the floor next to her. "Okay, okay I'm not here to talk about him anyway."

"Then why are you here?"

"I see you're wearing my gift," he observed avoiding her question.

She stopped shuffling for a moment. He caught her red-handed. "I tried it on again and just forgot to take it off. This doesn't change anything. Look I'm serious I have paperwork to finish. You can see your way out the front door."

He scanned the area around them. "Maybe there's something I could do to help. Remember how much fun we had when we spent the whole night working on the Mitchell account."

She thought he was actually a great help. He loved accounting in college, so the work on that account was a breeze to him. He picked up a stack of paperwork and began looking over them. She snatched the paperwork back. "I don't need your help. I'm fine by—"

"Maybe you should look at those figures again?" he interrupted her.

She frowned then scanned over her papers quickly. "What figures?"

He pointed towards some numbers. "These numbers right here on page ten, they're all mixed up."

She looked over the numbers quickly then groaned. "I can't believe this. I'm going to be up all night trying to fix this."

He took the papers from her hand. "Don't panic. We can fix this."

She raised an eyebrow surprised. "We?" she repeated.

He grinned, "Yes, we."

She snatched the papers back from him. "Look, I can't let you do this. This is my job, my problem."

He grabbed them back from her. "Monica will you stop being stubborn and let me help."

She sighed. She had no other choice but to consider his offer. Two heads were better than one. The thought of staying up all night made her sick to her stomach. "Alright, where do you want to start?"

Chapter Eight

"Dinner was great, Tina," Bryan commented after taking a sip from his drink.

"Yeah mommy, I like the way you make your chicken and mash potatoes," Joshua commented licking the last of his mashed potatoes from the side of his mouth.

Tina smiled. She took a napkin and wiped his face. "Thanks, you two. Now Joshua, it's almost time for bed. Go ahead upstairs and brush your teeth."

"Aw man, can I stay up a little longer?" he whined.

"Now you heard your mom little man," chuckled Bryan. "Go ahead and get ready for bed. I'll be there to read you a story in a little bit."

"Aw, okay."

Smiling, they both watched their son run upstairs. "I guess having dinner together has been working out well," Bryan observed speaking up. "Has his behavior improved at school?"

Tina got up and began clearing off the table. "Yeah, Ms. Johnson says he's doing a lot better. No acting out at all."

"That's good to hear. Hey, I got a call from Shauna today about a dinner party she's having," he told her while placing their dirty dishes into the sink.

"Yeah, I heard about it."

"Are you going?" he asked now taking the dirty glasses from off the table.

She began to rinse off dirty dishes before placing them in the dishwasher. "Yeah, she already has me on kitchen duty. What about you? Are you going?"

"I told her I would, that was nice of her to ask considering..."
She turned to look at him. "We're not together?" she supplied.
"Yeah."
"Yeah, I know. So, are you bringing Sharon?"
"Tina she *is* my girlfriend."
"You don't have to *keep* reminding me. It was just a question."
"Well then you understand that I have to bring her."
She shrugged. "And I have no problem with that. It's not like I won't have a date for the party."
He raised an eyebrow. "Date?"
She dried her hands with the kitchen towel. "Yes a date. You know when a man and woman go out. What, you think I don't have other men *checkin'* me out? You think I'm not pretty enough to get asked out."
"I think you're beautiful," he argued softly. For a moment their eyes locked. Finally he cleared his throat and looked away. "So... do I know the dude?"
Even I don't know the dude. "No. Does that matter?"
"Yes it does. I don't want some man I don't know around my son."
She got a little irritated. "Oh, but it's okay for *you* to have a woman I don't like around him? You're not making sense."
He stood his ground. "Look, for a woman it's different," he disputed.
"Whatever Bryan, why don't you just admit you don't want me dating someone else because you still have feelings for me?"
He moved away from her and gathered the silverware from the table. "I can't believe you're starting that again."
"I'm not starting anything," she told him stubbornly. "You're the one who's acting jealous. It's written all over your face. You don't want my attention focused on anyone else because you want it all on you."
"That's not true, Tina. I just want you to be careful."
"Oh, so now you start to care," she retorted.
He turned around instantly. "Woman you're being ridiculous. Of course I care about you. You're the mother of my child."
She didn't want the argument to be over. "So this has nothing to do with jealousy?" she pressed.
He was not able to look her in the eye. "No," he answered
"Bryan, for once just be honest with me."
"Tina, I don't know what you want me to say."
She glared at him. She knew he was lying. She saw the way he was avoiding eye contact. She had to make him see he was lying to himself. She stalked angrily over to the kitchen table and pulled out a chair. She put one leg on top of it and began to pull her skirt slowly up her leg. "So if I were to

wear a skin…tight…dress that was this short on my date," she asked while raising her skirt higher and higher. "You wouldn't care?"

He glanced at her gesture. He couldn't tear his eyes away. He swallowed hard then looked away uncomfortably. After seeing his expression, she stopped and put her leg down. *What the hell am I doing? Throwing myself at my ex! Am I that desperate?* She plopped herself onto the chair. She covered her face with her hands. "I'm sorry. I'm so embarrassed."

He came towards her. He placed a chair in front of her and sat down. "You have nothing to be sorry about. We're both just confused right now."

She took her hands away from her face and folded them on her lap. It was her turn to avoid eye contact. "Look, you can go. I'll read Joshua a bedtime story."

"No I'll—."

"Bryan, please," she pleaded softly. "Just go."

"Alright then," he sighed. Slowly he got up from his chair. He put on his jacket then headed towards the door. He paused. All of a sudden in one swift move he took long strides back towards her. He grabbed her by the shoulders.

"What are you doing?" she asked startled.

He didn't respond. Instead he kissed her firmly on the lips. His kiss caught her off guard yet she responded by kissing him back passionately. His tongue met hers eagerly ready to taste what he longed for. Her tears flowed quickly as she realized how desperately she missed him. He lifted her up from the chair without letting go of her lips. He placed her on top of the kitchen counter. She wanted this for so long; for him to love her again.

She unbuttoned his shirt gradually wanting to savor every moment. Her hands roamed over his chest. He moaned as she planted kisses along his neckline. She wanted him to remember the past, the nights they made love for endless hours. She wanted him to believe they were right for each other again. For a moment they gazed into each other's eyes. His body hungered for her. He began to unbutton her blouse never taking his eyes off hers. He finally admired her breasts in anticipation. He took one of her nipples into his mouth. "I've missed you," he murmured.

She moaned and closed her eyes. She ached for him painfully. She arched her back to meet his hunger. He bit her nipples lightly causing her to break down. "I want you Bryan," she cried. "I want to feel you inside of me again. Make love to me please."

Suddenly everything stopped. "Bryan?"

He pulled away. "Tina, we can't do this, I'm sorry."

She opened her eyes slowly only to face an apologetic look. "What's wrong," she asked confused.

He began to button his shirt. "This is not right. I shouldn't have led you on like this. I have a girlfriend."

She pursed her lips upset that she let him take advantage of her vulnerability. She immediately began to button her blouse in humiliation. "I can't believe this. You weren't thinking about her a moment ago."

He tried to hold her again. "I'm sorry."

She flinched and pushed him away roughly. "Don't" she snapped. "I get it. You don't want me." She got down from her counter and hugged her shoulders.

"Tina, that's not true."

She refused to look at him. "You don't have to lie. You know what, just go home. Go home to your girlfriend."

"Tina, please!"

"*Go*," she yelled this time her voice quivering. "Please, just leave me alone!"

Reluctantly, he headed for the door then pulled it open. "Believe me, the last thing I ever wanted to do is hurt you," he informed her remorsefully before leaving out the door.

"Well, I guess that's it." Monica yawned tiredly as she plopped herself back on the couch.

Michael lay next to her. He gave her a lazy smile. "Yeah, we calculated everything twice. It's perfect."

Monica had never been so drained in her life. It was three thirty in the morning. Her ex had surprised her once more. He could've been doing something else with his time, yet he chose to stay and help her. He was actually being sweet and decent. *This* was the Michael she fell in love with. If Sean didn't want to spend time with her, Michael didn't seem to mind taking his place.

"Why did you do this?" she asked getting up from her position. She entered her kitchen and took out wine glasses from her cupboard.

He sat up. "Do what?"

She shook her head and poured wine into both glasses. "You know what I'm talking about. You helped me big time. I've been a bitch to you for the last couple of weeks, even though you deserved it, yet you still helped me."

She headed towards him and handed him a glass. He took the glass and set on the lamp table next to him. "Monica, like I told you. I'd do anything for you."

She laughed as she set her own glass on the lamp table next to her. "*Monica I'd do anything for you,*" she mocked. "What are you up to?"

He grabbed her hand lightly. "Listen, I know I messed things up big time but you have to give me a second chance. I want to make things right."

She shook her head and sat back down on her couch. "I don't understand you. You're like two different men. You say one thing and do another. I'm sorry but I don't trust you."

"But I'm trying to make things right," he told her frustrated.

"Don't get mad because I'm on to your game. Why don't you say what you really mean, if this is just about sex just say it?"

"It's not about sex."

"Yes it is," she disagreed.

"Why do you keep putting words in my mouth? Don't you want to hear me out?"

"Of course I do, but only if it's the truth."

He got up and placed himself next to her. He took both her hands in his. Her heart began to pound as he stared deeply into her eyes. "First of all, I don't want to have sex with you. I want to make love to you but that's not all I want. I finally realized you're the only woman I know who can make me feel whole. Your smile captivates me. You're a passionate, determined, intelligent woman and that fascinates me. Your pain causes me pain. I love your style, your mind, your body. Without you I feel incomplete. I adore you, baby. I love you."

Damn diggity damn!!! She swallowed hard. She never thought those words would ever come out of his mouth. *What book did he get this from? Focus Monica! Focus!!* She shook her head. "Michael I—"

He intervened by quickly bringing his finger to her lips. "Let me make love to you," he whispered.

She quickly jumped off the couch. She began to feel hot. She rubbed her hands together. "I-I can't," she stuttered.

He stood up in front of her and rubbed her shoulders. "Relax," he whispered. Her body was unable to do so. It was screaming for him. She closed her eyes as her heart pounded in her chest. She he could feel him close. His kiss caught her off guard. It was gentle and soft. So different from his usual kisses which were always demanding. She opened her eyes once he pulled away.

She didn't know what to do next. She was so lonely yet there were doubts that still existed. Her body finally made the decision for her. *Shit, I'm horny as hell*, her mind decided for her. She pulled him roughly for another kiss.

This time her tongue explored his mouth like it was her territory. His tongue quickly played with hers longing for much more. As their kisses became more persistent, he picked her up and laid her gently on the couch. Her clothes disappeared quickly. He planted kisses on her body beginning from her legs unto her breasts. He sucked her nipples like a newborn baby occasionally blowing on them. She moaned with delight as her nipples grew hard.

"Damn, I've missed these," he murmured briefly pushing her breasts together to suck them simultaneously. She sighed with pleasure once more. When she no longer wanted him to have all the control, she moved from under him and climbed on top.

Instantly, she ripped his shirt open. His abs were striking. The man resembled a roman God. She returned the favor by licking his nipples teasingly. Her hand roamed down to stroke his pulsating dick through his pants. At last she unzipped his pants and pulled on his boxers. His dick popped out like a jack in a box. It was large, thick and ready to please. She giggled. "I see someone's glad to see me." She got off of him and went into the kitchen.

"Where are you g-going?" he asked anxiously as her warm body moved away from his.

She winked at him. "I think you need to cool down a little." She opened her freezer door and put some ice into a bowl. She quickly went back to him and began to rub the ice around the head of his pulsating dick.

"Hey, that's cold," he cried out.

She laughed. "Let me warm you up then," she murmured putting him into her mouth. She sucked him slowly making sure she relaxed her throat at first then finally put all of him in. He was definitely endowed in the right place. She gently rubbed the ice around his balls then sucked on them as well. He closed his eyes and threw his head back. He moaned repeatedly with pleasure.

It was all he could stand before exploding in ecstasy but he was not ready to do that just yet. His strong arms gathered her up and carried her over his shoulders into her bedroom. She squealed in delight at the act. He laid her softly onto her bed. Their eyes locked. His eyes put her in a trance. Slowly he pulled her legs apart. His warm tongue urgently dug unto her moistness. He devoured her repeatedly. She came instantly.

As she remembered, he always made sure he was in control during sex. This meant making sure she was satisfied before he could receive his pleasure. Just when she couldn't take anymore, he positioned himself on top of her. "We belong together," he told her before entering her. "I'm the only one you need."

Each thrust brought tears to her eyes. It was not because of pain, but because she began to fantasize it was Sean making love to her. At that moment she realized that Michael was no longer the man she wanted. It was Sean.

When she climaxed, she bit her lip to keep herself from screaming out Sean's name.

When it was over, he plopped down next to her. He rolled over and fell asleep. She on the other hand didn't. She couldn't get Sean off her mind. *What the hell is going on? Why are you thinking about him? He's with Simone so there is no way you could want him again,* her mind told her but she couldn't change what she felt in her heart.

She didn't remember when she fell asleep. When she awoke she found Michael still asleep next to her. She began to realize she made a huge mistake. Slowly she crawled out of bed and grabbed for her robe. She tip toed into her bathroom and stared into the bathroom mirror. She groaned and splashed some water on her face. *Shit shit shit, why did you let that man into your house??* A moment later she felt strong arms embrace her from behind. She jumped a little.

"Morning baby," he whispered into her ear.

She turned to face him. He was completely naked. "Oh my God," she gasped turning away. His bottom half was ready for seconds

His mouth cracked a smile. "What?" he asked innocently. "You're not turning shy on me now are you?"

"Michael, please go put some clothes on."

He chuckled. "You don't have to act shy. He's just happy to see you."

She reached for a towel. She handed it to him then walked back into her room to gather his clothes. "Look, you have to go," she stated bluntly.

He walked out after her and frowned. "Go? You still have time before work." He reached for her again. "Don't you want to go for seconds?"

She drew back. "No. This was a mistake. I wasn't thinking at all last night. I was tired and… and confused."

"Confused? Woman, what are you talking about? What happened was real and you know it. Just because you're a little scared—"

"I'm not scared," she interrupted. She gathered his possessions and handed them to him. "This shouldn't have happened and will *never* happen again. Michael, it's over between us. And I really mean it this time."

He glared at her. "Hold up, I show you how much I love you and this is how you treat me? Throwing me out like some whore? I don't believe this."

"Believe what you want. I thought this was what I wanted but I was wrong. I'm sorry but I'm not in love with you anymore."

"Y-You're not in love with me," he stuttered unbelievably. "So what… you'd rather be with that *kid*?" She remained silent. He shook his head disgustedly and began to put on his clothes. "Damn are you that desperate you'd rather rob the cradle than be with me? You don't need a boy, you need a man. "

She glared at him. "I don't need anyone." She stared him straight in the eye. "I can do fine all by myself." She headed for her front door then yanked it open. "Look, I don't even know why I'm explaining myself to you. You need to leave now!"

He fastened his pants and grabbed for his keys on her coffee table. He walked swiftly past her but then paused outside the door. "This is not the end Monica. I know you. I'm the best lover you'll ever have. I'm only going to give you one second chance and it's now."

She didn't hesitate. She shook her head. "No thanks, I'll take my chances elsewhere."

He shook his head then gave her devilish grin. He caressed her cheek. "Your mind can keep saying no but your body will always say yes," he told her then walked away with a satisfied smile. Finally the *real* Michael came out. She slammed the door behind him disgustedly. She went into her bedroom and picked up the picture frame she couldn't get rid of. Angrily she threw it into her garbage bin and groaned. *What the hell did I start now?*

Chapter Nine

Shauna began to get irritated as she tried to get pass the customers who rushed past her. Mimi's was packed. She was late for work but didn't care. She had to have a cappuccino to keep awake. She had awaken in a cold sweat around 3 a.m. and couldn't go back to sleep. She had another sexual dream about Pete. This one left her panties drenched. She began to get worried. No matter how hard she tried, she hasn't been able to get him off her mind.

"Excuse me miss... are you following me?"

She broke into a smile when she heard his smooth voice. She turned to find Pete standing next her. He wore a black suit. His hair was pulled back into a ponytail. She had never seen him look so handsome. He appeared even sexier than the first time she saw him. "Surely you're mistaken. I'm in line before you so you must be the one following me," she informed him with a giggle.

He gave her a sexy smile. "I guess you're right then. Maybe I am following you."

She laughed. Her heart fluttered as he gave her brief a hug. He smelled delicious. She was ready to have him for breakfast.

"Ma'am can I help you?" asked the girl behind the counter impatiently.

Shauna turned annoyed at the interruption. "I'll have two cappuccinos to go please."

"Add a coffee to that," he added placing money on the counter. He turned to look at her. "That's if you don't mind me paying. Man, two cappuccinos? I didn't know you liked those things that much."

"Ha ha, one is for my boss. You don't have to pay for this you know."

He winked at her. "Don't worry, I'm sure you'll make it up to me somehow."

She blushed then pulled a tendril in back of her ear. "Well, maybe I can. What are you doing Saturday night?"

He raised an eyebrow. "Are you asking me out on a date?"

She blushed again. "No."

"That's too bad. I was looking forward to spending time with you again."

The clerk placed the drinks on the counter in front of her. She picked up her two drinks and headed towards the nearest table with him following behind. She placed her drinks on an empty table. She found a pen and paper in her purse and began scribbling. "I'm having a dinner party at my house Saturday night. I would like for you to come."

"Let's see, a chance to see you dressed up again. That sounds like a plan to me."

"Great. Here's my address. It starts at seven o'clock."

"Thanks for the invite."

He reached out to take the piece of paper she handed to him. His hands brushed up against hers. Their eyes locked. Someone suddenly brushed past them breaking their moment. She snapped back to reality. She pulled her hand back quickly, "Um, no problem." She pointed to his tie. "So, um you look different from the last time I saw you."

He grinned and adjusted his tie, "That obvious? Do I look okay?"

"You look more than okay. As a matter of fact you look very handsome."

"Thanks, I have an interview this morning for an assistant principal position at my school."

"Wow, that's great. Are you nervous?"

"No and yes. I mean I really love the school and the kids. I've been employed at the school for some time now so I think I'm qualified for the position. I'm just going to answer the questions to the best of my knowledge. I'm sure I'll do fine."

"You'll do great."

"Thanks. Hey, did you mail off that application?"

He remembered! She nodded. "Yes I did. I guess I should find out if I got accepted in a couple of months."

"Are you excited?"

She flashed a smile and felt tingles all over. "Yeah, I guess I am," she answered excitedly.

"Good. Hopefully I'll be invited to the acceptance party."

"You'll be the first to get an invitation," she assured him.

He looked at his watch. "Wow, it's getting late. I have to go." He began to walk backwards. "Talk to you soon, okay?"

"Definitely," she murmured. As she watched him walk out the door she tried her hardest to look away but couldn't. *Please Lord, give me strength*, she prayed. She fanned herself off quickly before heading out the door.

Damn why did I let that man in my house? No, why did I have to be so horny? This has to be a nightmare! These were all thoughts that ran through Monica's mind on the way to work that morning. The account was finally done on time. It looked perfect yet she felt dirty. *How could you be so stupid? He came for booty and booty was what he got. I love you, Monica. Yeah right!! He knew what he was doing from the moment he stepped foot into my place and I fell for it again,* she thought repulsively. *Damn!*

When she got to work Mr. Dykes wasn't in his office but his door was open. She snuck in quietly and laid the portfolio on his desk. She then power walked back to her office. She let out a sigh of relief as she closed her door. She was not in the mood for a quick review. A moment later, there was a small knock at her door.

She rolled her eyes. *Shit!* "Come in," she called out. She braced for her boss's entrance. But no one came in. Instead a hand poked in waving a white handkerchief.

"I come in peace," Sean's voice muffled from behind the door.

She smiled to herself then fixed her face to look stern. "You can come in."

He walked in cautiously and closed the door behind him. "Hey."

She leaned back in her chair. "Hey."

He walked over to her desk. "Listen how about we start over. I'm sorry about the way I acted. I miss you."

I miss you too! She wanted to tell him but stood her ground, "Anything else?"

"Wait, don't you want this fight to be over?"

She turned back to her computer. "I have a lot of work to do."

He shook his head. "Damn girl, I just apologized and all I can get from you is attitude?"

"What's your point?" she asked still staring at her screen.

He sat in the chair in front of her. "What's up with you, Monica? I know you're stressed out, but lashing out at me won't make things better."

"On the contrary, it makes me feel a lot better. Or maybe I should find comfort in other co-workers like you did."

He frowned. "Other co-workers, you're not making sense."

She picked up her pen and twirled it around her finger. "It's funny how you seem to forget things like you… in Simone's office late at night… on each other like white on rice."

He shook his head confused. "Simone and I all over each other?" he repeated. "Man, where are you getting your information from?"

"Don't worry I have a very good, my eyes. I saw you in her office."

He shrugged. "So?"

She frowned. "So, it didn't look like you two were working. I see you couldn't even wait long enough for us to go out before you tried to hook up with someone else. Just in case you didn't get the memo, I'm not looking to get played, been there, done that and didn't like it. I hope you and Simone have a good time screwing each other."

For a moment they stared each other down. "Are you done?" he asked finally in calm tone.

She shrugged, "For now."

He stood up. "First of all, I'm not a player, a dog or whatever women continue to call all men these days. Yes, I was in her office and, yes, I was holding her—"

She cut him off quickly. "Look, I don't need to hear the details."

"*I was holding her*," he continued more firmly. "Because she just found out her father passed away."

Blood drained from Monica's face. "Wait….what did you say?" she whispered.

"He had cancer."

"Yes, I know but I thought he was in remission?"

"He was for a couple of years, but for the past couple of months he became sick again. The cancer began to spread throughout his body. The chemo wasn't working any longer. She just came back from seeing him in Baltimore last month."

"I can't believe this," she continued stunned. "I am so sorry. I just went by the office and saw you two and got jealous. The thought of you with someone else…I-I"

A moment later his hands wrapped around her shoulders; she turned to look at him embarrassed. "I can't believe I let my assumptions get the best of me." He remained quiet. She searched for a reaction but could not find one. She stood in front of him. "Please say something," she begged.

He sighed. "What do you want me to say?"

"I don't know, yell at me. Be angry. I deserve it."

He caressed her face. "Monica, all I want is to get to know you better. We've wasted too much time already."

She looked the other way. "I just feel so stupid. The thought of you two together drove me crazy. I couldn't even concentrate long enough to finish my work and took it out on you."

He gazed into her eyes. "Look, maybe some of the things you said the other day may be true. Maybe I need to take you more seriously. I know how much your work means to you?"

She shook her head. "No Sean, you're fine just the way you are. I jumped to conclusion so I have a lot of growing up to do. I don't think before I react."

He finally broke into a smile. He took her hand and kissed the inside of her palm. "Don't change too much. I like a woman with a lot of spunk. As a matter of fact, that speech you gave wasn't half bad."

She looked embarrassed. "I can't believe I said those things. What was I thinking?"

"You were thinking like a woman scorned. We all make mistakes. Stop being so hard on yourself, you're perfect."

She shook her head. "I'm far from that."

His voice became soft. "Maybe so, but you're perfect for me."

"Do you really mean that?"

He pulled her close. "I do. Is that a problem Ms. Stevens?"

She smiled and put her arms around his neck, "Well what if I don't believe you? How can you prove it to me?"

"Hmm, I have something in mind," he answered huskily. He kissed her passionately. She found herself melting in his embrace. "I can't believe I missed spending an evening with you," he murmured as they pulled away. "So did you finish the account?"

She bit her lip. Suddenly images of Michael sucking on her nipples crossed her mind.

"Monica?"

She quickly jumped out of her thoughts. "Huh?"

"I asked if you finished the account last night."

Again all she could picture was her moaning as she matched Michael's thrusts.

He waved his hand in front o her face. "Monica, snap out of it."

She snapped back to reality once more. "Yes?"

"What's wrong with you? Did you get the account done on time?"

She moved away from him. "Um yeah, I put it on his desk this morning."

"That's great. I knew you could do it. I wish I was there to help."

She smiled faintly. She felt so ashamed. They haven't even gone out on a date yet and she was already hiding things from him. "I wish you were there too but I got through it."

"I want to make it up to you."

"No, I should make it up to you. I started the argument. Listen my best friend Shauna is having a dinner party on Saturday and I would like for you to be my date. Will you come?"

His eyes lit up. "Wow, having dinner with friends. So I guess that means you're not embarrassed to be seen with me anymore."

"I guess I was acting paranoid, huh?"

"Maybe just a little but it's okay. You couldn't help how you felt."

She took his hands and entwined them with hers. "Well, all that has changed now. I can't wait to have dinner with you."

"Me neither but today, I'm going to treat you to lunch."

"Lunch sounds good. I know a nice restaurant over—"

He cut her off. "No, I've got someplace in mind."

She smiled, "Oh really, where?"

"You'll see. Hope you're appetite is ready."

She ran her finger up and down his chest. "Oh, it's always ready for you. You just better make sure you're ready for dessert."

* * *

"Shauna, pass me the garlic," ordered Tina mixing a large pot of pasta sauce on her friend's huge stove. "Monica, have you finished seasoning the Cornish hens?"

"For the millionth time, yes," answered Monica while rolling her eyes in irritation. "Damn Tina, I forgot how bossy you are when you're in charge of cooking."

Tina glared at her. "Look, I just want everything to taste good. Don't be jealous because I can throw down in the kitchen. Now did you put in parsley?"

Monica sighed. "Yes."

"Green pepper?" she continued asking.

"Yes," Monica answered again.

"Red pepper?" she asked once more.

Monica turned around and placed her hand on her hips. "Yes, yes, yes. *Gurl*, don't make me hurt you."

Shauna laughed as she cut up a red potato. "Maybe we should take a break," she suggested putting down the potato and knife. She wiped her hands and headed for the refrigerator. She took out a round cheesecake from her fridge and placed it on the counter.

"Isn't that for the party?" Tina asked eyeing the dessert eagerly. It was topped off with strawberries and dripping with syrup.

Shauna took out three forks from the drawer. "We deserve a break, besides there are six more of these in the fridge. It won't be missed."

"Thank God," said Monica. "I've been eyeing that cheesecake ever since Keith brought it in. Why didn't Keith hire a caterer anyway?"

Shauna placed the cheese cake on the table. "He wanted to but I told him no. He thinks I'm crazy. I don't know. I'm not used to living like this. I can't see someone beckoning at my call or me barking orders. It's just not me. I'm not going to turn into a snob like his mother."

"Shauna, you're so far from that," Tina disagreed. "Honey, if you don't need a maid, send her to my house. I need all the help I can get with Josh," she laughed.

Shauna laughed in return. "Look, we've been up slaving in this kitchen since six a.m. Are we going to eat this or am I going to have to eat it all by myself?"

Tina and Monica sprinted towards the kitchen table and took a seat. "Mmm, this is good," Tina smiled after placing a piece into her mouth.

"Man, I'm going to have to work double time in the gym tomorrow," said Monica licking some gooey syrup off the top of her strawberry.

"Oh, it won't be so bad," said Shauna

"Easy for you to say," Monica responded. "You eat like two grown men and don't even gain a pound whereas if I eat a piece of chocolate, I grow another piece of ass."

Tina snickered and Shauna gawked. "You need to stop. I don't eat like a—"

"I had sex with Michael," Monica suddenly blurted out of nowhere.

Shauna dropped her fork and Tina almost choked on her cheesecake. "H-hold on you did w-what?" Tina asked coughing this time.

Monica wiped her mouth then threw her napkin on her plate. "We hooked up, knocked boots, bumped booty."

"O Lord," said Tina. "How could you let that man break you down?"

"When did this happen?" asked Shauna.

Monica felt like crying. "He was the one that came over to my house the other night, not Sean. He ended up staying and helping me finish the account. Afterwards, he told me things I wanted to hear. How much he loved me and how beautiful I am. The next thing I knew I was naked and we were having sex. I thought he was what I needed but instead it made me realize how much I want to be with Sean." She groaned. "What am I going to do? If Sean finds out, he's not going to want to be with me anymore."

This time the tears did come. Her friends gathered around her and began to console her. "Wait, I'm confused," said Shauna. "I thought he wasn't interested anymore."

Monica filled them in on Sean's story. "You see," Tina began. "I knew it was all in your head. You need to figure what you're going to do about Michael. You know he's not the type to let things go."

"I know," she sniffled. "And if Sean finds out, things are over before they even start."

"Honey, you have to tell him yourself," said Tina handing her a tissue from her purse.

"Tina, it doesn't matter. He's not going to forgive me. If I had known the truth…," her voice trailed. "I can't believe I messed things up like this. There's no way he's going to understand something like this. I'm such an idiot."

"You stop that," said Shauna holding her hand. "We all make mistakes."

"He told me I was the perfect woman for him," Monica added. "How can I break his heart like this?"

"You have to tell him," Tina reinerated. "It's either he hears it from you or Michael."

Monica sulked in her chair. The thought of telling Sean really scared her but the thought of Michael telling Sean instead scared her even more. "You don't think I know that? I'm just scared of losing him. I guess I have to tell him before tonight. I invited him to the party. Shauna, did Keith invite Michael to the party too?"

Shauna nodded. "You know he did. You know they can't go anywhere without each other."

Monica pursed her lips. "Maybe I shouldn't come tonight."

Shauna straightened up quickly. "Don't you even think about it, I need you both here tonight? I can't do this by myself."

They both saw the nervous look on their friend's face and began to worry themselves. "You can't do what by yourself?" asked Tina.

"Nothing," she answered more calmly sitting back down. "It's just that I invited Pete tonight. I want you two to meet him."

"Are you sure you're doing the right thing by inviting him?" Tina asked watching her friend fidget in her seat. "You're talking about him now and can't even sit still."

Shauna rolled her eyes. "Pete's my friend. There is nothing between us remember."

"Except Keith," Monica retorted playfully. "Honey, are you sure you don't have feelings for him?"

"I-I'm sure," Shauna sputtered nervously. "I love Keith. I can't think about being with anyone else but him," she stated more firmly.

"All right girl. We believe you," Tina laughed. "Monica, she's right though. We all have to be here to hold each other's hands."

Monica narrowed her eyes at Tina. "Okay, your turn." she said.

Tina looked liked a small kid with her hand caught in the cookie jar. She finally sighed. "Alright, alright, Bryan and I sort of had a moment," she confessed.

"A moment," Shauna laughed.

"Nothing happened. We just kissed."

Monica raised her eyebrow. "Wait, you two didn't go past kissing?"

Tina wrinkled her nose. "We touched here and there but he chickened out on me *again*. I'm tired of it. If he thinks I'm going to sit back and watch him and that woman be all over each other all night, he's got something else coming."

"Well what do you plan on doing?" asked Shauna.

She grinned. "I have a date tonight."

"A date," Monica repeated curious, "With whom?"

"Remember that guy Alex, the one who valeted your car."

Monica threw her head back and hollered, "The waiter?"

Shauna gave them a confused look. "Who?"

"A cute waiter she gave her number to," Monica informed her. She gave Tina a high five. "That's my gurl. You fight back with a vengeance. Bryan won't know what hit him."

Tina giggled. "I knew that number would come in handy. I'm going to make Bryan regret he left me." She stood up and danced in place while her friends laughed. A moment later she plopped in her seat with a smile. "Man, I can feel tonight is going to be nothing but drama," she predicted. "Ladies we need prayer, because after tonight we'll need all the help we can get to keep us sane around these men. Can I get an Amen?"

"*Amen*," they said unison.

*   *   *

"Honey, can you get the door?" asked Shauna as she made sure everything was in place. Guests were starting to arrive. She began to get anxious. The thought of seeing Pete made her nervous. *I hope he doesn't look too good tonight.* Keith grabbed her waist from behind. He held her close

"Honey, will you relax. Everything looks great," he assured her. "It was a good idea to have this early. Now we can concentrate on each other as our wedding day approaches."

She nodded. "I know. I just hope that everything turns out okay."

He kissed her on her neck. "Did I tell you how beautiful you look tonight?"

She fixed some flowers in a vase. "Yes," she giggled. "At least five times."

She wore one of her latest creations, a white satin dress with a high bodice.

Sequins sparkled along the straps and backline of her dress. The doorbell rang again and she pushed him towards the door. "Boy, will you go get the door."

He groaned softly as he adjusted his tie. "We will definitely finish this later."

Within the next hour, more and more guests began to arrive. Bryan showed up without Sharon. He stated she wasn't feeling well. Shauna was relieved. Tina's plan would now definitely work without any distractions from his girlfriend. Michael also arrived alone. As soon as he walked in, he scanned the room. It was obvious he was looking for Monica.

In no time everyone began mingling with each other. Sounds of music and laughter filled the air. Tina finally arrived with her date looking stunning in her long silver fitted dress. There was one high split on the left side of her dress exposing a sexy leg. Shauna had to admit Tina was a pro when it came to making a man sweat.

"Dang girl, you are *working* that dress," Shauna laughed kissing her friend on the cheek.

Her date pulled her close. "Yeah, my *boo* looks real good, don't she?"

Shauna suppressed a giggle. *Boo?* Tina gave her a look as if to say *help me*!

Tina cleared her throat. "Shauna, I would like for you to meet Alex."

He nodded towards Shauna. "What up?"

Shauna smiled faintly. "Uh, nice to meet you." she returned. He was dressed like a hip hop star reject. He had a huge gold chain that hung on his chest, wore an oversized shirt and jeans that revealed part of his boxers. Shauna thought it was a shame because he was not hard to look at. She stepped to the side. "Come in and help yourselves to some hors d'oeuvres and the drinks are right over there."

Alex headed for the table practically knocking Tina out the way.

"Boo?" Shauna snickered as he was safely away.

Tina sucked her teeth. "Girl, don't even start."

"You did tell him this was a dinner party right?"

"Of course I did. He's been getting on my nerves from the time he picked me up in the hoopty he calls his car."

Shauna snorted. "Well, at least he has a car."

Tina rolled her eyes. "If you can call it that, do you know he drives in a lime green 1985 Cadillac. I almost fell to the floor. I hid my face the whole ride over here."

Shauna began to laugh hysterically.

"Shhh," Tina ordered hoarsely laughing along. "Thank God this is one date. He wasn't like this when Monica and I met him at the restaurant. How could someone so cute turn out to be a wannabe gangsta? Anyway he's only here for one thing and that is to make Bryan jealous. Is he here?"

Shauna nodded. "Yep and he's alone."

Tina raised an eyebrow. "Oh really, where's *Sharon, his gurlfriend,*" she drawled mocking Sharon's voice.

Shauna laughed. "I don't know, he said something about a stomach virus."

Tina scanned the room. "Hmph, w*hateva*, she's not here because she knows I'll whup her ass."

Shauna shook her head. "How about you go find him and show him what he's missing," she suggested.

Tina nodded. "Good idea." She quickly took out her lip gloss in her purse and refreshed herself. "Yep, it's time to make that man sweat."

Shauna watched her friend saunter sexily into her living room and smiled. Just as she closed her front door, someone pushed it back softly. She opened it back again to find a white woman before her.

"Hi, is this Keith Anderson's house?" she asked.

Shauna didn't respond. She couldn't stop staring at the beautiful woman who stood before her. She was the woman who was sitting with Keith at the hospital. Her long curly black hair cascaded around her face. Her green eyes sparkled as she smiled at her. Her voluptuous shape pissed Shauna off even more. Shauna could see right through her eyes. It was filled of deceit.

Shauna cleared her throat. "Yes it is, and you are?"

"Hey Marilyn, you made it!" Keith had come between them. He brushed Shauna aside and led Marilyn inside. Shauna frowned then closed the door with a slam. Keith turned when he heard the slam. He walked back towards her. "Oh honey. Where are my manners, I would like for you to meet Marilyn Goodman. Marilyn this is Shauna."

His fiancé. Shauna wanted to shout but instead held out her hand, "Nice to meet you."

Marilyn's smile resembled a venomous snake. She gave Shauna's hand a short squeeze. "Shauna I've heard so much about you. And you're right Keith, she is beautiful."

Shauna's anger began to diminish slowly but she still remained cautious. "Thank you."

Keith tugged on Marilyn's arm. "Hey, Max and Steve are here already. Let's go say hi."

Shauna raised her eyebrow. *Why the hell I wasn't invited to come along?* It was like he had ESP. "Honey, do you want to join us?" he asked her before turning to walk away. •

She shook her head. "Um, maybe later, I want to greet some more guests."

He didn't look disappointed. "Okay. Pass by when you're done," he told her. He walked away with Marilyn chattering along the way. Her blood began to boil again but she kept calm. *Two can play that game*, she mumbled to herself. She picked up a glass filled with champagne from the table and gulped it down quickly. She then waited anxiously for Pete to arrive. Now all the doubts she had about inviting him had suddenly disappeared.

Tina sat on the couch next to Alex barely listening to what he was saying. He had already had six glasses of champagne and was slurring with his words. *Damn why was he sitting so close?* She felt like she was going to pass out. His breath was like an inferno and she was getting impatient. Unfortunately she could not move from the couch. Bryan was staring at them from the far corner of the room. Suddenly she let out a high pitch giggle. "Oh Alex, you're too funny."

"Thanks, baby girl," he murmured as he moved closer to her. She shifted her position quickly. His breath was still hot against her face. *Lord, please help me find a tic-tac for this man.* "Hey, how about after the party we head out to my crib for a night cap," he drawled.

She shook her head. "Sorry, I have to be home soon. I have a babysitter with my son, maybe some other time."

He picked up his drink from the table and guzzled it down while spilling some on his shirt. He wiped his mouth with the back of his hand. She became very disgusted at this point. She stood up with a fake smile. "Um, I have to go to the ladies room. I'll be right back."

He grabbed her hand then brought it to his mouth. He placed a sloppy kiss on top. "Don't keep me waiting," he warned.

She pulled her hand away. "Don't worry, I won't."

She headed for the bathroom at a fast pace. She let out a sigh of relief once she closed the door behind her. She cursed herself for inviting that fool and prayed the night would end soon. She looked in the mirror and began to play around with her hair. She was disappointed that Bryan hadn't approached her yet. Suddenly a knock at the door interrupted her thoughts.

"Someone's in here," she answered loudly.

In seconds there was another knock. This time she became irritated and yanked the door open. "I said someone's in here."

Without giving her time to think, Alex walked in past her holding an open bottle of champagne. He pulled her hand away from the door knob then locked the door. His body blocked the door. He stared at her seductively.

She frowned and crossed her arms against her chest. "What the hell do you think you're doing?"

He drank from the bottle sloppily then placed it on the floor. "I stole a bottle from the kitchen. I just thought that maybe we can have some privacy in here. So do you need help *unzipping* anything?"

She laughed nervously. "Unzipping, um I don't think so." She tried to walk around him but he blocked her path. She frowned. "Can you *move* please?"

He grabbed her by the waist. "Come on baby, relax. I brought this champagne for us. We can stay here and have our own party. We can get our groove on right here."

She pulled away from him, "I said no." Her words went in one ear and out the other. He grabbed her again but this time held her real tight. She put her hand on his chest to push him away but he would not budge. "Alex, let go. You're holding me too tight."

He ignored her complaint and tried to kiss her. She turned her face to the side. She shut her eyes and struggled as his hands began to roam all over. She began to think quickly. She had to get him out of the bathroom. "Look, boo I want to be alone with you too, but not in here. We can go somewhere else," she persuaded.

His face came close. "Naw, I like it right here." He planted a trail of sloppy kisses on her neck. "Mmmm, damn you smell good and you're fine too. How about we do a little one on one in here?"

She became furious. "If you don't let me go, I'm going give you something to cry about," she threatened angrily.

He just laughed and kissed her hard on the lips. She pushed him away in disgust. "Alex, this isn't funny. You're drunk and I don't want you to do something you'll regret."

His eyes looked evil. "Relax boo. There will be no regrets tonight."

"*Alex let go!*" she shrieked. She tried to lift up her leg to kick him in the groin but he was too quick for her. He blocked her leg with his then placed her in a different position. He frowned. "There's no sense in fighting me." He turned her around and pinned her against the wall. He began to fondle her through her dress. "You know you want this. How do you expect me to act with you dressed like that anyway?"

She felt numb. She was tired of struggling. Her eyes filled with tears. "Why are you doing this?" she cried.

"Doing what boo?" he whispered into her ear. "We're just having a little fun. Move again and it'll just hurt even more. Just relax."

She wanted to scream but her throat went dry. Tears began to stream down her face. She couldn't believe she invited this lunatic into her friend's home. She had never felt so helpless in her life. Suddenly there was a knock at the door.

"Tina you in there?" a muffled voice asked from behind the door.

It was Bryan. Alex put his hand over her mouth so she couldn't answer. All of a sudden she remembered a self defense strategy she had learned while watching Oprah a couple of months ago. She never dreamed that she would be in such a position. With all her strength, she stepped on his foot with the heel of her high heels and put her whole weight on it. She then hit his chest with back of her elbow aiming for his heart. As he doubled up in pain, she unlocked the door and opened it quickly. She ran straight into Bryan's arms.

He held her tight. "Tina you okay, baby? What happened?" he asked. His comfort made her cry even more.

"He...he..," she began unable to control her sobs any longer.

She didn't have to say another word. He let her go and sprinted into the bathroom. He grabbed Alex by the front of his shirt while he struggled hard to stand up. He punched him hard in the stomach. Alex quickly buckled over. Bryan grabbed him up again and threw him against the wall. He began to punch him repeatedly. He was going to continue until Tina stopped him. She couldn't stand to see anymore.

She pulled him back. "*Bryan stop!*" she yelled. "That's enough."

He turned back to look at her full of rage. "I can kill this dude right now if you want me to."

She shook her head. "He's not even worth it."

He grabbed Alex by the collar. "Oh, this would really be worth it."

She had never seen him so angry. "Bryan please, just let him go. He's drunk and I'm okay now."

He frowned. "He needs to be taught a lesson."

She wiped her tears away. "I just want to forget all this."

He finally nodded then dragged Alex by the collar into the living room. He headed towards the front door with lots of surprised looks and gasps from guests.

Keith came up in front of them mortified at the scene. "Bryan is everything okay here," he asked

"Yeah," Bryan answered, "Just taking out the trash."

Tina walked up behind them and hugged herself tight. Shauna was by her side in seconds.

"Honey, are you okay?" she asked. Tina nodded her eyes full of tears. Shauna gave her a hug. "What happened?" she asked again.

Tina didn't answer. She could feel everyone staring at her. Bryan threw Alex out on the front lawn but it didn't seem to have an effect on him. He just rolled over and laughed loudly. "Look dawg, I was just doing that bitch a favor anyway. Ho's like that like it rough. You have to show them whose boss to get what you want."

Bryan ran up to him and punched him hard in the jaw. He was knocked out instantly. He rubbed his hand then walked back to Tina. He stroked her face. "Are you sure you're okay?"

She nodded. "I-I need to g-get out of h-here," she stammered between tears. "Can you take me home please? I don't have a ride."

"Tina did that guy hurt you?" Keith asked her from behind.

She shook her head frustrated. "I'm okay. I don't want to talk about this anymore. I-I just want to go home."

He placed his jacket around her shoulders. "I'll take you now."

She gave her friend a faint smile. "Shauna, I'll talk to you later."

"No problem, honey," Shauna assured her. "Just be safe."

As soon as Tina was safely in the passenger side of Bryan's car, he climbed into the driver's seat next to her. "Are you sure you don't want to go to the police?" he asked placing his key into his ignition.

She shook her head again. "He didn't rape me," she insisted. She felt like she was trapped in a nightmare and couldn't wake up. Tears begin to well up in her eyes again. "How could I have been so stupid?"

"Tina this is not your fault. The bastard took advantage of you."

She began to cry for several more minutes. He remained quiet and held her tight. For the first time that night she felt safe. She didn't want to go home. "Bryan, I don't want to be alone right now. Can we go somewhere for a little bit?"

He started the ignition immediately. "Just tell me where to go and I'll take you."

Chapter Ten

Monica giggled as Sean nibbled on her earlobe. They were parked in his car a block away from Shauna's home and making out like crazy. She felt like she was in high school again. She was having the best time of her life. "You know we're at least an hour late," he whispered kissing her one last time. "Maybe we should get going."

"Just five more minutes," she told him. "I just like being here with you."

He raised his eyebrow. "You haven't changed your mind about introducing me to your friends have you?"

She caressed his cheek. She was avoiding the party as much as possible but not because she was embarrassed. She was avoiding Michael. She just didn't feel like dealing with his temper tantrums tonight. If Sean found out her secret through Michael's mouth, she knew she definitely wouldn't stand a chance with Sean. Hopefully Michael would think she wasn't coming to the party and leave. "No I'm not changing my mind about anything. I meant what I said. I want this to work between us."

He grinned. "Good. I really care about you."

"I care about you too."

He took her hand in his. "Before we take things further, I want to make sure of something."

"Okay…what is it?"

"Are you're over your ex?"

She stared at him tenderly and stroked his cheek. "Yes," she answered truthfully. "He's my past. You're the one I want to be with."

"Are you sure?"

She nodded. "I want nothing to do with him. I know you have doubts and—"

"It's not that," he interrupted. "I wanted to make sure because I need to tell you something."

She raised her eyebrow. "Is it good or bad?"

He scratched his head. "That depends on how you take it," he paused. "This is kind of hard for me to say."

Her heart pounded. *Lord, please don't let this man tell me he has kids or he's gay or...* "Sean just spit it out. You're making me nervous."

"Okay. Look... I've never been with a ..."

"A what?" she prompted.

"I've never been with a woman before."

She looked at him confused. "What do you mean you've never been with a woman before?"

"I mean I've never *been* intimate with a woman before. I'm a virgin."

She stared at him for a moment. "Come again?"

"I'm a virgin," he repeated.

She laughed out loud. "Boy, stop joking around. Tell me what's really going on."

He shook his head. "It's not a joke. I've never had sex before."

She gazed into his eyes. They were telling the truth. She was at a loss for words. "But you...we were just... are you sure?"

It was his turn to laugh. "Of course I'm sure. This is not something I tell just anyone. It's embarrassing."

She could not believe what she was hearing. "But you don't act like a virgin. Sean, you know the right places to touch... I don't understand this."

"Remember how I told you that my dad ran out on us?"

She nodded. "Yeah."

"Well like I told you, I had to become the man of the house so didn't have time to go out or have a girlfriend in high school. When I got to college, it was definitely a different scene, I dated but I still hadn't found what I've been looking for. My ex was my first relationship, if you even want to call it that."

"So you two never..."

He shook his head as her voice trailed. "No. I told her I didn't want to do anything until we were on the same page. She was a freak though. She showed me other ways to pleasure a woman without actual intercourse being involved. I guess she got tired of me brushing her off. Anyway she wasn't on my level. But you," he paused then kissed her hand softly. "You're a different story. There's a connection with you I can't deny. I've never felt like this about anyone. I'm really feeling you Monica. I want us to take the next step."

She was speechless. She turned to look outside her window. *Awww damn damn damn! A virgin, what the hell was she supposed to do now? Would it really be right to take his virginity?* He pulled her to look at him. "Baby please, say something."

She shrugged. "What do you want me to say?"

"I don't know something. Are you angry with me?"

"Why would I be angry? Being a virgin is a blessing."

He sat back in his seat embarrassed. "It's a shame. I'm twenty-two years old."

"So? You have nothing to be ashamed of." She grinned. "As a matter of fact, I think it's sexy."

He smiled then moved towards her for kiss but she drew back. "Um I think we should get going. Shauna must be wondering where we are."

He was taken aback by her response. "Okay. Hey, are you sure you're okay with this?"

She opened the passenger door. "Yeah of course, I'm getting hungry, are you ready to go?"

He opened the driver side door. "Yeah sure," he answered with a little uncertainty in his voice.

As they walked towards Shauna's home her mind raced. She didn't want to enter the party just yet but she could no longer stay in the car either. Everything was different now. She didn't deserve his virginity. Once Sean finds out she slept with Michael, she was sure he would change his mind about wanting her to be his first. Part of her also had to question, could he actually forgive her? As they headed towards the front door, she silently prayed that Michael wouldn't make a scene. Sean rang the doorbell, a moment later Keith answered the door.

"Monica, you made it," he smiled giving her a hug.

Monica smiled in return. "Sorry we're late."

Keith moved over to let them in. She quickly scanned the room behind him. She was relieved Michael was not in sight. "It's okay," Keith replied. "Dinner is just about ready. So is this your little brother?"

Monica blushed profusely. Sean felt her tense up against him. He quickly wrapped his arm around her waist. "No. I'm Sean, her date," he stated proudly.

Keith looked stunned for a moment. "Oh, I'm sorry. Nice to meet you man. Come on in and join the party. Drinks are at the bar."

"Do you want me to get you anything?" Sean asked her as she now searched the room for Shauna and Tina.

She nodded with a smile. "Rum and coke please."

He excused himself and headed for the bar. "Monica, I'm sorry about that. I just assumed...," his voice trailed.

She shrugged him off. "It's okay. Where are Shauna and Tina?"

"Shauna is around here somewhere and Tina left already."

"Left already? Why?"

"There was a small altercation. Her date was drunk. I don't even know the full details, but Bryan took her home."

Monica's eyes grew large. "Is she okay?"

Keith had already lost interest in the conversation. His eyes were somewhere else. She followed them and frowned at its destination. He was staring at a white woman who didn't have a problem staring back. "Bryan is with her, so she'll be fine," he stated finally. "Listen, you have a good time, I'm going to check on some other guests."

She gave a quick nod then watched him head towards the other woman. "What happened? Babysitter didn't show?" a voice asked behind her.

She cringed. She turned around to find Michael with a smirk on his face. She frowned. "Excuse me?"

"Damn Monica, I can't believe you really showed up with that guy."

She glared at him. "Why are you *sweatin'* me so much? Who I'm with is not your concern. Stop acting jealous."

"Jealous?" he laughed. "Of that guy, please. He's got nothing on me. You're just using him to make me jealous. Maybe you should try plan B."

She crossed her arms against her chest. "You need to get over yourself. You're not worth my time."

He gave her an evil smile. "You seemed to think so the other night."

He came close but she moved back. "Shows what little you know. I may have had sex with you but I was thinking of him the whole time," she hissed. He grew quiet. She was happy she put him in his place but she quickly remembered he could be an ass and rat her out right in front of everyone. She sighed. "Look, Michael. I don't want to fight with you."

"No, what you don't want is for me to tell your boy toy what went down the other night."

"What went down the other night?" Sean asked interrupting their conversation

Shauna had the sudden urge to throw up. She couldn't stand to hear Marilyn brag about herself any longer. *Okay,* she put together an organization to help fight breast cancer? *Okay,* she volunteered in Asia to help the Tsunami victims for several months. So maybe she was a saint, but did she have to tell the whole world? *Saint my ass.* She kept a plastered smile on her face. *More like the Devil Wears Prada!*

"So Shauna, what university did you graduate from?" asked Marilyn interrupting her thoughts.

"Well I—" Shauna began.

"Columbia University," Keith cut in. "She has a degree in Business Administration. Shauna has great fashion sense. She's going to own her own boutique real soon, right honey?" He pulled her close but she frowned and wrenched away from him.

"Excuse me, I'm going to check on dinner," she told them furiously heading towards the kitchen.

Keith excused himself as well and walked into the kitchen behind her. "Shauna I'm sorry," he began apologetically.

She spun around angrily. "What the hell do you think you were doing out there? Making up some story like that, what I'm not good enough for you and your colleagues?"

He shook his head. "Look, the words just came out the wrong way."

She glared at him. "Don't give me that. You flat out told them I graduated from college."

"Okay I did, but there's a good reason why I did it. Our Chief of Staff is retiring in the next couple of months and I want to apply for the position. This could mean big things for us. I spoke with Marilyn about it and she thinks that I should do whatever it takes."

She gawked at him. "Wait, hold up Marilyn? I can't believe you spoke to her about this before me. And I'm going to be your wife," she stated as her voice rose.

He looked towards the living room. "Shauna, calm down. Someone might hear you."

She shook her head unbelievably. "I don't care who hears me. This is *our* house so I don't give a damn who hears me." She paused for a moment to take a deep breath. "Tell me, Keith. What's really going on between you and Marilyn? Are you cheating on me?"

He rolled his eyes. "Shauna, let's not start this again."

She frowned. It was not the answer she wanted to hear. "Answer my question. Or, wait, maybe I should be more specific. Are you *fucking* her?"

He looked appalled at her vulgarity. "What has gotten into you? She's my co-worker and my friend and that's it. I mentioned this to her because she—"

She covered her ears. "You know what? I don't even care anymore," she interjected. "There shouldn't be any excuses when it comes to her. You can tend to the food. I'm going to get some air."

She stormed out the French doors leading to their newly renovated deck. The front displayed a half acre of a well maintained garden. Her thoughts wandered towards her current situation. This was what she wanted, a dream house, a successful, handsome fiancé and a chance to go back to school. So why did she feel like something was missing? She leaned on the railing and let out a deep sigh.

She could feel her relationship falling apart. Who was this Marilyn? Why was she slowly moving into their lives messing everything up and why hadn't Keith come after her yet? She was not only angry at Keith, she was angry at herself for letting that woman get to her. She shivered at the thought of them having sex. She clenched her fists angrily. *I'll kill them both!*

Suddenly she felt warmth on her shoulders. She looked at her sides and saw that it was a man's jacket. "Look, I really don't want to talk about this right now," she stated tiredly.

"We don't have to talk. We could just stand here quietly."

She smiled. It wasn't Keith's voice she heard. She turned around. His smile met hers. She gave him a hug. "Pete, you made it." *Thank God.*

"Sorry I'm late. I had a late class tonight. I'm working on this still-life project with my college kids. They were really getting into it."

She nodded understandably. "Sounds like fun."

"Yeah…" he paused. "Are you okay?"

She turned away from him and held the railing tight again, "Yes, why?"

"I heard you two arguing in there. I wasn't eavesdropping. Someone let me in and told me that you were in the kitchen."

"So you heard everything?"

"Not everything. You sounded really upset. Are you sure you're okay?"

She didn't answer. She sighed and grabbed his hand. She led him out into the garden. He walked next to her in silence. "This party has turned into a disaster," she said finally coming to a halt in front of a garden bench. She let go of his hand and sat on the bench surrounded by a bed of roses. It's aroma consumed the air around them.

He sat down next to her. "Talk to me. What happened?"

"Everything is going wrong, Pete. My friend Tina was violated tonight in my home, my fiancé is gawking all over another woman, and—". Unable to control herself any longer, she burst into tears.

He pulled her towards his chest. "Whoa hey, it's going to be okay."

His embrace was comforting. She began to calm down a bit. "I can't believe my fiancé is ashamed of me," she sniffled.

He stroked her hair as she lay on his chest. "Why would he be ashamed of you?"

"He told his co-workers I graduated from college. I guess he has a reputation to maintain and having a wife with no degree does not fit into that picture."

He winced. "Damn. I don't know what to say."

She pulled away from him and wiped her tears away with the back of her hand. "You don't have to say anything. Just listening means a lot."

"I will always be here for you, you know that."

She nodded and was quiet for a moment. "Do you mind me asking what happened with your marriage?" she asked.

He shifted in his seat. "There's not much to tell. We met a couple of years ago at a concert. We dated for a year and on our one year anniversary she proposed."

She laughed out loud. "She proposed?"

He chuckled. "Yeah, it surprised me too. I mean I accepted but I don't think we were ready for marriage. We were both fascinated with the concept. You know, the house, white picket fence, the cute dog. Throughout the first year we argued about the stupidest things like taking out the trash and whose turn it was to feed the dog. Then we began to argue about when we should have children. She wanted to concentrate on her career and I wanted to start a family. It all went downhill from there."

"Wow, that's crazy. But you know what's funny? Keith and I have never talked about when we would like to have children. I just assumed we would start having children right after we're married."

"Well, now is definitely the best time to bring it up."

She nodded. There was another awkward silence. "So did you love her?"

"I thought I did. I realized later on I wasn't *in* love with her. Sounds messed up, huh?"

She shook her head. "I'm not here to judge. So…" she paused. She picked out a yellow rose from her garden. She began to pluck off its petals. "Have you ever been in love?"

He was silent for a moment. "Once," he answered finally. "I was in love with someone from a while back but we lost touch. I don't think I ever stopped loving her."

She mistakenly pricked herself at his response. "Ouch," she winced holding her finger. Instantly she put it into her mouth.

He pulled her finger out her mouth. "Let me take a look at that."

He examined her finger as if he was a physician. She giggled. "So what's the prognosis doctor?"

He didn't reply. Instead he placed her injured finger into his mouth. Her heart stopped beating. She couldn't breathe as she watched him slowly pulled her finger out of his mouth then put it right back in again. The warmth around her finger sent shivers throughout her body. She closed her eyes for a moment. She began to imagine his mouth her on her breasts instead. "Does that feel better?" he asked.

Her eyes fluttered open. She drew her hand back and blushed. "Um yeah, thank you." She stood up uncomfortably. "I think we should get back to the party. Are you coming?" she asked starting to walk away

He stood up and caught her arm. "Shauna, wait."

She turned around. "Yes?"

"I just want you to know that I'm glad you're back in my life again."

She smiled. "Me too, thanks for listening." All her worries about Keith and Marilyn, his colleagues, and the wedding had vanished.

He came close then gazed into her eyes. "I'm here for you whenever you need me."

She nodded. The wind blew around them. The leaves on the ground began to rustle. A tendril fell onto her face. He reached over and placed it behind her ear. He stroked her face gently. Everything that happened next happened in slow motion. His lips were on hers and her arms went around his neck. His kisses became demanding as his tongue roamed her mouth. A moan escaped her lips as he kissed her neck. She could feel his heart pounding against hers.

"It's you Shauna," he breathed. "I fell in love with you the first time I saw you. I never stopped loving you."

His words brought her back to reality. She pushed him away softly. "I-I can't do t-this," she stuttered breathing rapidly.

He tried to hold her again. "Shauna..."

She moved away. "No, this was a mistake. I'm getting married in a couple of weeks. I have never cheated on Keith and I don't plan on starting now."

"I'm sorry. It's just that—"

She didn't wait for him to finish. "I'm sorry. I have to go," she told him. She gathered her dress and raced back towards the house.

"You can stop right here," Tina told Bryan as he drove alongside a secluded area of the beach. She looked out the window as she remembered the many nights she and Bryan spent making love under the stars. They were silent for a couple of minutes. "Bryan, what happened to us?" she asked suddenly. "We were so right for each other. I don't understand how my pregnancy changed all that?"

He sighed. "I don't know what to tell you, Tina. We were just too young."

"Too young," she repeated. "We were in college. It's not like we were sixteen years old. We were old enough to make decisions like having to take care of a baby."

He stared straight ahead. "Tina, I don't want to dwell on the past tonight."

Her eyes began to fill with tears. "Well, I do. How could you let this happen to us? You told me you would never hurt me. You told me you loved me. Was that all a lie?"

He turned to look at her. His eyes full of remorse. "I loved you with all my heart. You've got to believe that."

She wiped her tears away. "How can I? You left me alone for the remainder of my pregnancy. How do you think that made me feel?"

He gripped his steering wheel. "I just felt so pressured and confused."

She frowned. "Pressured? Bryan I never pressured you into anything. We had unprotected sex and I ended up pregnant. It was our mistake but something beautiful came out of it."

He leaned back into his seat. "I know that now. You're taking everything I say the wrong way. Why do we have to talk about this right now?"

"We have to because this has been bothering me since you left. You don't understand what I've been through." She didn't want to get even more upset but couldn't help herself. If she and Bryan were together, the whole episode with Alex would never have happened.

He was quiet for a moment. "Tina, I'm sorry. I'm sorry for not being with you during the pregnancy and for leaving you to take care of my son alone for the first couple of years of his life. But, baby, right now I want you to make sure you're okay. Some asshole just took advantage of you back there and you're avoiding the situation."

She hugged her shoulders in shame as she remembered Alex's hands all over her. "I can't believe I let that happen."

He shook his head. "You didn't let this—"

"I did," she cut in. "I didn't even know the guy. I met him at a restaurant and only asked him to be my date tonight to make you jealous." She groaned in frustration and looked out her window. "God, you must think I'm some crazy woman who needs to get a life."

He took her hand. "On the contrary, you're a smart woman whose plan worked to the T."

She turned to look at him. "What do you mean?"

"Tina my eyes have been on you all night," he admitted. "I've never seen you look so beautiful. From the time you walked into the house with that dude. I knew he was trouble. I watched him drink alcohol like it was water. When I saw him follow you to the bathroom, I knew something was up." He gazed into her eyes. "If something had happened to you..."

"You don't have to worry about me. I can take care of myself."

He smiled. "And you proved that tonight. That guy took a good ass whuppin' before I got a hold of him."

She smiled in return. "I did do a good job, didn't I?"

He chuckled. "A very good job, maybe I should watch my back?"

She laughed and poked him in the chest. "Yep or your ass is next."

He held his hands up in front of him and laughed in return. "Hey, I'm on your side."

She punched him lightly on the arm. "That's what I thought."

"Oh, so it's like that?" he challenged. "How about I give you a can of whup ass right now?"

She narrowed her eyes and made a karate pose. "Bring it on then. I will go Jackie Chan on you real quick."

He laughed at her gesture and she burst out laughing. "I really miss this," she told him as their laughter died down. "Hanging out and laughing with each other."

"I miss it too," he confessed. "I just—"

"How about we play a game?" she interrupted.

He raised an eyebrow. "A game?" he repeated. "What kind of game?"

"Truth or Dare."

He looked at her as if she was crazy. "Wait, you really want me to play a middle school game with you?"

"Stop being such a party pooper. I'll start first, truth or dare?"

He laughed. "Okay, okay."

"Well, truth or dare?" she repeated.

"Truth."

"Do you still love me?"

"I can't answer that."

"That's too bad. That means you have to do a dare."

"Hey, that's not fair," he protested.

"Sorry that's the rule."

He nodded. "All right, what do you want me to do?"

She pretended to think for a moment then pointed in front of her. "I dare you to go skinny dipping."

"You want me to go in the ocean butt naked?" he inquired unbelievably. "You've got to be kidding me."

"No, I'm not. You know the rules."

"You want me to get into the water?"

"Butt naked," she added with a giggle. "Now hurry up. Take those clothes off."

"All right, all right," he sighed defeated.

He got out the car and she followed behind him. It was a half moon yet it shined brightly over them. She was able to watch him undress very clearly. His muscles flexed as he took off his shirt and pants. She fought a smile as he stood there half naked. He still had his boxers on. "Everything needs to go," she warned loudly. "It's either you take it off or I'll take it off for you." He shook his head and smiled. He took off his boxers and quickly ran towards the water. She cracked up as she watched his buttocks disappeared into the water.

The water was warm as he jumped in. He hadn't been to the beach in a long time. He and Tina used to go all the time and would sometimes stay until the sun came up. He dove again into the waves then pushed his head out the water. He looked for Tina on land but she was nowhere to be seen. He frowned. *Where that hell is that girl?* Suddenly he felt a pinch on his buttocks and jumped. Tina popped up from under the water laughing. She was completely naked.

"You looked like you were having fun, so I decided to join you," she laughed staying afloat.

He stared at her remembering the woman he fell in love with. He had never seen her look so stunning. He cleared his throat. "It's my turn to ask a question," he told her.

She nodded breathing heavily as a wave hit her. "Go ahead."

"Truth or dare?"

"Truth," she grinned.

"Do you still love me?" he asked.

She shook her head. "I don't think I *should* answer that."

"Okay, now you have to do my dare."

She rolled her eyes. "Oh, so now you're all into the game," she laughed. "Okay what is it?"

"I dare you to kiss me."

She raised an eyebrow then shook her head. "Um, the last time we kissed you left me high and dry."

"This time it's different."

"Are you sure? I mean I don't want you to have any regrets."

He swam closer to her. "Trust me. I want this."

She nodded then stared into his eyes. She held his face tenderly then kissed him on the tip of his nose. He laughed as she pulled away. "What was that?"

She winked and swam away from him. "You didn't say what type of kiss."

"Oh, so now you got jokes?" he yelled swimming after her. He splashed her as he got close. She splashed him in return and tried to swim away. He was too fast for her and grabbed her waist from behind. She giggled as she felt his manhood against her back. She turned to face him. He pulled her close. She could feel his heartbeat against hers.

"You're heart is beating fast," she observed.

"Yours too," he whispered.

In the next moment his lips met hers. "I want you so bad it hurts," he told her as his hands roamed all over her body.

His fingers fondled her nipples. "Bryan," she whispered. "I don't want to get hurt."

He held her face and stared into her eyes. "Baby, do you trust me?"

She paused but then nodded slowly. "Yes," she answered finally. He smiled at her lovingly. He took her hand then began leading her back to shore. He picked her up once his feet were placed firmly on the ground. She immediately wrapped her legs around him. He carried her back to land in long strides, kissing her along the way.

"Stay here," he ordered as he placed her on the ground. He ran back to his car and retrieved a blanket. Slowly he laid her shivering body down on it. He stared at her for moment. He saw doubt in her eyes as he caressed her face. "Trust me," was the last thing he told her before his lips came towards hers once more.

His tongue roamed her mouth as if they were still lovers. Her breasts were swollen by the time he was finished with them. She was surprised he remembered all her right spots and even created new ones she never knew existed. Memories of the love she possessed for him now resurfaced fully. She held him tight as he entered her. That night he was no longer seen as just her son's father. He was the man she longed to spend the rest of her life with. He was the man she loved.

Chapter Eleven

Monica turned to find Sean frowning. She and Michael remained quiet. "What went down the other night?" Sean repeated this time with a little edge in his voice.

"Nothing sweetie," Monica answered finally taking her drink out of his hand. "We were just talking about that Clipper's game the other night. I kinda made a small wager and lost."

There was an awkward silence as she sipped her drink cautiously. "Monica, aren't you going to introduce me?" Michael asked breaking the silence.

She gave him a dirty look. "Uh yeah, Sean this is Michael."

Sean held out his hand. Michael shook it firmly. "So you're the infamous *ex*?" Sean declared. Monica smiled discretely. The way he stressed *ex* was no doubt a threat.

"And you're the new *kid* on the block?" Michael returned.

Monica cleared her throat. She was not in the mood to stop a fight. Let alone give Michael the chance to tell Sean the truth. "Sean, I'm really hungry. I think everyone is getting ready to sit down. Are you ready to go?" Before he could answer, she pulled him towards the dining area. Just then she saw Shauna walk in from the kitchen. She told Sean to have a seat then excused herself. She walked towards her friend.

"Where have you been?" she asked pulling her aside. Shauna did not answer her. Her face was flushed. "Honey, what's wrong?" Monica inquired.

Keith came up to them both. "Everyone is sitting at the table. Are you ready to join us?" he asked Shauna.

She nodded. He led her to the dinner table aimlessly with Monica following behind. Monica cursed under her breath when she saw Michael sitting in the seat on the other side of hers. Sean didn't look too happy with the arrangement either. She sat across from Shauna and gave her friend a *'help me'* look but it seemed like her friend's mind was somewhere else.

Once everyone was seated, Keith stood up and picked up his glass. "I would like to say a few words before we eat. I just want to say thank you for joining us in the pre-celebration of our life together."

Just then Pete walked in from the kitchen. He stood in the corner and watched Shauna intently. When Shauna spotted him, she blushed profusely. Monica caught her friend's facial expression and looked towards where she was looking. She could see a man watching her friend from the shadows in the kitchen. *Damn he's fine,* she thought.

It seemed like Shauna could not tear her eyes from him either. She kicked her friend lightly from under the table. Shauna looked at her embarrassed then immediately went back to eating her food. *Uh oh, that's not a good sign*, Monica thought.

Dinner to Monica was a blur. She had lost her appetite completely. Sitting between her ex and her soon to be man was overwhelming. Through peripheral vision she could see them exchange dirty looks. Other times, they'd constantly stare at her throughout the meal as if she was a prize piece. She couldn't stand the tension. She had to wake up from this nightmare. She looked at her friend from across the table and could feel the same tension. "Shauna can I speak to you for a moment," she asked.

Shauna nodded in relief and followed her friend into the living room. "Honey, you look like you're in another world. What's up?" asked Monica taking a seat on the sofa.

Shauna shook her head. "I'm fine. I just have some other things on my mind."

Monica gave her a sly smile. "Could a sexy man with the dreads be one of those things?" she questioned.

Shauna sat on her sofa and sighed. "I don't know what's wrong with me. Ever since Pete walked back into my life, I can't stop thinking about him."

Monica's jaw dropped. "Wait, that's Pete?"

"Yeah."

"Girl, I was only joking. What other secrets have you been hiding? You never told us he was that sexy."

"Monica, I'm not even concentrating on that," she laughed. "He's just so easy to talk to. And he's—".

"Sexy?" Monica interrupted with a smile.

Shauna burst out laughing. "He is, isn't he," she finally acknowledged. "His physical features have changed so much."

"I figured that because there was no way you would've let that man go if he looked like that." She stood up and looked into the kitchen once more then sat down. "Man how do you keep yourself from jumping his bones?"

Shauna rolled her eyes. "Can we stop focusing on his looks for one moment?"

Monica laughed, "Okay, okay."

Shauna took a deep breath and continued. "Now like I was saying, a couple of weeks ago I was thinking about going back to school. I was skeptical at first so I tried to talk to Keith about it but he blew me off with work. I bumped into Pete at Mimi's. We talked and when I told him what I was doing, he thought it was great idea. He told me he was proud of me. That's all I wanted to hear from Keith but he hasn't had time for me these days. Anyway, I applied and now I'm waiting for hopefully an acceptance letter. Keith is always at the hospital. Pete gave me his time and helped me realize that I made the right decision. It just feels so different."

Monica hugged her friend. "Honey, I'm happy that you're going back to school but you know you could have talked to me or Tina about this."

She smiled. "I know that, but I was embarrassed. You two are college graduates with successful jobs. You can't understand how it feels to be a clerk at a boutique. I want to own my own boutique someday and having a business degree is a start."

Monica nodded. "I understand and I'm very happy for you. So now let's get back to you and Pete. Do you have feelings for him?"

Shauna sighed. "I don't know what they are. But things got even more complicated tonight."

Monica raised her eyebrow, "Complicated?"

Shauna bit her lip. "Um, yeah," she paused. "We sort of kissed. It's no big deal."

Monica's eyes grew large. "Not a big deal? Are you crazy? If Keith found out he'd think it's a big deal."

Shauna looked distressed. "I don't know how it happened. First he started sucking on my finger…"

"Sucking your finger?" Monica gawked. "Damn, all this happened tonight?"

Shauna groaned and covered her face with her hands. "Girl, what am I going to do? I don't know what's gotten over me."

"Alright, calm down, before you start to panic, let's just analyze this. Did you want this kiss to happen?"

"Well, I wasn't looking for it."

"That's not what I asked you."

Shauna groaned. "No...I-I don't know."

"You don't know?" Monica repeated.

"I'm so confused."

"Well, did you stop it at least?"

Shauna winced. "Yes...after he told me he loved me."

Monica's shook her head unbelievably. "Hold up!! Love you? I don't understand. Shauna, what is it you're not telling me? How long have you known this man?"

Shauna wasn't ready to tell what happened between her and Pete. "Like I told you we knew each other in high school. We had feelings for each other back then but things didn't work out. We lost touch."

"So you never had closure."

"I don't need closure. Those feelings are no longer there."

"Are you sure?"

Shauna frowned. "What do you mean am I sure? How could you ask me that? I'm engaged, remember?"

"Shauna, your mind has to be clear of all doubts before you jump over that broom. Now what did you say to him after he told you he loved you?"

Shauna looked at her hands. "I panicked. I told him the kiss was a mistake and that I didn't want to ruin my relationship with Keith. I can't hurt him like that."

Monica rubbed her back. "Honey, you did the right thing. You said it yourself. Keith is a good man. Isn't that what you want?"

She looked at her friend. "It is. Look, I'm just going to forget this ever happened. I just need to get myself together."

"You're going to be okay," Monica assured her. "Look, maybe you should stop seeing Pete for a while...at least until after the wedding."

Shauna looked skeptical. Staying away from Pete seemed like the hardest thing she ever had to do. "I guess your right."

Monica sensed her hesitance. "But if you have feelings for him, you need to resolve them before the wedding."

"Trust me, that kiss will never happen again."

Just then Pete walked into the living room. Shauna stood up quickly. "Hey."

He looked uncomfortable. "Hey, um I just wanted to say good-bye."

"Leaving so soon?" Shauna asked.

"Yeah, I have to be somewhere early tomorrow morning."

Monica cleared her throat. Shauna looked at her friend. "Oh. Excuse my rudeness. This is my best friend, Monica."

Monica smiled. "Hello."

Pete nodded towards her. "Nice to meet you."

Suddenly, Keith walked into the living room. He gave Shauna a nervous look. "Honey, I've been looking all over for you. Guests are starting to wonder where you are. Are you okay?" He saw Pete and quickly put his arms around her.

Shauna smiled faintly. "Yes, I'm fine. I was just saying good-bye to a good friend of mine from high school. Keith this is Pete, the one I wanted you to meet. Pete this is my fiancé, Keith."

They exchanged handshakes. "Always nice to meet a friend of Shauna's," said Keith rubbing Shauna's shoulders lightly. "Are you sure you want to leave? We were just about to bring out some dessert."

Pete stared at Shauna. "I'm sorry but I really have to go."

Keith saw the stare and raised an eyebrow. "So, were you two close back then?" he prodded.

Pete finally broke the stare and looked at Keith. "You could say that."

Keith now held Shauna by her waist. "Was she just as beautiful back then?" he asked.

Shauna blushed uncomfortably. "Keith."

Pete finally broke into a smile. "Nothing compares to what she looked like back then. She had her own sense of style. All I can say is, Keith you're a very lucky man."

"I know. I tell myself that everyday," he boasted. He turned and gave her a light kiss on her forehead. She avoided any eye contact with Pete. For the second time she felt embarrassed about having a fiancé.

Pete cleared his throat. "Excuse me, but I have to get going, it was nice meeting you both."

"Um, I'll walk you out," said Shauna suddenly. She moved away from Keith's embrace. "I'll be right back," she told them. Monica nodded. She led Keith back into the dining room before he could protest.

Shauna walked him out the front door then closed it behind her. They were quiet for a moment. "Look Pete—" she began.

He held his hand up to stop her. "If it's okay with you I'd like to speak first."

She nodded. "Sure."

"I want to apologize for my behavior back there in the garden. I disrespected you. I don't want to do anything to jeopardize our friendship. I hope you can forgive me."

She shook her head. "You don't need to apologize. Old feelings came back and overtook our emotions. Let's just forget it happened, okay?"

He smiled. "Okay. Well, I hope this doesn't make things awkward between us because I would like to invite you to an art gallery I'm hosting for my kids in two weeks."

She quickly forgot about the suggestion Monica gave her. "I would love to go."

"Great, well I'm going to let you go."

She felt relieved and disappointed at the same time. She gave him a hug. Part of her didn't want to let go. "So, I guess I'll see you around?"

He hugged her in return. "Yeah, see you around."

As he turned to walk away, she had a sudden urge to call him back but she stopped herself. Instead she walked back into her house. She closed the door behind her and leaned against it. She smiled as she remembered his words. *It's you Shauna... I'm in love with you.*

"You better take that look off your face before Keith sees it," said Monica interrupting her thoughts.

Shauna glared at her friend who watched her from her sofa with a goofy grin on her face. "What look?" she asked innocently.

"The look of *sprungliness*."

Shauna crossed her arms against her chest. "Sprungliness? Girl you need to get your eyes checked. And what the hell is sprungliness?"

Monica laughed. "You know exactly what I mean. Look in the mirror and you'll see exactly what I'm talking about. It's written all over your face."

Shauna rolled her eyes. "What you need to do is stop analyzing me and concentrate on those two men in the other room who's getting ready to fight over you."

Monica fidgeted in her seat. "Damn, don't you think I know that? I just don't want you to end up in the same situation as me. I don't want Pete to take advantage—"

Shauna cut her off. "He would never take advantage of me. You don't know him. He's not like that."

"I don't know him but what I do know is that you want him really bad."

Shauna gave her a poison dart look. She hated the fact that she could read her so easily. Did Keith see it the same way? "I'm not going to stand here and let you continue to analyze me when I can pay a therapist for the real thing."

"I'm just saying to be careful."

Shauna placed her hands over her ears. "I don't want to talk about this anymore." She sat down next to her friend. "Honey, I know you're concerned, but I love Keith and I'm going to spend the rest of my life with him. Now can we can we please change this conversation around to you? What are you going to do about Sean and Michael? I can't believe you left them alone in there. What if Michael tells Sean the truth?"

"I checked on them already," Monica told her. "They're on different sides of the room. Besides, I don't think he's going to tell him. We've been here for a while now and he would've said something already. He's probably going to blackmail me or maybe even something worse. I have to tell Sean the truth."

Shauna grimaced. "Are you ready for that?"

Monica stood up from the sofa. She looked through the kitchen opening where she could visibly see both men clearly. Sean looked up and caught her watching him. He winked at her and she smiled. She then looked towards Michael who also grinned at her as if to say 'I've got you right where I want you'. She gave him a disgusted look then turned back to her friend.

"Oh yeah, I'm sure. I'm tired of Michael thinking he can control me. I need to get him out of my life now so I can start a new one with Sean but I can't do that with this secret on my head."

"You're right about that," Shauna agreed. "But what if he wants nothing to do with you? What do you do then?"

Monica gave her a sad look. "Hopefully he won't feel that way. I'm trying to think positive."

"Well if he does, then it's his loss. So when are you going to do this?"

Monica crossed her fingers, "Tonight."

Tina opened her eyes slowly as a light wind softly brushed her shoulders. She looked up to find the stars staring back at her. She looked to her side and saw Bryan sleeping soundly. She was wrapped safely in his arms. She could hear the waves crashing in the background. She closed her eyes again. *Lord if this is a dream, please don't wake me up,* she prayed.

She snuggled closer in his arms wishing she could stay that way forever. She couldn't believe they made love on the beach for several hours. He took his time loving her from head to toe. She shivered at the thought of him doing it all over again.

"Hey," he whispered interrupting her from her thoughts.

Tina looked at him and smiled. His handsome face smiled back at her. "Hey, sleepy head," she answered.

He took his arm from around her and stared at the stars for a moment. "I can't believe we fell asleep." He looked back at her. "Are you okay?" he asked.

"Yeah, I'm fine," Tina responded disappointed that he took his arm away. "And you?"

He nodded. "I'm good." He took a deep breath. "Man, what time is it?" he asked again.

"I don't know," she responded irritated. *Why was he so concerned about time?* "Why?"

"What about Joshua? The babysitter might get worried."

"Don't worry, I told her that I might be real late. She said she didn't mind. I told her she could use the spare bedroom to lie down. She's a college student. He'll be okay."

"Oh."

Suddenly there was a moment of silence.

"Bryan—"

"Tina—"

They both chuckled. "You first," she gestured.

He hesitated then began to gather his clothes. "Maybe we better get going. The sun is starting to come up. We don't want to get caught out here exposed."

Tina got upset quickly. He was acting like nothing had happened between them. She sat up and dressed herself. Tears stung in her eyes. She stalked back to the car and climbed into the passenger seat.

As Bryan placed himself into the driver seat, she felt like she was about to explode. Just when he was about to put his key into the ignition, she put her hand over his to stop him. "Listen Bryan, I want to you to get something straight. I am not going to be some booty call you can call anytime you want some ass."

He frowned. "Is that what you think?"

She took her hand away. "Well, that's how you're making me feel right now. You seem uncomfortable about what just happened. Do you feel this was a mistake?"

"Don't *you* think this was a mistake?"

"No, I don't. Making love is never a mistake."

"What about Sharon?"

She frowned. "What about her? I asked you if this was what you wanted and you said yes." He didn't reply. He stared at the waves crashing in front of him. She reached over and began to stoke his manhood. She could feel him already getting erect. His breathing increased as she came close. "Your body does not lie. You want me and you know it," she whispered into his ear.

She began to nibble on his earlobe. "Tina, why are you doing this to me," he groaned. She took his hand and placed it on her breast. He no longer could fight his urge to touch her. He pushed his seat back and pulled her onto his lap. He began to savor her nipples hungrily. She arched her body closer to him. "Damn, no matter how hard I try, I can't say no to you?" he continued.

She gave him a sexy grin then leaned in a kiss. "I love you, Bryan," she told him between kisses.

Suddenly he pushed her away softly by her shoulders. She began to get aggravated. "What's wrong now?"

He shook his head. "I can't keep doing this to you. This is wrong."

"What do you mean wrong?"

He closed his eyes. "I can't give myself to you fully. I'm not being fair to you."

She pulled herself off him and sat back into her seat. There was an awkward silence. "Do you love me?" she asked after a while. He didn't answer her. She laughed embarrassed. "I guess I have my answer."

"You haven't given me a chance to respond," he argued.

"It shouldn't take you so long to give me an answer."

"Why are you being so difficult?"

"Why are you avoiding my question?" she countered. "Just tell me the truth."

"I never stopped loving you, Tina," he confessed. "Especially after making love to you again, I now know my heart and body belongs to you..." his paused. "But there are some things beyond my control that—"

She was tired of his excuses. "Beyond your control, so what you're really saying is that you used me?" He tried to hold her but she cringed at his touch. She gave him a hard look. "Don't...I don't need you to feel sorry for me."

"I don't feel sorry for you and I didn't use you. It's just that everything is so messed up. I don't want you to be mad at me and for things to go back to the way they were. All that fighting we were doing before was getting ridiculous. We've both moved beyond. We're finally becoming a family."

"A family?" she repeated. "A family consists of parents who love each other."

"And I told you I do love you."

"I don't understand what the problem is," she persisted.

"Maybe we shouldn't talk about this right now?"

"Bryan, be honest with me. Was this just about sex or did we make love back there."

"We made love."

Her heart ached. "Then why can't we be together?"

"It's complicated."

She rolled her eyes. "Complicated? You don't even love her. She's ghetto, rude and doesn't even care about Joshua."

"I don't believe that," he told her defensively. "I would never stay with someone who doesn't accept my son."

"Look, all I know is that Joshua doesn't feel comfortable around her and that says something."

He placed his hands on the steering wheel and stared at the waves in front of him. "Tina, I already went over this with Joshua. It was all a misunderstanding. Everything is fine now."

"Everything is not fine. Why can't you be a man and just tell her the truth?"

"I can't…"

"I can't believe this," she exclaimed. "What the hell is holding you to her?"

"She's pregnant," he blurted finally.

Tina's heart dropped. For a moment she stopped breathing. "S-she's w-what," she sputtered when she was able to catch her breath.

"She's pregnant," he repeated with a sigh. "She took a test a couple of days ago. It was positive. She has a doctor appointment next week to confirm everything. This was not how I wanted to tell you."

Tina sat there astounded. She felt pain. It was as if her heart was just ripped out from her body.

"I can't leave her," he proceeded to explain. "You've got to understand. I can't make that same mistake again."

She couldn't believe what he was saying. "So it was okay for you to leave me but not her."

"That's not what I—"

She shut her eyes tightly as tears rolled down her cheeks. "Just take me home please," she interrupted.

"Tina—"

"*Take me home now!!*" she cried out hysterically.

Bryan put his keys into the ignition and started the car miserably. He wanted to wait for the right time to tell her about Sharon's pregnancy, but she didn't give him any choice. He wasn't thrilled about the news either. He had finally realized that he never stopped loving Tina. He had decided to break things off with Sharon but now things were different. He just didn't have the heart to abandon another child.

Monica rustled in her bed trying not to wake up to the sound of ringing in her ears. She opened one eye to look at her alarm clock. It was 7 a.m. She heard the ringing again. When she finally realized it was the doorbell, she groaned. *What the hell? Who is at my door this early in the morning?* She crawled out of bed and grabbed for her silk robe. She walked slowly towards her door. The doorbell rang again.

"I'm coming," she yelled. She looked through her peephole and found Sean staring back at her. He held a red rose in front of him. He placed it under his nose then smiled at her sexily. She smiled in return. The past couple of weeks had been unforgettable for her. They spent every waking moment with each other. He treated her like a queen while she felt guiltier by the minute. It was only because she hadn't found the courage to tell him the truth. At one point she did find the courage but lost it once she gazed into his sexy eyes.

She didn't want to lose him. Finally last week he asked her to be his girlfriend. She was thrilled. He was finally her man!

"Morning beautiful," he murmured as she opened her door. He pulled her close and gave her a long sweet kiss.

She smiled as he pulled away "Nice wake up call," she laughed. He grinned and handed her the flower. He then bent down and picked up a grocery bag that was hidden from her view. "What's all this?" she asked as he walked past her.

"Just a little breakfast I'm going to put together for you," he informed her huskily. He put the bag on the counter and took out a couple of items. "Wow, a cook too?" she smiled impressed. "If I had known, I would've brought you a cute little apron."

He smiled in return then stared at her as if seeing her for the first time. Her cheeks grew hot. "What?" she asked shyly. 'Why are you staring at me like that?"

"Nothing," he answered. "It's just that I've never met a woman who can look so sexy this early in the morning."

Her cheeks heat up. She wrapped her robe tighter and pointed a finger at him. "Don't start something you can't finish," she giggled.

He winked at her. "Oh, I'll finish it alright."

She had promised herself she wouldn't take the next step with him until she told him the truth. It was hard though. Every night he left her wanting him more and more. She and Michael had sexual chemistry but with Sean it was different. It wasn't about sex. She had fallen in love with him.

She pulled him for another kiss. "I'm going to take a shower. Make sure my breakfast is ready when I come back," she told him as she headed for her bathroom.

"Yes ma'am," he answered eyeing her behind as she walked away. "I'll be right here making you my famous sausage omelet."

"Mmm, sounds good, I'll be right back."

"Don't keep me waiting or I'll come after you."

She giggled as she turned on the hot water in her shower. She couldn't stop smiling. Sean was in her kitchen making breakfast for her. No, *her man* was in her kitchen making breakfast for her. She couldn't remember the last time she was ever so happy. She disrobed and climbed into the shower. She closed her eyes and as the hot water hit her back.

With her eyes still closed, she reached out to grab the bar of soap, but it wasn't there. She opened her eyes and gasped. She instantly used her hands and arms to cover herself. She was at a loss for words. Sean stood naked in front of her. He held the bar of soap in his hand. "Looking for this?" he asked with a sexy grin.

Her eyes grew large. "What are you doing in here?" she exclaimed when she was able to speak. Her eyes gradually roamed his body. She hadn't seen him completely naked before. His legs were thick just like his manhood which stared at her.

"I didn't mean to scare you. I just wanted to give you a back scrub," he pouted. He came towards her. She took a step back.

"Boy, what has gotten into you?" she asked nervously remembering her promise.

"You," he answered then moved behind her. He began to wash her back. "Relax," he whispered into her ear. Despite the objections her mind threw at her, her body did otherwise. She did as asked and let him do as he wanted. Each movement was graceful. As his hands roamed over her breasts, he paused slightly at each nipple until they grew hard. She moaned in satisfaction. "We can't do this," she argued softly yet not able to move.

"Do what?" he asked kissing her neck softly.

"Sean, you're driving me insane," she cried as he placed himself in front of her. Her breathing became rapid as his mouth met hers.

"Baby, I want you so bad," he told her between breaths. She could feel her heart ready to burst. Her body ached for him badly, but she knew in her heart she couldn't take the next step, not just yet.

She held him back. "Baby, we need to talk."

"Talk?" he asked breathing hard, "Now?"

"Yes, now," she answered nervously. "Look, I need to tell you—" She was interrupted by pounding sound. She paused for a moment to listen closely. "Did you hear that?" she asked him.

He paused for a moment then went back to planting kisses along her neckline. Nothing was on his mind except for her. "I didn't hear anything."

The pounding continued. "Shhh, wait," she ordered. They remained quiet for a moment. The pounding grew louder. "Someone's at the door," she told him relieved. She pulled away from him and reached for her robe.

"Hey, where are you going?" he asked trying to holding her back. "Just let them go away."

She hit his hand lightly. "It may be important. I promise I'll be right back, baby." She stepped out the shower and grabbed her robe. She closed her bathroom door behind her in relief. The pounding had now become persistent. "Damn, hold on," she yelled.

Without thinking, she opened her front door. Michael barged in without giving her a chance to react. He grabbed her by the waist and forcefully planted a sloppy kiss on her mouth. She pushed him away roughly and wiped her mouth with the back of her hand. "What the hell do you think you're doing?" she said angrily. "Are you crazy?"

"Monica, I want you back," he stated stumbling towards her. "I can't let some little *boy* take you away from me."

His breath reeked of alcohol. She moved away from him. "Michael you're drunk, get out." She tried pushing him towards the door but he held his ground. She got irritated. "Look, I'm not playing. Why can't you just leave me alone?"

"Hell no I'm not leaving you alone. This is bullshit," he yelled this time. "That dude doesn't deserve you. We made love. It meant something to me and I know it meant the same to you."

She looked towards the bathroom door frantically. *He was going to ruin everything*. "Will you please keep your voice down?"

He shook his head. "I'm not leaving until you listen to me."

She rolled her eyes. "We have nothing to talk about. Nothing you're going to say will change my mind about us. It's over Michael. Get over it."

He clenched his fists. "It's not over. How could you just throw away our relationship like that?"

She frowned. "*Me?* You broke up with me remember? Just because we had sex it didn't mean I was going to take you back." She couldn't understand where all this was coming from. He actually sounded sprung. She had to laugh. He looked so pathetic.

"So this is a joke to you?" he seethed.

At that point she realized that maybe laughing was the wrong thing to do but she didn't care. She had enough. "No, you're a joke. You're drunk and I don't feel like dealing with you right now."

"I'm a joke? You're the one who's seeing a dude half your age. What can you two possibly have in common?"

"That's not your concern. Face it Michael, you don't want me. You just can't stand the fact that I don't want *you* anymore. Someone else has my attention and it's killing you. And FYI, we have a lot of things in common, *especially* in the bedroom."

Her last comment put a bad taste in his mouth. Just when he was about to retaliate, Sean came out the bathroom smiling with only his pants on. "Hey baby what's—" His smile faded quickly when he saw Michael. He glared at Michael. "What the hell is going on?"

Michael laughed hysterically. "Well, well, well so that's why you wanted me to stay quiet. I guess you two were trying to get your groove on, oops my bad. Hey man, we were just talking about you."

She tried pushing him out the door again. "Sean, he was just leaving," she explained. Michael pulled away from her and went up to Sean's face. Monica felt like disappearing. She could feel an explosion coming on and Sean was caught in its path.

"Yo man, my girlfriend asked you to leave, so either you do it or I'll help you out physically," he warned.

She came between them. "Okay, let's just try to calm down," she suggested. They both ignored her completely.

"Oh, so now she's your girlfriend?" Michael repeated. He looked at Monica. "Man you work fast," he told her. His eyes turned back at Sean. "Don't worry I know where the door is, especially the bedroom door. Your *girlfriend* spent many nights screaming *my name* right through that door."

"Sean, do not listen to him," she pleaded. "He's drunk. If I had known it was him at the door, I would've never opened it."

Michael snickered sloppily. "Oh yeah and she was also telling me how good you are in the bedroom."

Sean glanced at Monica confused. She looked like a deer in headlights. He now stared Michael down. "Look man, I think you should leave now."

"Yeah man," he cackled. "But I *know* you couldn't top a couple of weeks ago."

Sean frowned. "A couple of weeks ago?" he repeated now curious.

"Sean, do not listen to him," Monica repeated frantically trying to push them apart. She turned angrily towards Michael. "*Will you just get the hell out,*" she shrieked.

Michael smiled at her wickedly. "Baby, don't be shy, you might as well tell him the truth."

Sean was getting angrier by the second. He pulled her to look at him. "What the *hell* is he talking about?"

Michael chuckled happily at the scene. "I'm sorry I have to tell you this man, but your girl ain't *feelin'* you."

"*Liar!!*" Monica lashed out.

"Because if she was," he smirked ignoring her outburst. "She wouldn't have *fucked* me."

Sean didn't say a word. He just continued to stare at her. His jaw was tight. He looked both furious and betrayed at the same time. Monica covered her face with her hands. She felt like sinking through the floor.

"She's even wearing the diamond bracelet I brought her for her birthday," Michael continued. "Sorry man…" He came close to Monica and tried to embrace her but she fought his touch. "All this right here is *mine.*"

Suddenly it was like a bomb hitting Hiroshima all over again. Sean threw the first punch and it was hard. Michael fell to the floor and knocked over her coffee table. He got up and hit Sean back in the face. Sean did not flinch. It was like someone had taken over his body. He hit Michael back in the stomach several times. "*Sean, stop please,*" Monica yelled hysterically.

She did not know what to do. They were tearing her place apart. Michael stumbled when he got up and tried to throw another punch but missed. In seconds Sean throw another punch and knocked him out. Monica was at his side immediately. She stroked his face. "Baby, are you okay?" she asked.

He didn't answer. He pulled away from her. "Is it true?" he asked calmly between breaths.

"Sean, just let me explain," she began.

She tried to hold him but he flinched. *"Is it true?"* he shouted this time. His tone made her jump. She didn't answer. She bit her lip. She never felt so dirty and ashamed in her life. Tears began to well up in her eyes as she nodded slowly.

He shook his head unbelievably. *"Are you fucking kidding me?"* he barked. "I can't believe this. He treated you like shit and you went right back to his cocky ass. So that's why you don't want to make love to me."

She shook her head as her tears flowed. "No. S-Sean you don't u-understand," she babbled. "Just let me explain please. That's not how it happened."

"I don't give a damn how it happened."

"I wanted to tell you but…" She ran her hands through her hair. Her sobs overtook her. Things were so out of control and there was nothing she could do to stop it.

He wasn't affected by her crying at all. "But what, Monica, you forgot? You forgot to tell me that you *fucked* your ex?" He stormed back into the bathroom and grabbed his clothes. He pushed past her and headed for the front door.

She ran behind him. "Sean, please don't leave me. I need you. Don't do this to me," she begged pulling his arm back.

He wrenched his arm away. "Don't do this to you? You did this to yourself. How could I have been so stupid? A gift from an old friend my ass! You've been lying to me the whole time. I asked you if you were over him and you said yes. I can't believe I trusted you," he yelled angrily.

"I am over him," she cried. "I don't want him. I want you."

"Me? Oh, you don't need me. Your man is right there on the floor. He can give you all the diamonds you need. Apparently I was wrong about you. You're not a woman who wants to be treated right. "

She grabbed a hold of him again. "It was a huge mistake."

"A huge mistake?" he repeated angrily. "No, I made a huge mistake by thinking you were a good woman. I guess I have a lot to learn after all."

"Sean, no I—"

He yanked his arm away and stared her down hard. "Stay the hell away from me," he snapped then stomped out her door.

Chapter Twelve

"What time will you be home tonight?" Keith asked for the third time as Shauna put on her favorite pair of silver earrings. He sat on their bed and watched her slip into her black flowing dress.

Shauna sighed annoyingly at his interrogation. "I don't know. The art show starts around eight and they're having a reception afterwards."

He came up to her and placed his hands around her waist. "How about you make up some excuse and stay home tonight," he suggested. "We could watch a movie, I can order in from our favorite restaurant and later on..." his voice trailed as he planted kisses along her neckline.

She pulled away from him and went into the closet to retrieve her shoes. "Honey, you know I already promised Pete I'd be there," she told him coming back into the room.

He pouted. "So tell him you're sick or something. I'm in the mood for a little role play tonight."

She smiled faintly and she slipped on her shoes hastily. She was ready to leave and fast. "Now you know I can't do that. He's a good friend."

He crossed his arms against his chest. "How long have you known this guy anyway?"

"I told you since high school."

"Well, how come you've never mentioned him before."

"We lost touch. What's with the third degree?"

"I don't know. I just feel uneasy when my sexy fiancé is around another man without me there."

She rolled her eyes and smiled. "Baby, you have nothing to worry about okay?"

Ever since their party, Keith has been sticking to her like glue. He's stayed home more often and no longer had any excuses about being on call at the hospital. He apologized again about the incident with his friends the night of the party. She accepted only because she felt so guilty about Pete. She just prayed that no one saw them in the garden.

The kiss they shared was unbelievable, exciting and scary. She couldn't help it, but the old feelings she had in the past were resurfacing. She decided that Monica was right. It was best not to see Pete any longer. She had planned on telling him once she saw him. She could no longer place her relationship with Keith in jeopardy. He deserved her whole heart and Pete was standing in the way. When she was finally ready, she walked up to Keith and kissed him fully on the lips. "I promise, I won't be too late," she assured him before heading out the door.

When she arrived at the art gallery, the place was packed with students and families. She looked around in awe. The walls were plastered with murals, paintings, and a couple of exhibits were displayed on the floor. She spotted Pete immediately. Once he saw her, he broke into a smile and headed towards her. He greeted her with hug. "Hey, you made it, you look stunning as usual."

"Thank you and thanks for inviting me," she smiled hugging him in return. His cologne consumed the air around her. She closed her eyes and took an opportunity to inhale his aroma. "Pete, these exhibits are amazing. I can't believe these were all done by students."

He nodded proudly. "They are so talented. All I told them was to create something from the heart and this is the result."

"The influence you have on these kids is wonderful. You've accomplished so much. I'm so proud of you."

He took her hand. "Thank you. That means a lot coming from you."

Her heart fluttered. She swallowed hard. She pulled her hand away. "Look... do you have time to talk for a minute?"

He looked around. Everyone was busy admiring the exhibits. "I can spare at least five minutes."

"Here he is mama. That's Mr. Morris," she heard a girl's voice state loudly from across the room. They both turned and saw a young girl pulling her parents towards them. "Oh, that's Tamika Shorter, my most improved student. Her exhibit is that painting on the wall."

"Very nice," she observed. "Listen, you go talk to them. I'm going to walk around for a little bit," she informed him beginning to walk away.

He grabbed her hand softly. "Don't go too far," he warned softly with a smile. She smiled in return then nodded.

Fifteen minutes later, she placed herself by the punch table and watched him from afar as he spoke to the family. She couldn't think straight. Just watching him was turning her on. She shook her head and began to walk far away from them. She needed to clear her head. She found refuge on a bench outside. The night air felt nice. She closed her eyes and exhaled.

"There you are." She opened her eyes and found Pete taking a seat next her. "I've been looking everywhere for you. Why are you sitting here alone?"

She hugged her shoulders. "I just needed some air and some time alone to think. Should you even be out here? I don't want to take you away from your gallery."

"Hey, I'm allowed one break. So what are you thinking about, me perhaps?"

She blushed and bumped her shoulders with his. "Don't you start," she warned playfully.

"I'm just kidding," he laughed. "Anyway, you wanted to talk. Are you and your fiancé arguing again?"

She shook her head. "No, we're fine. As a matter of fact he's been great. He's on his best behavior." She laughed. "He probably thinks I don't want to go through with the wedding."

"Are you?"

"Am I what?"

"Going to go through with it?"

She got off of her seat so he would not see the look of uncertainty on her face. "Of course, why wouldn't I? Keith is a good man and he loves me. I just can't believe time has gone by so quickly. And who would've thought I'd be marrying a surgeon."

"Yeah, go figure."

She turned to look at him. "What's that supposed to mean?" she asked defensively.

"Nothing," he returned. "I just thought….nothing, forget it." There was an awkward silence. "Shauna, are you sure this is what you want?" he asked speaking up again.

She nodded. "Yes."

"Are you sure?"

"Yes," she answered in an exasperated tone. "I'm a grown woman. I know what I want."

He heard the irritation in her voice and backed off a little. "Okay, I hear you. I just don't want you to make a mistake like I did."

"Just because you've made mistakes in your marriage, doesn't mean that I will. This is my life not yours."

He stood in front of her. "I'm not saying—"

She cut him off. "Then what are you saying?"

"I'm just asking you just to think for a moment. Do you two have anything in common? Are you able to be yourself when you're around him? From what I see you're not."

She turned away from him. "Why are you doing this?"

He placed his hands on her shoulders. "I'm not doing this to hurt you. You're an incredible woman, Shauna. I just want you to make the right choice."

His closeness was too much to bear. "And what other choice is there?" she whispered.

"Me?" he disclosed finally. "Let me be the one to make you happy."

She turned back around. "I can't believe this. You've been planning this the whole time haven't you?"

He looked confused. "Planning what?"

"All this, you invited me here to talk me out of marrying Keith didn't you? You don't even know him. He's a great man."

"He may be but he doesn't respect you. You said it yourself he's ashamed of you."

"He made a mistake and apologized. We've bypassed all that."

"Shauna, you're not being fair to yourself. He's *not* what you need."

She narrowed her eyes at him. "And you are? How can you stand here and judge him like that?"

He sighed. "Look, I didn't want to upset you tonight. Let's just go back in and forget about this," he told her beginning to walk away.

She pulled him back. "No," she told him stubbornly. "I want to finish this once and for all. You can't start something like this and just leave."

He turned to look at her. "I don't want to argue with you. I don't like seeing you upset."

Her anger began to diminish a little. "I don't like arguing either," she said softly. "But you're still stuck in the past."

He headed back towards her. "Is that so bad? Shauna, I love you and something inside me keeps telling me you love me too. I don't want you to marry Keith. I'm the one who understands you. There has to be a reason why we found each other again."

She gazed into his eyes for moment. Her heart beat loudly in her chest. She shook her head. "Pete, I'm not the same person I was in high school. I've grown up. I've changed a whole lot."

He smiled then took her hand. "You may have changed physically but you're still the same sweet, beautiful, ambitious woman I fell in love with. You still crinkle your nose when you're confused, you bite your bottom lip when you get nervous, and you still wear those charm bracelets you love so much."

She smiled a little. She couldn't believe he remembered distinct things about her. She began to wonder if Keith knew as much. He never liked her bracelets. He always thought they were childish. She pulled her hand away and shrugged. "Okay, so maybe you know a little more about me than him. That doesn't mean I should cancel my wedding."

He shook his head frustrated. "I'm not telling you what to do. I just want you to be happy. You deserve someone who will love you unconditionally."

She became stubborn again. "Well Keith *does* love me unconditionally. He gives me everything I need. He's there for me a-and…"

He took a step closer. "And?" he murmured. Suddenly her mouth went dry. She couldn't think. He was too close. His cologne surrounded her nostrils again. She wanted to stand her ground but felt weak. She moved back a little but he held her arm from going any further.

"And?" he repeated.

"He…" she began but didn't finish. His face proceeded towards hers and she moved in without thinking. In seconds her lips were on his and her arms went around his neck. She wanted to tear him apart. Urgently, her tongue roamed his mouth desperately searching for something she longed for. Her body ached for his and his actions showed her the same.

He moved her against the tree further away from the school. He sucked on her neck softly. With one hand he cupped her breast. Gently he played with her nipple through her dress causing her to whimper softly. Immediately she pulled down the straps to her dress. She needed his mouth on her breasts.

The coolness of the night made her nipples grow hard. He quickly warmed them with his mouth, sucking and licking simultaneously. She moaned in satisfaction. His other hand lifted up her dress and stroked her behind through her lace panties. Instantly she became wet. His manhood now poked against her. "Baby I want to make love to you so bad it hurts," he groaned.

"Mr. Morris? Mr. Morris, are you out there?"

He held her close and gestured for her to be quiet. She nodded. She closed her eyes and prayed they weren't found. Moments later Pete let out a sigh of relief. He stroked her face. "It's okay, no one saw us."

She moved away and fixed her composure. Things were spiraling out of control. "I-I should go."

"Please don't go," he pleaded softly. "I really want you to stay. We can go back inside and join the others."

He tried to hold her but she pulled away. "Please don't make this harder than it needs to be," she told him. "I can't be around you anymore. I've tried to avoid doing this but now I realize that this is how it has to be. I'm cheating on my fiancé and that's not me. Every time I'm near you I want you more and more."

"Well doesn't that tell you something? Why are you so afraid of being with me? Just admit we feel the same way about each other."

She shook her head. "No, I'm just confused. I'm nervous about the wedding," she informed him as if trying to convince herself.

He looked at her irritated at her excuses. "You're kisses tell a whole different story."

"Look, I'm sorry if I led you on," she apologized. "But this has to stop. I can't lose Keith."

He suddenly became angry. "Are you worried about losing Keith or his money?"

Offended, she slapped him across his cheek. *"How dare you say that to me!"* she declared furiously.

He rubbed his jaw. "I'm sorry. I didn't mean that. I know you're not that type of woman."

Tears stung in her eyes. She really didn't want to lose him but had no choice. "Listen just stay away…it's for the best."

"Shauna—" he began.

"I'm serious, Pete."

He shoved his hands in his pockets and looked sad. "Okay, if that's what you want. You won't see me ever again."

Tears began to fall without her consent. "It's the right thing to do."

He turned to walk away. When he was a few steps away he turned around. "Just remember, when you're ready to face this, I won't be there for you with open arms." With that said he walked his way back into the building.

*   *   *

"You guys, I'm freaking out," said Monica tearfully as she sat in Shauna's attic. The attic was just recently converted to a sewing room so Shauna could continue to work on her designs. All three friends were there for a last minute dress rehearsal. "He won't return any of my phone calls. He makes sure he's not alone at work so I can't talk to him. I really messed up big time."

"I don't know what to tell you girl," said Tina trying to stand straight as Shauna zipped up her bridesmaid dress. "He's upset. You have to give him time."

Monica looked distraught. "But he needs to let me explain. I thought he hooked up with Simone and moved on; ugh why didn't I just tell him when I had the chance?"

"There's no need in going back with shoulda's coulda's or woulda's," said Shauna smoothing out some wrinkles in Tina's dress. "You just have to find some way to make him listen. We all make mistakes and regretting doesn't make it better," she sighed thinking of Pete. For the past couple of days she was beginning to have regrets of not telling Pete how she felt about him since high school. Her life would've probably been different.

Tina raised her eyebrow. "What regrets do you have, Shauna?"

Shauna rolled her eyes, "This is about Monica not me." She turned towards Monica. "Why don't you just go back to the Moonlight? I'm pretty sure he still works there. See if you can get through to him there?"

Monica frowned. "Hell no, I already told you I'm not going back to that club again. What would I look like begging him to take me back?"

"Like a woman who desperately wants her man back," Tina told her.

Monica shook her head. "I can't do it."

"Well then I don't want to hear any more whining from you from now on," said Shauna firmly.

Monica gave her a dirty look. "Dang Shauna, you don't have to be a bitch about it?

Shauna returned her look. "I can be a bitch whenever I want. Now get your ass over here and let me fit this dress on you."

Monica went to her reluctantly and stood on top of a stool. She gave Tina a worried look.

"Monica is right, Shauna. What's up with you?" Tina asked.

"I'm fine," she mumbled. She was tired of everyone asking her that. So what if she was a little cranky? She had a right to be. What if she made a mistake about her decision with Pete? Was she going to live the rest of her life with more regrets? "I'm just tired. I want to get these dresses done and out of the way," she lied.

Suddenly Tina's cell phone rang. She took it out of her purse and looked at her caller ID. She sucked her teeth and threw it back in her purse.

"Who was that?" asked Monica

She rolled her eyes. "No one important, just Bryan."

"No one important," Shauna repeated. "You could've fooled me. From what happened at the dinner party, I thought he was you're knight in shining armor. It sounded like you two were getting back together again?"

"You and me both," she sighed. Tears stung in her eyes. "He told me he still loved me."

Monica's face brightened. "Well, that's a good thing right?"

Tina nodded. "I thought so too... but then he told me that Sharon's pregnant."

Both Shauna and Monica's mouths dropped open.

"You've got to be kidding me," said Monica stunned.

"You're joking, right?" added Shauna.

"No joke," she continued as her tears began to flow. "We made love that night and I thought this is it, I'm going to have the family I've always dreamed of but then it all came crashing down on me when he said he couldn't leave her. He doesn't want to make the same mistake he did with me. I feel…I feel like a punching bag," she wept. "First he says the right things; I fall for them then get punched in the face all over again."

They both came to her quickly. Shauna hugged her tight while Monica stroked her hair. "It's going to be okay," Monica consoled her. "He doesn't deserve you. Trust me, it's his loss."

"Yeah," Shauna agreed feeling tears well up in her eyes. "You're going to meet a good man who will love you unconditionally." She repeated Pete's words and burst into tears. She sat next to Tina and began to sob uncontrollably.

"What the hell?" said Monica out loud, "Honey, what's wrong," she asked Shauna trying to hold both her friends.

"Everything," she cried. "I told Pete I never wanted to see him again."

Monica held her hand. "We talked about this remember, this was something you had to do right?"

She shrugged. "Yes…no…I don't know anymore. I'm so confused. I love Keith, I really do, but Pete is on my mind day and night. I think I'm still in love with him."

"What do you mean still in love?" Tina sniffled. "You never told us you dated him."

Shauna calmed down a little. "We didn't exactly date…he was my first. My first time was on prom night."

"Oh Lord, Shauna why didn't you tell us?" asked Monica.

She sniffled. "I don't know. I guess I didn't want you guys to judge me."

Tina held her hand. "Judge you? Honey, you know us better than that. Who are we to judge you?"

"Yeah," Monica chimed in. "Why don't you just start by telling us how this all began?"

Shauna nodded. "Well, in high school he got picked on constantly. I finally got to know him in one of my art classes when were paired up for a project. We made a connection quickly. As months went by, I began to develop feelings for him." She took a deep breath and continued. "The day he asked me to prom, I was surprised. It turned out to be the best night of my life. I lost my virginity and fell in love that same night. He told me he loved me afterwards. I wanted to say it back but all I kept thinking was what would everyone else think? How shallow was that?"

"Shauna, you can't blame yourself for the past," Tina consoled her. "It was years ago. That's not you anymore."

She wiped her last tear away. "Right now I'm not so sure. I'm still hurting him by pushing him away. Part of me can't stop thinking how different my life would be if I had told him how I felt."

"Shauna, you can't do this to yourself. The only thing 'what if' questions will do is drive you crazy. So does this mean you don't want to marry Keith?" asked Monica.

She shook her head. "No, I just have to keep reminding myself that Pete is my past and Keith is my future."

"But, honey, if you have to keep doing that then maybe you should think this over," Tina disagreed. "Make sure this is what you want. Marriage is for life."

Shauna got up slowly. "I know that and that's why I have to make this work. Look at us. A bunch of pathetic women pining over men, we need to get ourselves together."

Tina stood up as well. "You're right. And I think I know how we can do that. Shauna, don't make plans this weekend."

"Why not," she asked with curiosity.

"You have a bachelorette party to attend," Tina winked.

Shauna squealed in excitement, "Oh hell yeah."

Monica and Tina laughed in unison.

As Tina drove up into her driveway that afternoon, she found Bryan sitting on one of the stairs leading to her doorstep. He looked a mess. His eyes looked tired and it looked like he hadn't shaved for days. Once Tina put her car into park, Joshua quickly unbuckled his seatbelt and ran out the car to greet his father. "Hi, daddy," he exclaimed. Bryan's sad face quickly turned into a smile.

Tina rolled her eyes. She was not in a mood for a fight. She got out of the car and stood in front of them. "What are you doing here?" she asked him.

"Why haven't you been answering my calls?"

"I've been busy."

"Too busy to answer your phone, I just wanted to make sure you we're okay."

"I think you should focus on your girlfriend and not me."

He looked dismayed. "Come on, Tina, you're not being fair."

"Are you two fighting again?" asked Joshua in the middle of their argument.

Tina took out her house key from her purse. "No honey, this is a disagreement," she answered opening her front door. "Now you go on inside and get ready for dinner."

"Aw man," he complained before heading on his way.

"Tina, listen to me, I never meant for this to happen," Bryan explained after his son went in. "I don't want this to change things between us."

"Listen I don't want to get into this right now. I have to get dinner ready."

He frowned. "So this is this how it's going to be? What happened to our family nights?"

She shook her head. "We don't need them anymore. We're no longer a family."

"Mommy can I ride my bike for a little while?" interrupted Joshua again.

She waved him away. "Yes, just don't go near the street."

Bryan stood in front of her. "How can you say were no longer a family? Just give me a chance to figure everything out."

She glared at him. "Oh, so now were supposed to just sit here and wait for you? Well sorry, that isn't going to happen."

"Tina I'm stuck."

"Look mommy. One hand!" yelled Joshua.

"That's good baby, just be careful," she yelled behind her but did not look his way. "Bryan, you're not stuck," she continued. "You just don't want to get caught. You're a coward. I'm sorry but you're not the person I fell in love with." He tried to hold her but she moved away. "There's nothing you can do to fix this. You have a new family to take care of. Don't worry about us. We'll be fine."

He looked frustrated. "How can you say that?"

"I'll just find a good man who wants to be with me."

"Tina, I love you. Just the thought of you with someone else breaks my heart in two."

She threw her hands in the air. "Well, whose fault is that? How do you think I feel when you're with her? What do you want me to do, tell you I love you and that everything is going to be okay? Well, I'm sorry but it's not reality. You're going to have a new baby. Joshua and I do not fit into that picture."

"You're wrong, we can make this work."

"No, you're wrong. Nothing you do or say will change things. You no longer have an obligation to us. You're free to do as you please."

He looked hurt. "I can't believe you're saying this."

Her heart ached but it was for the best. There was no way they could be a family with Sharon pregnant. "Look I have to go. It's getting late and Joshua hasn't eaten yet."

She yelled for her son to get into the house. She tried to walk past him but he stopped her. "Tina this not over, I'm not going to lose you both again."

"Bryan—"

He held her face and stared into her eyes. "No," he interrupted. "You two are my life. I won't let you do this." He embraced her. She finally broke down and embraced him in return. He drew her back and gazed into her eyes. Slowly he leaned towards her for a kiss but before their lips could meet, they heard tires screeching loudly to halt.

She wrenched away from his embrace and scanned the road for Joshua. He was close to the road waving frantically at them. "*Joshua!!*" she screamed. Bryan had already sprinted across the driveway to get to his son but it was already too late. A lime green car had hit their son and sped away.

In seconds, Tina was by her son's side pulling him into her arms. He was not moving. Neighbors began to gather around. "Somebody please call 911," she yelled frantically to the crowd. Several people pulled out their cell phones and began dialing. Suddenly Joshua began to squirm a little.

"Josh, don't move," Bryan ordered softly kneeling beside him.

"It hurts, daddy."

Bryan stroked his hair. "I know son. But you have to be strong. The ambulance is on its way."

He moaned then smiled a little. "I'm going to ride in an ambulance... c-cool."

He drifted off for a moment and Tina shook him gently. "Baby, don't close your eyes," she choked. "Y-you have to stay awake for me, okay?"

"But... I'm so ...sleepy," he whispered hoarsely trying to keep his eyes open. "My stomach hurts."

"I-I know baby, but please just keep your eyes open for mommy. E-Everything is g-going to be o-okay," she stumbled with her words unable to control her crying.

"Mommy, I'm sorry I went... into the street."

She stroked his face softly. "It's okay baby, don't talk. I just want you to lie still." He closed his eyes again. She shook him frantically. "Joshua, wake up honey." He did not respond. She began to sob and held him tight. Bryan buried his head onto his son's chest and began to cry as well. Their cries were drowned out moments later by sirens heading their way.

Chapter Thirteen

"I can't believe you talked me into coming here?" Monica complained for the third time as she and Shauna made their way to the front of The Moonlight. They spent an hour in line trying get into the club so she was already annoyed enough.

"Well, there's nothing we could do now," Shauna commented while showing the bouncer her ID. "We're already at the door and were here on a mission." She took hold of her friend's arm as she pushed through a crowd of people.

Monica sucked her teeth, "You're on a mission not me," she grunted as people continued to push by her. Suddenly a bolt of nervousness came upon her. She began to sweat profusely. "Shauna, I don't think I can do this."

Shauna spotted Sean at the bar and pointed at him. "Yes you can. There he is over there. Now go get your man!" she ordered.

When Monica spotted Sean at the bar her heart pounded loudly in her chest. She felt like a teenager all over again anxiously waiting to see her crush. She fell in love with him all over again. Her nervousness became more intense. "Shauna, I really can't do this. What if he ignores me or tells me to go screw myself?"

Shauna held her by the shoulders. "Honey, you won't know until you try."

Monica shook her head. "But don't you think it's wrong that we came here without Tina? Maybe we should do this another time."

"Monica, stop playing games. You know good and damn well Tina wanted us to do this. She couldn't find a babysitter on such short notice. You have to do this."

"I know, I know. I'm just so scared he's not going to want me back."

Shauna held her friend's hands gently. "Then it wasn't meant to be."

Monica nodded and looked towards Sean again, "Alright. Wish me luck."

She wandered over to the bar and sat on the stool closest to him. His back faced her as he poured and mixed drinks. She cleared her throat. "Um, can I have a rum and coke please?" she asked loudly.

Sean paused for moment but didn't turn around. He continued to mix drinks then placed a glass in front of a woman who sat next to her. He gave the woman a sexy smile. "Here's your sex on the beach," he told her.

The woman placed some bills on the bar table then took a cherry from a bowl in front of him. "Damn, you sexy," she drawled as she played with the cherry in her mouth. "My number is on that bill, make sure you use it." He smiled at the woman while she continued to flirt with him. Her heart sank even though it was obvious he was trying to make her jealous.

"Rum and coke please," she repeated loudly interrupting their flirting.

He rolled his eyes in irritation and mixed her drink. He slid it in front of her. "Six dollars," he snapped.

"Sean, I need to talk to you," she began. "There are some things I—"

"The drink is six dollars," he interjected loudly this time.

She retrieved some money from her purse and placed it on the bar. "Can we talk please?"

He glowered at her. "I have nothing to say to you."

"Look, sweetie, *let it go* the dude said he *ain't* interested," stated the woman next to her.

Monica turned and eyed the woman down. She wore a blonde wig but it sat on her head lopsided. The cat suit she wore was plastered on her. The woman was at least a size sixteen but squeezed herself into a size ten. *Damn, bitch can you breathe?* She wanted to ask but remained calm. She was on a mission and only Sean's name was on that list. "Um, this conversation doesn't include you so, please see your way out of it?" Monica warned. She turned back to Sean. "There are some things I want to say to you. Can we talk on your break?"

"Oh, I know your *bougie* ass ain't talking to me like that," the woman bellowed standing up. "What you need to do is walk your desperate ass outta here before I kick it out the door."

Monica stood up as well. She was not in the mood for any bullshit. She took off her earrings and placed them on the counter. "I wish you would *bitch*, I'll beat your ass right here *right* now," she yelled.

"Ladies let's just calm down," Sean interrupted.

The woman came in front of Monica and smacked her gum loudly. She sized her up and down. "Naw, if this bitch thinks she's all that, let her try to whup my ass."

Monica had enough. Without time to think, she lunged at the woman and yanked her wig off. The only thing left after that attack was a cap on her head. Laughter surrounded them quickly. In seconds they were at each other like cats and dogs. She pulled on Monica's hair as Monica grabbed for her throat. The hooting and hollering of 'take it off' from men in the club made her even angrier. Two bouncers finally approached and wrenched them apart. They were both escorted out of the club.

"Monica, what happened?' Shauna huffed running up to her. "One minute I saw you talking to Sean and the next minute you were choking some woman. I tried to get to you but I couldn't move through the crowd. Are you okay?"

Monica ran her fingers through her hair and paused to catch her breath "I-I knew coming here was a b-bad idea," she stammered tearfully. "This is not me. I don't fight random women in clubs and I don't run behind any man."

Shauna gave her a hug. "Well, what do you want to do now?"

She pulled away and headed towards her car disappointedly. "Go home. I'm through. He didn't even want to talk to me."

"Are you sure?"

Monica rubbed her aching shoulder. "I'm not deaf. It's over." Shauna held her friend as they began to walk away.

"*Monica!!*" yelled a male voice behind them. They both turned around to see Sean running towards them.

Monica frowned confused. "What are you doing out here?" she mumbled as he got closer. She was not in the mood for another fight.

"That woman had no business putting her hands on you," he answered. "I just came out here to see if you're okay and to give you these." He handed her earrings to her.

"Um, I'm going to wait in the car," said Shauna.

"I'm embarrassed and pissed but I'm okay," she answered as Shauna walked away.

She flinched as he touched a swollen spot on her face. "You have nothing to be embarrassed about," he told her. "You were defending yourself and you did a good job at that."

She smiled a little. "I have to thank my four older brothers for that." She paused for a moment. "Why did you really come out here? You made it quite clear you didn't want to speak to me."

"Like I said I came out here to make sure you're okay. Just because I don't want to talk to you it doesn't mean I don't still care."

She brightened up a little. "Do you really?"

"Yes, but that doesn't mean I want to be with you either," he added quickly. "I'm sorry Monica but I don't trust you."

"Will you please just let me explain," she pleaded.

"I don't think that's going to help."

"Just give me a chance. Hear me out and whatever you decide, I'll deal with it."

There was a moment of silence. He finally nodded. "Okay, explain."

She exhaled slowly. She did not know where to start. She decided to just speak from the heart. "Sean, when I first met you, I was a wreck. Michael had just broken up with me and my self-esteem was low. I never thought a sexy young man like you would ever be interested in me. I tried to get you out of my mind because of the age difference but you brought passion out of me I never knew existed. The more I got to know you, the deeper my feelings got."

He looked unimpressed with what she was saying. "So what happened then?"

Her eyes began to well up with tears. "When I saw you with Simone I thought you had moved on. I thought you were no longer interested in me. I was devastated."

He frowned. "So you slept with your ex to get back at me?"

"No, no, I had no intentions of sleeping with him. He came over unexpectedly and ended up helping me with the Hutchinson account. I was vulnerable and he said some things I needed to hear and one thing led to another. I didn't mean for this to happen. If I had known the truth about you and Simone, I wouldn't have ever done anything with him."

She waited for him to respond but he remained quiet. "Can you say something please?"

He glared at her. "What do you expect me to say? You never trusted me from the beginning so you never really gave us a chance. You brought nothing but lies into our relationship. You told me you didn't want anything to do with your ex yet still you accepted that bracelet from him. Do you know how stupid I looked in front of him?"

She looked towards the ground. "I know and I'm sorry. I wasn't thinking." She proceeded closer to him and entwined her hands with his. "Baby, please believe me, I'm over him. What happened was a mistake. I want to be with you and only you. I can't eat, I can't sleep, I think about you all the time...," she paused. "Look, what I'm basically telling you is I'm in love with you Sean."

For a moment they stood there eyes locked. Just when she thought she made a break through, she heard Shauna yell out her name behind her. She turned around irritated but her expression quickly changed when she saw Shauna's face. She looked white as a ghost. Monica ran to her and held her by the hands.

"What is it, honey? What happened?" she asked anxiously.

"It's Joshua," she croaked. "We have to get to the hospital."

"Keith, please tell me Josh is going to be alright," said Tina hysterically holding onto his arm. Joshua was taken to Eastside Hospital where Keith worked. The hospital had a reputation of being one of the best in the country. When Joshua was rushed to the emergency room, he had just completed his last surgery for the night. "I can't lose my baby, I just can't. He's all that I have," Tina wept to him.

He pulled her to sit down in the closest chair. "Tina, we will do the best we can. The good news is that he's stabilized."

"So he's going to be okay, right?" inquired Shauna.

Keith shook his head. "Right now, I can't answer that. They are getting him prepped for surgery and—"

"Surgery," Bryan interrupted. "Why the hell does he need surgery? I thought you said he was stable."

"He is but there is some hemorrhaging from his left lung." Keith answered.

"Oh God," Tina cried almost falling to the floor. Bryan tried to hold her but she cringed at his touch. *"Don't touch me!!"* she screamed. "This is your fault. If you didn't come by today, I would be putting my baby to bed right now."

Blood slowly drained from Bryan's face. "Tina, you don't mean that."

She looked him dead in the eye. "Like hell I don't," she stated bluntly. "Just stay the hell away from me."

He held up his hands finally giving up then walked away quietly to the other side of the waiting room. Monica and Shauna both held Tina steady in her chair while her sobs continued. Keith squeezed her shoulder. "Tina, he will be okay. He's in the best hospital in the city and in my care. I promise you he will pull through."

She finally looked up with tears streaming down her face. "Thank you Keith. Please just bring him back to me."

He nodded then left the room quickly. The waiting room remained silent for over an hour. Both Monica and Shauna did their best to help Tina remain calm. After the third hour, Bryan and her friends went to the cafeteria to retrieve some coffee. Tina was happy to be alone. She walked to a window and looked out to see a full moon. A tear slid down her cheek at the thought of her son not living to see another day. "Tina, drink some tea," said her mother softly interrupting her thoughts. "It'll help calm your nerves."

She turned as her mother handed her the hot cup. She took it and reluctantly took a sip. "Thank you for coming, mama."

"Oh hush, he's my grandson. Why wouldn't I be here?"

"I know but you and daddy live miles away."

She gave her a stern look. "Tina, now I don't like you speaking that way. We would do anything for him and you know that. I don't care if we lived in Timbuktu, your daddy and I would be here."

She gave her mother a hug. The last time she saw her parents they didn't leave on good terms. They argued constantly about her relationship with Bryan. She had a great relationship with her parents, but Bryan was the one thing they could not agree on.

"I can't lose him mama," she whispered putting her cup down. "He's my life."

She rubbed her daughter's back. "Baby, it's going to be okay," she consoled her. "The Lord is watching him right now. Our prayers will help him pull through."

Tina tried to be optimistic. "I hope so."

"Honey, Josh is a strong boy. He's a fighter. Do you remember when he first learned to ride a bike?"

Tina laughed a little. "Yeah, he fell so many times."

"And what did he do?"

"He got right back on that bike and rode it until he never fell again."

Her mother chuckled. "He has your stubbornness and Bryan's ambition."

Tina's smile faded. She faced the window again.

"Tina, you can't blame him for this."

"Yes I can," she argued. "Look mama, he's the last thing I want to talk about right now. I just want to focus on Joshua."

She nodded. "I understand that but I just wanted to let you know that your father and I trust your judgment. If you plan on rebuilding a relationship with him again, we'll stand by you."

Tina turned to look at her. She couldn't believe what she was hearing. Her parents were always against her rekindling a relationship with Bryan. "What changed your minds?" she asked surprisingly.

She smiled. "Ever since the three of you've been spending time together, you've changed. You sounded so happy the last time I talked to you on the phone. Baby, you're still in love with him and that's a good thing."

Tina rolled her eyes. "How is it good when he's with someone else?"

"But he loves you."

"And how do you know that?"

She looked across the room at Bryan who paced up and down restlessly. "Trust me, a mother knows. I finally see he's grown up."

Tina sighed. "He has changed in some ways," she agreed. "But things are different. If you knew the rest of the story," she hesitated. "Let's just say, he and I are really over for good this time."

"I don't believe that," she disagreed.

Tina's eyes moistened with tears as she finally faced the truth. "Well, believe it mama. He and I are through. I really wanted to make things work but they can't."

She put her hand on her daughter's shoulder. "Then maybe you should try harder. Nothing is set in stone. You're not the type to give up." Tina turned away as her tears fell. Her mother rubbed her back softly. "Honey, does being with him make you happy? Are there days when you wake up and can't wait to see him? Does he make you laugh when you're sad or make you feel like you're the only one that matters?"

Tina turned around then sniffled. "Mama, even if I told you yes to all those things, it doesn't mean much. Things have changed. Everything is so messed up. I..." Her voice trailed as she saw Keith walk into the waiting room.

She rushed up to him and braced for the worse. She tried reading his face at first but he just looked tired. "Keith, what happened? Did everything go okay? Is he going to be alright?" she asked anxiously. Her heart beat rapidly awaiting for his answer.

He finally broke into smile. "The surgery was a success. He is resting comfortably. You all can see him soon."

The room cheered and Tina began to cry happily. She gave him a big hug. "Thank you," she whispered.

He hugged her in return. "It was my pleasure."

Once she pulled away from Keith, she turned and bumped into Bryan. "Oh sorry," she mumbled instantly moving away. His eyes were also full of tears. She closed her eyes as her tears of joy continued to come through. Moments later she felt his strong arms embrace her. Her mind was telling her to draw away but her heart told her to hold on to him forever. She decided to listen to her heart.

*   *   *

"I would like the baked salmon with steamed vegetables please," said Shauna handing over her menu to the waiter. She took a long sip of her Martini and tried to look interested in the conversation Keith and his mother were having. She hated having dinners with his mother. From the first time she met the woman, she had made it clear that no woman was good enough for her son. When she approached Keith about her remarks, he blew it off.

"She's just looking out for my best interest, she probably didn't even mean anything by it," he told her. Shauna rolled her eyes in distaste. There was no use in arguing with him. He was definitely a mama's boy. His mother was always right and everyone else was always wrong.

Mrs. Anderson was a beautiful fair-skinned black woman. Shauna could see why many men would adore her back in the day. "So Shauna, are you almost done with the preparations for the wedding?" his mother asked interrupting her thoughts.

Shauna put on a fake smile. "Yes, as a matter of fact, I just finished the last touches on my dress."

His mother rolled her eyes in annoyance. "Seriously dear, are you sure you don't want to buy your dress at Antoine's? His work is superb. He's well known all over Europe. It's not too late to change your mind, you know?"

Shauna clenched her fists under the table. "I'm sorry to disappoint you Mrs. Anderson, but my dress is done and I love it. It's unique and simple. It may not be extravagant for you but it's my creation."

The old woman shrugged her shoulders. "I guess if that's what you want. Just don't make it look too…oh what do you young folks call it again… ah yes ghetto. There will be many high society individuals at this wedding. I don't want my son's wedding turning into a circus. We Andersons have a status to maintain."

Shauna glared at her. She wanted to jump across the table and yank the woman's long dark hair that hung on her shoulders. Her light brown eyes stared back at her as if they were provoking her. Shauna opened her mouth to tell her off but Keith cut her off.

"Mother, will you stop worrying. Everything is going to be fine. Shauna has done a great job with all the preparations."

His mother smiled exposing wrinkles around her mouth. She caressed her son's cheek. "I just want to make sure you have the finest wedding possible, honey. My son deserves nothing but the best."

Shauna rolled her eyes again and gulped the last of her Martini. The scene was a little too sickening for her. She decided to escape to the bathroom. She threw her napkin on the table and stood up. "I'm going to the ladies room," she announced. They barely even looked at her. She walked away in a huff not watching where she was going and walked smack dab into someone. "Sorry," she apologized. She looked up and saw Pete. Her heart raced. Seeing him again reminded her of how much she truly missed him.

"P-Pete," she smiled. "What are you doing here?"

He didn't return her smile. "Having dinner," he answered coldly.

"Oh," she answered surprised by his tone. "So…how have you been?"

He suddenly looked past her. "Good. Look I have someone waiting for me. I don't want to be rude so can we do this another time?" he asked impatiently.

Her heart sank. "Um, sure, sorry I took up your time."

He nodded and swiftly walked away from her. Embarrassed, she went on her way to the ladies room but didn't go in. She wanted to see who he was dining with. She peeked through a palm tree that was displayed next to the rest area. Her heart ached as she watched a beautiful young woman sit across from him.

Suddenly she felt sick to her stomach. *How could he move on so quickly?* Suddenly Pete looked towards her. She dashed into the ladies room immediately. She entered one of the stalls and leaned her back against it. She fought back tears as she grabbed for a roll of toilet paper.

Back at the table, Pete sat quietly playing with his food in front of him.

"Hey, what's up with you?" asked the woman in front of him. "Your whole attitude changed ever since you came back to the table."

He did not answer her.

"Hel-lo Pete, I asked you a question. And who was that woman you were talking to?"

He finally looked and gave her a small smile. "No one you need to know lil sis. You just better hurry up and eat so I can kick your butt at the pool table tonight."

She raised an eyebrow. "Hold up, kick my butt? Oh, it's on tonight. By the time I'm done with you, you're going to wish you never said that."

He chuckled, but he was dying inside. He had seen Shauna watching them from afar. She looked hurt. He knew she probably thought he was on a date. He wanted to run to her and tell her the truth, but decided against it. He decided to respect her wishes and leave her alone.

Chapter Fourteen

It was a beautiful day for a wedding. Shauna looked out of her balcony only to find their garden transformed into a wedding extravaganza. Keith's mother had indeed intervened by ordering an ice sculpture, expensive caviar, and an orchestra of violinists. Shauna did not even bother to argue. She just wanted the day to be over with. She had to admit though. Everything looked amazing.

A large tent covered a large area of the garden. Three hundred white chairs were lined up single file ready to be seated by the elite. Each chair had a large light blue bow carefully wrapped around it. An arch surrounded by a floral of white lilies was placed up front where the justice of the peace was to stand. On the other side, tables were set for the reception dinner. Expensive china and sterling silverware were placed in front of each seat. The floral arrangements on each table were shipped from all over the world.

She sighed and turned around to walk back inside. She looked at herself in a full length mirror. Her dress was perfect, the weather was perfect, and the garden was perfect, so why didn't she feel so perfect?

"Shauna, you look like an angel," Tina breathed staring at her in awe.

"You really do," Monica agreed. "Man, that dress looks amazing. Honey, you have talent."

Shauna turned to her friends and grinned. "Thanks. You two don't look bad yourselves. And our make-up is on point, considering we were up until four o'clock this morning. I can't believe you two dragged me to a strip club last night."

Tina laughed as she stood in front of the mirror to touch up her lip gloss. "Joshua's accident pushed your bachelorette party to the side but there was no way we were going to let you get married without your last night of freedom. Besides, you weren't complaining while putting dollar bills in Dark Chocolate's G-string."

Shauna giggled as she put on her pearl earrings. "He was fine, wasn't he?"

"Hell yeah," they agreed in unison and cackled.

"That ass was tight as hell," Monica stated between breaths. "And the front didn't look too bad either. All I can say is Mandingo ain't got nothing on him."

Shauna sat on her bed to catch her breath. "You two are off the chain," she giggled. "But really, thank you for last night. I really needed it. I'm so happy you two are here to share this day with me."

Tina grinned. "We wouldn't want it any other way."

"That's right," Monica confirmed.

Shauna motioned them to sit next to her. They came over and sat on each side. She held both their hands. "After my parents died, I thought that I would never feel the love of a family again. But after meeting you two, I was proven wrong. You both have brought nothing but happiness into my life. I thank God every day for giving me two more sisters to share my life with. I love you both so much."

Teary eyed, they all hugged each other tightly. For a moment they remained silent. Finally, Shauna stood up and walked to her dresser. She came upon her trinket bracelet. It reminded her of her argument with Pete.

"Shauna, are you okay?" asked Monica coming up behind her.

Shauna gave her a quick nod. "I'm fine. I just want to make sure I have everything." She began to think. "Now, let me see, I have something old which is my great grandmother's pearl earrings. I borrowed my sister's bracelet. My garter belt is blue and my wedding dress is new. Well…I guess that's it. All that's left is for me to say my I do and I will be Mrs. Keith Anderson. Is everyone in the wedding party ready?"

"Ready when you are," Tina assured her. "Joshua keeps asking me when he's supposed to give the rings to Keith."

Shauna smiled. "I am so happy he's okay. I was worried he wasn't going to be able to walk in the wedding."

Tina nodded. "Me too but he's been doing great since the surgery and eating like a pig. I never want to go through that again. I'm just happy to have my baby back."

"We all are," Monica piped in. "Did they find that loser yet?"

Tina nodded. The police showed up at the hospital while Joshua was in surgery. Tina identified Alex's car as the one who hit her son. She would never forget what his car looked like. It was the ugliest lime green she had ever seen. "He was arrested a couple of days ago as a matter of fact," she informed her. "Can you believe he's been hiding out at his mama's house? He finally confessed to the whole thing. He told the police he had been drinking. He didn't remember how he got into his car. Anyway he's sitting in a jail cell without bond."

"Man, when it rains it really pours," Monica commented. "Who would've thought that asshole would be back to haunt you like this. Hopefully everything will turn out okay."

Tina gave her an assuring smile. "I have a good feeling it will. I hope he rots in jail."

Shauna placed her veil on top of her head. "I second that. Hey Tina is Bryan here?"

Tina came up behind her to help her pin her veil straight. She shrugged. "I haven't seen him, not that I was looking for him anyway."

Monica made a face towards Shauna and mouthed, *'yeah right.'* Shauna giggled while Tina caught a glimpse of Monica's gesture in the mirror. Tina pointed her finger accusingly at Monica. "Don't you even go there? What about you? Like you weren't you looking for Sean?"

Monica stuck her tongue at her. "No I wasn't. He's not coming. I haven't spoken to him since we talked at the club so I'm accepting the fact that it's over."

Shauna turned and gave her a sympathetic look. "I'm going to be fine," Monica told her confidently before she could comment. "Look, today is your day. I'm not going to let my drama get you down. Let's just focus on you today. "

"Yeah," Tina agreed. "Today is not the day to discuss *our* drama. All you have to do is relax."

Shauna nodded. *Relax*, she repeated to herself. She let out a deep breath as Tina put in her last hair pin. *You can do this*. She began to tremble. Her nerves were starting to get the best of her. She turned towards her friends. "Um, is it okay that I have a few minutes to myself?"

"Honey, are you sure you're okay?" Tina asked.

"I'm fine, I promise."

Monica stood up and headed for the door as Tina followed behind. "Okay, we're going to tell everyone you'll be ready in a few," Monica told her. "If you need us, just give us a holler."

She nodded as they left the room. When the door closed, she went towards her bed and pulled out an envelope from under her pillow. Feldman University was displayed on the front in bold letters. She tore it open slowly. Her heart beat rapidly. Her eyes grew large as she read the first sentence. *We are happy to inform you of your acceptance to Feldman University...* She placed her hand over her mouth as tears of joy formed in her eyes.

She now sat down on her bed contemplating on whether calling Pete was the right thing to do. *What are doing,* she scolded herself. *You're going to walk down the isle in a couple of minutes.* But she just wanted to hear his voice. She picked up the receiver and slowly dialed his number. She had his number memorized ever since he gave her his card. Her heart raced as she waited for him to pick up. Part of her prayed he wouldn't answer.

"Hello?" a woman's voice answered.

Her heart stopped.

"Hello?" the woman repeated.

She hung up the phone with a slam. Her eyes began to fill with tears again but she fought them away. She took out a pen and paper from the drawer next to her and began to write. When she was done she placed the letter in an envelope and put it with other letters to be mailed. She finally realized it was time for her to move on just like he did. She looked in the mirror one last time and freshened up her makeup around her eyes. She placed a bright smile on her face before she lowered her veil. She erased all doubts from her mind and headed downstairs to get ready for her wedding march.

"Who was that on the phone, Charise?" asked Pete as he came through his front door with two bags of groceries.

His sister shrugged. "I have no idea. The person didn't say a word."

Pete frowned as he placed the bags on the counter. *What if that was her,* he wondered. He knew today was Shauna's wedding day and had put it out of his mind until now.

His sister gave him a questioning stare. "Bro, what's up with you? You've been acting weird lately. What's on your mind?" He didn't answer her. She came to him and put her hand on his shoulder. "Pete, you know you can always talk to me."

"I'm in love with a married woman," he told her finally.

She frowned. "Married?" she repeated.

He looked at his watch. "Well, she will be within the next hour."

"Wait a minute, I don't understand."

"I've known Shauna since high school," he began. "We just recently met up with each other again and it's been like a dream come true. I haven't seen her since we graduated. Seeing her again brought back feelings I thought I left in the past but I'm still in love with her."

"Does she feel the same way?"

"She keeps denying it. I know it's wrong but we've kissed. I know we both felt something, but she won't admit it."

"Well, how can you be so positive?" she pressed.

"Trust me, I know. She was the woman I spoke to at the restaurant."

She looked at him impressed. "I remember her. Dang bro, when did you start pulling women like that?"

"Charise," he warned.

"Just kidding," she laughed. "Why did she look so upset after you spoke to her?"

"I think she thought I was on a date with you."

She looked horrified. "Wait a minute. She thought you and I were together? Ewww."

He rolled his eyes. "*Anyway*, why would she look so devastated if she didn't care?"

"Pete, you need to talk to her."

"I can't. I promised her that I would leave it alone. And I'm definitely not going to break up a marriage."

"I know but you may not be too late. You need to stop her from doing something she may regret."

He shook his head and began putting some cans into the cupboard. "It's out of my hands, Charise."

"How can you say that?" she disputed. "If you love her like you say you do then you need to go to her. That probably was her on the phone."

"I doubt it."

"You don't know that."

He ignored her and continued putting away the groceries. She went up to him and stopped him from what he was doing. "Look, you need to tell her she's making a big mistake."

"But I did all that."

"Are you sure or did you back her into corner?"

He remained silent.

"That's what I thought," she concluded. "Go to her Pete. Do it before it's too late."

Tina took a deep breath as she waited for her cue to walk out through the French double doors leading into the garden. When sounds of instrumental music filled the air, she held her bouquet tightly. She turned around to look for Shauna and found her flashing back a smile. She turned back around and began to walk forward. Slowly she came face to face with a large audience. Instantly she scanned the area for Bryan.

And there he was staring at her intently at the end of the third row. She looked to see if Sharon was with him but she wasn't. She sighed in relief. She could not bear to see that woman with him knowing she was carrying his child. While Joshua rested in the hospital after surgery, she and Bryan spent lots of time together talking about how they could make things work. They decided to take things slow for now. He never brought up the subject of Sharon's pregnancy and it seemed like everything was fine again.

She could not tear her eyes off of him. He looked so handsome in his dark navy blue suit. He smiled at her as she got closer. She blushed and smiled in return. She walked to the other side from where the groomsmen stood then watched Monica walk down the isle. She looked towards Michael who gawked at her friend. She hid a smile. He was literally drooling over her. The last person to walk in was Ciara, Shauna's little sister. She was an exact replica of Shauna only younger. The flower girls were adorable as they created a red carpet of rose petals along the ground.

When Joshua began to walk down the isle, her eyes filled with tears. He looked so handsome in his suit. He proudly carried the rings on a white pillow. He grinned, revealing two missing front teeth. Tina giggled as she wiped away her tears. Finally Shauna stood at the doorway accompanied by her brother, Andre. Everyone stood up at their presence.

Shauna's wedding dress shimmered in the sunlight. Two straps hung on her shoulders then crossed in the back. Every lining was filled with sequins. The dress was followed by a long train. As she walked down the isle, her heart pounded loudly in her chest. She kept her smile frozen even though she was scared to death. She held her brother's arm tightly as she proceeded forward. "Are you okay?" he whispered in her ear. She nodded and gave him a faint smile. She stared ahead at Keith who could not tear his eyes off of her. As she got closer she could see tears in his eyes. She suddenly felt guilty for thinking about hurting him. When they finally got to the front, he proudly took her from her brother's arm.

They stood in front of the justice of the peace quietly as everyone else took a seat. "Today I will be joining this man and this woman in holy matrimony," he began. "Marriage is a sacred vow exchanged between a man and woman. When two people truly love each other, no one can tear that love apart. Marriage is hard work but when two people put their heart and soul in it, it will last forever."

He took both their hands and placed them on top of each other. "Shauna Knowles and Keith Anderson, you both stand here today before God stating that you want to spend the rest of your lives together as husband and wife."

Shauna gulped and felt faint. *Rest of our lives?* She glanced at Keith and found him sweating profusely. She herself couldn't stop trembling. She looked forward again and shut her eyes for a moment. All she could picture was Pete standing happily in Keith's place. When she opened her eyes, reality hit her. She was about to make the biggest mistake of her life.

"Wait, I can't do this," she announced out loud.

Keith looked at her confused. "What did you say?"

She turned to face him. "I-I said I can't do this," she repeated pulling her veil off of her face.

"Wait, are you serious?"

She nodded slowly. "Keith, I can't marry you. I'm not ready for this."

He frowned. "What do you mean you're not ready? We've been planning this for almost a year."

She was close to tears. "I know and I'm sorry but this isn't right."

"What do you mean this isn't right?" he repeated frustrated now. "Don't you love me?"

She held his arm. "I do but…look, can we talk in private please." She definitely did not want to explain things to him in front of everyone.

He wrenched his arm away. "But, what do you mean but?" he asked loudly.

She glared at him when she began to hear whispers from the audience. "Look do you really want to talk about this in front of everyone?"

He glared in return. "Hell yeah I do. It's not like you haven't embarrassed me enough anyway."

Tina walked up to the both of them. "Keith, she's right. You two should talk in private."

"Tina, stay out of this," he barked. "This is between me and Shauna."

"Don't you dare talk to her like that," Shauna spat at him. "She has nothing to do with this."

"No, she doesn't," he agreed. "This has everything to do with you. Why the hell are you doing this now?"

She sighed. "Keith, it's time that I be honest with you and myself," she paused. "I love you but I'm not in love with you. I'm in love with someone else."

He began to laugh uncontrollably. "You've got to be kidding me," he told her between breaths. "This has got to be some joke. Am I on television? Where are the cameras?"

She gave him a serious look. "This is not a joke," she assured him.

His smile faded. "You've been cheating on me?"

"It's not like that," she argued. "I swear Keith, it was not my intention to hurt you like this…" her voice trailed as she saw the fire in his eyes. She stared at him now terrified. He looked ready to explode. Both his hands were clenched into fists. She had never seen him so angry before.

"*You're nothing but a dirty whore,*" he growled. "I brought you into my house, treated you like a queen and this is how you repay me? I would never disrespect you like this. If you think I'm going to let you do this, you've got another thing coming."

She bit her lip and looked around her. Some of the guests gave her ghastly looks while others shook their heads. She never felt so dirty in her life. *Did I do the right thing,* she asked herself.

"You don't deserve all this," he continued angrily. "I can't believe I trusted your sorry ass."

"Now hold up," Monica began, but Shauna held her hand up to silence her.

Her fear had suddenly disappeared. Yes, he was upset but that didn't give him the right to disrespect her. She stared at him hard. "Look," she began her voice quavering. "I'm sorry this all came out like this but…" her voice trailed once more as she spotted a dark bruise on the side of his neck. She narrowed her eyes to get a closer look then frowned. It was a hickey. She did a double take. "W-Wait, what the hell is that on your neck?"

His expression quickly changed to a dumbfounded look, "Huh?"

"Did I stutter?" she asked sarcastically. "I said, what the hell is that on your neck?"

He quickly turned his head the other way trying to hide the evidence. "What are you talking about? There's nothing on my neck."

She laughed out loud. "Oh really, I'm not stupid Keith. Either that's a really big mosquito bite or some bitch has been sucking the hell out your neck. How dare you accuse me of cheating when you've been the one cheating all along?"

He came towards her. "Shauna, it's not what you think."

She moved back before he could touch her. "You just called me a whore in front of everyone while you turned out to be the *whore* all along. But wait," she hesitated.

Suddenly everything became clear. When she got home last night she found a note on her pillow. It stated there was a ten car pileup on Highway 6. He was called to the hospital for several emergency surgeries so he'd be there all night.

She shook her head furiously as she came to one conclusion. Slowly she looked out into the audience and searched for Marilyn. Once she spotted her, her blood began to boil. She looked white as a ghost. She turned back to Keith. "I knew it. I knew something was going on between you and her. Did you *fuck* her last night?"

She heard gasps from the audience but she didn't care. He shook his head. "I'm not going to discuss this with you right now."

As soon as she heard his words something clicked inside of her. She nodded calmly. "Okay, I'll take that as a yes." Slowly she dropped her bouquet on the floor and took off her earrings. She quickly handed them to Monica. "Hold this girl," she ordered.

"Shauna what are you doing," Tina hissed at her.

"I'm gonna do what I should've done a long time ago, *whup that bitch's ass*," Shauna answered furiously gathering her dress together.

Both Tina and Monica lunged forward to hold their friend back. Marilyn quickly jumped up from her seat and ran towards the exit. Some people began to laugh while others looked horrified. Her wedding was turning out to be an episode of The Jerry Springer show yet she didn't give a damn at this point.

"Shauna, you need to calm down," Monica insisted. "Honey, this is not the right time. If this had been any other day, I would have been right behind you but he's not worth it."

Shauna was unable to control her emotions anymore. She burst into tears. Monica hugged her tight. Tina quickly announced to everyone the wedding was off. Guests began disappearing but some lagged behind looking for more drama.

"I knew it," Shauna heard Keith's mother say. "I knew that woman wasn't good enough for my son. She is nothing but trash."

"Mother stay out of this," yelled Keith.

Shauna turned around angrily and gave his mother a hard look. "No, let her speak. I've got some things I've been meaning to say to her for a long time."

"No," he told her. "This is between you and me and your infidelities."

She was taken aback. "My infidelities," she gawked. "I can't believe your turning this around on me. I haven't slept with anyone but you. Can you say the same?"

"Now is not the time to dig up skeletons in our closets," he retorted avoiding her question.

"Did you or did you not sleep with her last night?" she interrogated again.

He didn't answer her. He scratched his head and looked the other way.

"You're nothing but a dirty dog," Monica lashed out at him.

He rolled his eyes at Monica. "I know you're not talking. I heard about your little night with my boy, Mike. What are you, an accountant by day and a freak at night? Besides, I'm not the one searching for dates at the playground."

Michael came forward and pulled Keith back. "Yo man, that was so uncalled for. You leave Monica out of this."

Monica gave him a dirty look. "I don't need you to stick up for me," she informed him. "I can take care of myself."

"And so can I," Shauna concurred. "This is my fight and I'm ending it right now." She clenched one hand into a fist as tight as she could at her side. She went up to Keith and gave him a hard look. Instantly, threw the hardest punch at his groin area. Since she was so short, she had a perfect aim. He loudly cried out in pain and he fell to the ground. His body curled up like a newborn baby.

She took off her veil and flung it to the ground. She snatched off her ring and threw it at him. "Have a nice life," she told him with a satisfied smile. She gave her friends a quick hug then ran down the isle out the door. She knew exactly where she was headed yet prayed she wasn't too late.

Chapter Fifteen

Keith had never been so angry in his entire life. *How dare she embarrass me in front of my family and colleagues? And professing her love for another man on our wedding day? What the hell was she thinking?* He did in fact cheat on her a few times, but the other women meant nothing. He was in fact attracted to Marilyn, but nothing more.

When he first met her in medical school, the attraction was evident. They went out and ended up having sex on their first date. The sex was great but he wasn't in love with her. They continued to have a sexual relationship throughout their residency but Keith had made it clear there would be nothing more and she agreed.

After he finished his residency he moved to Los Angles to start a new job and look for a serious relationship. When he first laid eyes on Shauna he had already decided he wanted her as his wife. He was serious about being faithful from the start but then lost control when female interns began throwing themselves at him, he just couldn't resist temptation. Then Marilyn came into the picture again.

Her transfer caught him off guard. She surprised him at lunch and told him she was here to stay. There was fire in her eyes as she spoke of her divorce. She was still beautiful. He began to grow hard as he reminisced of the nights they shared. At that moment he decided to stay clear from her.

The first couple of weeks were fine. He kept his distance as much as possible. The plan finally came to an end when she cornered him in the employee lounge one night. She stopped him abruptly outside the door and made some excuse about needing to talk to him about a patient.

"Keith, it's important. It's about Mrs. Cohen in room 403."

He looked at his watch. "Can't this wait till tomorrow?" he asked hurriedly. "I'm having dinner with Shauna. I don't want to be late."

"This will only take a second," she insisted pulling him back into the lounge. She closed the door and came in front of him. She eyed him seductively.

"Okay, what was so important it couldn't wait till tomorrow?" he asked impatiently.

She responded by pushing him against the wall. She grabbed him by the groin. He frowned and held her back. "Marilyn what the hell—" She stopped his words by a kiss. Her tongue plunged into his mouth with urgency. He held her back again. "What the hell are you doing? Have you lost your mind?"

"I'm just trying to make you feel good again baby," she purred. "Don't act like you don't want me. It's like old times again you know, sneaking around, having sex on hospital beds. We've always had a connection and I don't think that went away. I know you've been dodging me but don't you think we've held out long enough?"

"Marilyn, I'm engaged," he reminded her.

She giggled. "And that makes it even more exciting." She rubbed herself against him. She could feel him get hard. She licked her lips. "Come on," she whined. "I just want a little taste. Please?"

He began to feel hot. He groaned as she took his hand and ran it over her left breast. He sighed. He couldn't help but stare at her large round breasts. "What if someone comes in," he asked finally feeling defeated.

She smiled sexily and ran her finger up and down his chest. "We can go in that broom closet over there. Don't worry, I promise to be very quiet."

He grinned at her then swiftly pulled her into the closet. In seconds they were at each other. He tore her shirt open quickly. His mouth covered her breasts. She moaned as his tongue played with her nipples roughly. His then mouth moved from her breasts to her mouth. He sucked her tongue as his hands traveled towards her backside. Her hands sought for his pants. She unbuckled it and got down on her knees. Eagerly she placed his large dick into her mouth. She sucked him gradually. He moaned repeatedly with pleasure. *Shauna, please forgive me,* he groaned feeling guilty for just a split second. He truly loved his fiancé but he craved sex more.

Keith tightened his grip on the steering wheel while flashbacks of what just happened flooded his mind. He began to get angrier as he remembered all the board members he invited to boost his reputation. His chances of being nominated were ruined. *Great! Now I'm definitely going to be Monday morning's gossip,* he thought furiously. *How could I show myself at work again? What if I get fired?* The hospital had an outstanding reputation. The board would definitely find today's event unacceptable. He slammed his fist down on the steering wheel of his car.

Instantly, he reached over to the glove compartment and yanked it open. A gun was exposed in clear view. He had purchased it six months ago when there was a series of robbery incidents happening late at night in the hospital parking lot. He picked it up, kissed it and placed it back in the compartment. He continued to stare at Shauna's car which was in clear view several yards away.

He knew exactly where she was going. He knew Peter Morris was more than just a friend. He saw the way they looked at each other the night of the party. It was evident that he loved Shauna as well. "She's mine," he stated out loud. Suddenly something clicked in his head. *If I can't be happy, neither will you Mr. Morris*, he muttered. He pressed hard on the gas pedal and followed closely behind making sure he did not lose her car.

Pete could not concentrate on teaching his class that night. He kept looking at his watch and repeating himself from time to time. He began to regret not listening to his sister about stopping the wedding. Part of him wanted to do just that and shake some sense into her but he couldn't face rejection once more.

He sighed as he watched his students work on the class assignment he gave at the beginning of class. He had to get her off his mind. He got up and began to examine his students work. Suddenly a knock on the classroom door interrupted his concentration. He looked towards the door and saw Shauna standing behind it through the window of the door. He did a double take. He thought he was dreaming. He looked again and this time she gestured him to come outside.

He excused himself and anxiously headed towards her. He opened the door only to find her in distress. Her eyes were puffy with black smudges. Tears streamed down her sad face. Immediately his strong arms embraced her. He let her cry for a little bit then drew her away from him.

"Shauna, what are you doing here? What happened? Aren't you supposed to be at your reception?"

She shook her head and sniffled. "I couldn't do it."

"Couldn't do what?"

She gazed into his eyes. "I couldn't marry him, Pete."

"Wait, I don't understand."

She shook her head. "I-I told him that m-marrying him was a big mistake. He went crazy. He even called me whore"

His face turned angry. "Where the hell is that bastard?"

"Who knows," she cried. "But wait, that's not even the best part, I found out he's the one that's been cheating all along."

He was baffled by what he was hearing. "Wait, are you sure?"

She nodded. "Oh yeah, I'm very sure," she confirmed. "He made me feel so ashamed…when h-he's been doing …"

He hugged her again. "I'm sorry you had to find out something like that on your wedding day. No one deserves to be treated that way."

She pulled away from him. "I need to apologize…"

He shook his head. "Shauna—"

She cut him off quickly. "No, I should've been honest with you from the beginning. You gave me so many chances but I kept pushing you away."

"You don't have to do this," he insisted again.

"No, I have to. If I had told you I loved you since high school, who knows how things would've turned out."

He stared at her stunned. "Since high school," he repeated slowly.

She smiled faintly. "Since the first time we made love."

"Wait, are you serious?"

She nodded as her eyes began to water some more. He moved away from her. There was dead silence as he tried to gather his thoughts. "How could you…," his voice trailed. "Why wouldn't you tell me something like that back then?"

"I was scared," she admitted.

"Scared of what? What, you thought I'd hurt you? You know I would never do that. I told you I loved you that night and that meant I wanted to be with you."

"I did know that, but that wasn't why I never told you the truth. I was scared of what other people would think if we became more than friends."

He stared at her for a moment then turned his back towards her. "All these years I've thought about the life I could've had with you and you blew me off because of other people opinions?"

"Yes, and I'm very ashamed of it. For years, I've had to live with that decision and regretted it since."

He turned around. "How can I make sure your not going change your mind about us again? Are you sure you're thinking clearly right now? I'm not some ping pong ball you can bounce in and out your life. I just can't keep letting you play with my heart like this."

She shook her head. "I am thinking clear. I stopped my own wedding today. I told my fiancé in front of everyone that I was in love with you." He closed his eyes for a moment trying to brush away anymore uncertainties. She finally went to him and held him tight. "I know you have doubts and I will do anything to make them go away. I came here today to tell you the truth. Even if you don't want to be with me, that's fine. But I thought you had to know. Just like you told me, it's always been you, Pete. I'm in love with you."

His arms finally wrapped around her. "You don't know how long I've waited for you to say those words."

"It feels good to say it," she laughed softly. "While I was walking down the isle today, all I kept wishing was that it was you waiting there for me instead of Keith."

He caressed her hair. "You had a chance to avoid all this, but you didn't, why?"

"I don't know how else to explain it. I guess I was protecting Keith. I didn't have the heart to hurt another man again. If I had known what I know now..." her voice trailed.

He sighed and kissed her forehead. "I guess some things happen for a reason."

She continued to hold on to him tight. She didn't want anything else to come between them ever again. Suddenly she remembered the other woman from the restaurant and her phone call to him from earlier that day. She pulled away from him. "Look, I know you've met someone. I saw you two together at the restaurant. I don't blame you. I would do the same if the tables were turned. I don't want to make things more complicated for you. Maybe I should go."

She tried to move away from him but he held her close. "Hold on, you have your story twisted. I want to set the record straight. The woman I was with—"

"You don't owe me an explanation," she interjected.

"Is my younger sister, Charise," he continued. "She's home from college for a couple of weeks."

"Oh," she commented relieved. "So you're not with anyone else?"

"I can't think of being with another woman except for you."

"So do you still want me to be a part of your life?"

"Only if you say it one more time."

"Say what?"

"Say you love me."

She grinned. "I love you, Peter Morris, with all my heart, body and soul."

Their lips at last met for an unforgettable kiss. She waited for this moment for so long. She let out a sigh of relief as they pulled away. She placed her head on his chest; being in his arms felt so right. She closed her eyes in anticipation at the thought of making love to him again.

When she opened her eyes again a shadow had caught her eye. She froze. She blinked several times to make sure she was registering what she was seeing. The evening had settled in, so it might've been her eyes playing tricks on her. But unfortunately it wasn't. There stood Keith a distance away looking angry and distraught. The look in his eyes was deadly. Her eyes grew large as she noticed a gun in his hand. It was aimed at Pete.

"*No!!,*" she screamed as a shot rang out. With no time to think, she pushed Pete out of the way and stood in his place. Within seconds she felt a burning sensation in her stomach and her knees buckle from under her. Instantly her body fell to the ground. Pete regained his balance from the push then immediately threw himself on the ground. His eyes grew large when he saw Shauna's body a few feet away. Immediately he crawled towards her. He used his body to shield hers just in case there were more shots. He scanned the area carefully. He saw and heard nothing.

A moment later he yelled for his students to stay inside and call the police. He rolled off her. "Oh God, no!" he stated out loud. Her eyes were closed and there was no response. He quickly felt for a pulse but it was slow. Her white dress was now stained with blood. He ripped off the sleeve of his shirt and applied pressure to her wound. "*Baby, wake up for me, please,*" he shrieked.

His heart pounded as he tried to remain calm. He was in a state of shock. She saved his life. She had taken a bullet for him. He began to cry. He pulled her into his arms carefully and cradled her. "Shauna, listen to me. You're all that I have. I can't lose you again. I need you in my life. Baby you can't do this to me. I love you."

"Mr. Morris is she okay?" asked someone behind him.

"Did someone call 911?" he asked harshly ignoring the question.

"Yes sir," the voice answered.

"Good, now everyone get back into the room and stay there," he yelled.

Shauna moaned softly as she opened her eyes. She felt like she was hit with a bolt of lighting. She was in excruciating pain. "W-what happened?" she whispered.

Pete sighed in relief. "Oh God, I thought I lost you," he murmured happily stroking her hair. "You were shot."

"S-shot?"

"Yes. It came out of nowhere. I don't know—"

"I-It was K-Keith," she interrupted as everything came flooding back to her.

He held her steady. "Wait, are you sure?"

She nodded. "Yes." Her mouth grew dry. It was getting hard for her to speak. "I-I saw him holding the gun…he aimed it at you… I-I never thought he would do something like this…his eyes looked so…" She cried out in pain and began to shiver. She could feel her body get cold.

"Baby, don't speak," he pleaded. "Just hold on. The ambulance is on its way."

She began to cry. Her vision was getting blurry and she began to get scared. She was not ready to die. Just when she thought her life was finally coming together, Keith had taken it all away in just seconds. She reached out and stroked his face. "I-I never meant to h-hurt you...I love y-you," she whispered.

Blood drained from her face. She looked pale. His eyes grew large. "Please don't say that," he told her in an alarming tone. "Don't make it seem like this will be the last time we will see each other. We're going to get married and have lots of children. I can't do this without you."

She shivered. "I-I'm just so cold..." Her voice trailed as she closed her eyes once more.

"Baby, wake up," he pleaded tearfully. He shook her frantically but her body felt limp. He checked her pulse again. This time he could not find one. "*No, no, no,*" he wept as he gathered her tightly into his arms.

By the time Monica got into her car that evening she was exhausted. She couldn't believe her friend had just canceled her own wedding. Shauna was the last person she thought would ever do such a thing. *Now Tina on the other hand is another story,* she chuckled. She giggled as she remembered how Shauna took off her shoes ready to fight. She would've loved to see it happen but she strongly believed a woman should never fight over any man. She wished she had listened to her own advice a couple of weeks ago at the club. The real shocker was Keith turning out to be a dog. It goes to show that dogs come in all types of packages; rich, poor, tall, short, fine and even ugly.

She was very worried about Shauna though. She called her several times but her calls went straight to voicemail. Keith had disappeared quickly after Shauna took off. His groomsmen tried to talk to him but he was fuming. They decided to just let him go to walk off some steam. Her thoughts then wandered towards Sean. She was disappointed that he didn't show up to the wedding. She sighed as she picked up her cell phone. She quickly browsed through her missed calls. His number was not one of them.

She finally decided to just give up. If he wanted nothing to do with her then she had to accept that. Just as she placed her key into the ignition, a knock at her window startled her. It was Michael. She rolled her eyes then rolled her window down impatiently. "Look, I'm not in the mood for you right now. It's been a long day."

He pushed his hands into his pocket. "I'm not going to take up your time. I just wanted to know if you've heard from Shauna."

"No, I haven't. I have to go." She quickly rolled her window back up and started her car.

He knocked on her window again. "Wait, can you please at least let me apologize," he pleaded loudly through her window.

She gripped her steering wheel and frowned at him. "You can't be serious. You don't even know what it means to apologize," she said loudly through the window.

"Look, Keith had no business putting you out like that."

She continued to frown but then rolled down her window. "And you had no business telling him what happened."

"He's my best friend. Besides I never thought he would take it that far."

She sucked her teeth. "Whatever."

"And I know you don't want to hear this but I'm also sorry about how everything that went down between you and what's his name?"

She glared at him. "His name is Sean and I'm sure you're devastated about the whole thing."

"No, really, I acted like an ass."

"That's not the word I would exactly use."

He winced. "Ouch, I guess I deserved that one."

"Yeah, you do," she agreed. "And a whole lot more. I think you better leave before I tell you how I really feel."

"Is that what you really want?"

She gawked at him. "Do you want me to say it in a different language?"

He looked grim. "Why do things have to be like this?"

"Excuse me? Michael because of your big ass ego, I lost someone very special to me. Yes, I was wrong for keeping our *dirty* secret, but I was going to tell him when I was ready. He didn't need to hear the details from you."

"You're right but for what it's worth, I really am sorry."

She looked at him closely and for the first time he actually looked remorseful. "Your apologies won't fix things but if you're *really* sincere about it then I guess I can accept it for now. "

He broke into a smile. She quickly held up a finger. "That doesn't mean that there's a chance for us either," she added quickly.

"I know but maybe…"

"No," she stated firmly. "There are no maybes so don't even think about it. I'm done with the drama Michael. I really mean it."

He held up his hands and laughed. "Alright, right now I'll take anything I can get. So where are you off to?"

"Home and I'm going *alone*."

He grinned then backed away cautiously. "I hear you. I hear you."

She put her car in gear as soon as he was a few yards away. As she drove off, she smiled to herself. It was the first time she ever felt she had control over their nonexistent relationship. She had a gut feeling that he would continue to be a part of her life whether she liked it or not.

As she approached the front door to her apartment she tiredly fumbled for her keys in her purse. When she opened her door, she was taken aback. The inside of her home displayed an oasis of lit candles. Slowly she walked in and placed her purse on the table. Her heart raced.

What the hell?! "Hello?" she called out. "Is someone here?"

There was no answer. *Who would do this?* She then thought of Michael and got angry. He told her he had no other set of keys to her place, what if he lied? *Does he not understand the concept of no*, she thought irritably. She shook her head and opened her bedroom door swiftly ready to put him in his place but what she saw stopped her in her tracks.

Red rose petals showered her bed while vanilla scented candles were displayed throughout her room. She had never seen anything so beautiful. "Do you like it?" a deep voice asked behind her.

She gasped and turned around quickly. "S-Sean?" she said surprisingly. He was wearing a suit. He looked so handsome. His face was clean shaven which made him look a lot older. She wanted to jump his bones but held her composure. "W-What are you doing here?"

He took her hand. "I'm here to see you. I hope it's okay that I did all this."

She shook her head. "I don't understand…I thought you didn't want anything to do with me."

He came close. "Well, I've been thinking about us a lot lately. I thought about my life without you and realized something would always be missing." He took the hand he held and brought it to his lips. "I can't get you out of my mind."

She was baffled. "I-I don't know what to say?"

He stroked her face gently. "I don't want you to say anything. Just know that you're a hard woman to get rid of."

She smiled as her eyes filled with tears. "I'm so sorry."

"I don't want to hear anymore apologies. There's other things I'd rather do right now."

She swallowed hard. "Other things?" she repeated, "Like what?"

"Like this." He moved towards her for a slow kiss. His tongue plunged into her mouth searching for her hers. He found it waiting and wanting. Her arms went around his neck. She missed him terribly. This time she was not going to let him go. He drew her back softly. "I want too see you naked," he ordered. There was hunger in his eyes.

"What?" she giggled surprised. She really loved this side of him, intriguing and exciting.

"I want to see all of you *right now*."

She smiled. She was no longer going to play the shy role. If he wanted her naked, then that was exactly what she was going to do. Get naked. Gradually she began to disrobe until she resembled the day she was born.

"You're so beautiful...," he commented. He beckoned her to come to him. "Come, I have another surprise for you." She went to him and he picked her up into his arms.

She giggled as she held him for support. "Where are we going?"

He began to walk with her in his arms. "I'm going to show you what love is supposed to feel like."

"Love?"

He smiled. "Yes, love."

"Are you saying that you love me?" she pressed.

"Do you want to hear me say it?"

"Only if you mean it."

He didn't respond. Instead he took her into her bathroom where a bubble bath awaited her. Her tub was also surrounded by lit candles. There was also a large bowl of chocolate covered strawberries placed on the side. She licked her lips in anticipation. "I can't believe you did all this. How did you even get in here?"

He laid her into the tub gently. The water was warm and exhilarating. "Just relax and let me take care of you," he told her. "Oh and by the way, I love you, Monica." After that he bathed her delicately. It was the most sensual experience she ever encountered. She and Michael had fun in the bedroom but what she was experiencing right then was real, it was real love.

He took one strawberry and teased her lips with it. When he placed it in her mouth, she sucked on it tenderly. He placed his mouth on the other end and did the same until their lips met for a kiss. She smiled as they pulled away. It was the sweetest kiss she ever received. She pulled him towards her. "I want to make love to you," she announced softly. "I want to show you so many things."

He smiled at her. "And I'm ready to learn, but I'm not done with you just yet." He finally pulled her to stand and he dried every inch of her; at times used his tongue in various places. "Now it's time for a massage."

"A massage," she laughed. "Boy, are you trying to torture me? Where did you learn to be so romantic?"

He chuckled. "I listen well."

He carried her into her bedroom and laid her onto the bed. He poured some massage oil on her and began to massage her gently. As he stroked her breasts, a moan escaped from her lips. He planted butterfly kisses from her breasts to her stomach taunting her with each touch.

"Do you want me?" he asked finally.

"Y-yes," she gasped and he pulled her legs apart.

He kissed her inner thigh. He stroked her wetness slowly with his finger. "Who does this belong to?"

"You baby…only you," she smiled.

His finger was replaced with his tongue. He explored her hungrily. Making sure he tasted every inch of her. She came immediately. Once he was done with her she pushed him off playfully and positioned herself on top. "I think it's time for me to take over. I want to taste you too."

She unbuttoned his shirt exposing his rippled chest she missed so much. Her tongue played with his nipple teasingly while her hand stroked his groin area through his pants. He was already hard. She ran her tongue over his bellybutton while she unzipped his pants exposing his shaft. She made circular motions with her finger on the top of the head. His breathing became rampant as she licked his tip slowly.

"And who does this belong to?" she asked a moment later.

It was his turn to smile. "You baby…you and only you," he answered.

She tasted him over and over until he exploded. She only let him relax for a few minutes. She began to rub his shaft softly. He grew hard again quick. She resumed her position on top then slowly put all of him inside of her. "Oh God…Monica are you trying to kill me," he cried out as she began to ride him steadily.

She placed his hands on her behind. "No," she murmured. "I'm just trying to love you. Trust me this will be a *first time* you will never forget."

They spent the rest of the night making love exploring each others fantasies and desires. She introduced him to some positions she read about in her favorite book *101 Ways to Achieve an Orgasm*. He caught on quickly. They even invented a new one of their own. When they were finally exhausted, they laid in each others arms. "Happy Belated Birthday," he whispered into her ear as she fell asleep with a smile.

He watched her sleep for a while before dozing off. The night had been amazing for him. It all started with Michael coming through the night club a couple of nights ago.

"What the hell do you want?" Sean barked at him.

"Look man, I'm not here to fight. I came to apologize," Michael answered.

Sean frowned. "Don't expect me to return the favor."

He slid a key across the bar table. "Go to her," he told him. "She is an amazing woman and loves you man. I let her slip her away. Don't make the same mistake I did."

And that was it. He thought long and hard about the whole thing. There was no doubt he was in love with Monica. The thought of losing her to another man again would be painful. He finally decided if Michael can be the bigger man and admit his mistakes than he can be the better man by forgiving her.

"This day was something else," Bryan commented as his car pulled up into Tina's driveway. He had offered her a ride home after everyone left. Monica was supposed to take her home since they rode together. Before she could decline his offer, Monica gladly accepted his invitation for her.

"Yeah," she agreed. "I hope Shauna's okay. I've been calling her cell but she's not picking up."

"She'll be fine. She probably wants to be alone. But Keith, I've never seen him so angry before. He sped off in his car like a madman."

Tina looked concerned. "I know. I just hope he doesn't do anything stupid."

"He's a smart man."

She raised an eyebrow, "So smart that he cheated on my best friend."

"Well she wasn't so innocent either."

She sucked her teeth. "Neither are you so don't even go there." She opened her door and let her son out. She turned to face him. "Thanks for the ride."

"No problem."

"Do you want to come inside for coffee or tea?"

He smiled. "I was hoping you would say that. As a matter of fact, I've been meaning to talk to you."

Once inside he insisted on putting Joshua to bed. She took that time to take a quick shower and change into more comfortable clothing. When she came back down surprisingly he had prepared her a cup of tea and was seated patiently at the kitchen table. She sat down across from him. "Well, this is nice," she smiled. She took a sip. "I see you remember how I like my tea," she commented as she placed her cup down.

"Yep, a little bit of cream and lots of sugar."

She nodded. There was an uncomfortable silence. "I never got the chance to tell you how amazing looked today," he said speaking up.

She smiled. "Thank you, you didn't look so bad yourself."

There was another awkward pause.

"Bryan."

"Tina."

They smiled in unison. "You first," he gestured.

She took a deep breath. "Bryan, I love you," she began.

"I love you too," he returned.

She paused. "And after you left, I never thought those words would ever come out my mouth again. I was so hurt but I can't hide how I feel any longer. I really want to be with you but I can't sit here and share you with another woman. I understand she's pregnant but that doesn't mean you're obligated to her. Your only obligation is to that baby."

"You're right," he agreed.

She raised her eyebrow. "Wait, you're agreeing with me?"

"Sharon and I are no longer together," he finally admitted.

She shook her head confused. "B-But...the baby?"

"There is no baby," he stated irritably. "She lied about the pregnancy."

"Are you serious? How did you find out?"

He looked tense. "I caught her bragging about it to one of her girlfriends on the phone. I couldn't believe she would go so far as to lie to me about something like this."

"I can believe it." At that moment she wanted to stand on top of the table and chant *"Ding dong, the bitch is gone"*. He looked dismayed. "Look I'm sorry you had to find out that way," she told him honestly.

He shook his head. "I can't believe I couldn't see through her lies. I wasted my time with her when I should've been here with you and Joshua."

She placed her hands over his. "Bryan, she lied to you. This is not your fault."

He took her hand and kissed its palm. He gazed into her eyes. "When I was with Sharon, I didn't feel complete. Something was always missing. My heart wasn't there. You took it the day we met and never gave it back."

She looked the other way as she fought the tears that stung in her eyes. "Bryan, I've been hurt so much."

"Please look at me," he persuaded. She sighed then turned to look at him. At that moment he stood up then knelt in front of her. "Baby, I know I put you through so much. If only I could turn back time, but I can't. Give us a chance to become a real family again. You and Joshua are my heart. I was confused at one time but not anymore. What I'm really saying is..." he paused then smiled. "Baby, I want to play Truth or Dare with you every night and wake up every morning with you in my arms."

She burst out laughing as her tears came. She wiped them away then stroked his cheek lovingly. "You got me at Truth or Dare."

"Daddy, are you ready?" interrupted Joshua loudly behind her.

She turned around. "Honey, what are you doing out of bed? It's past your bed time."

Joshua came next to his father and giggled. He hid something behind his back. She raised an eyebrow. "What are you two up to?"

Bryan nodded towards his son. "Yes Josh, right on time." Joshua finally pulled out what he was hiding behind his back. It was a velvet ring box. Tina's mouth dropped open. Joshua opened it and stated proudly. "Mommy, will you marry us?"

She covered her mouth with her hands. She began to cry. "I-I can't b-believe this. I-I don't know what to say."

Bryan smiled at her. "Baby, there is no doubt in my mind that I want to spend the rest of my life with you. Please say yes."

"Yeah," Joshua agreed. "Say yes, mommy."

She laughed. "*Yes!!*"

"Yes?" Bryan repeated.

"Yes, yes, yes," she confirmed. She squealed as he picked her up from her seat and swung her around enthusiastically. He then took the ring out of the box and placed it on her ring finger. She admired it happily. She finally had her man and the family she always dreamed of. She pulled him for a long passionate kiss.

"Ewww," Joshua stated loudly as he watched them.

They both pulled away and laughed. Her prayers were finally answered.

Epilogue

Nine months later...

"Alright this is it. I see the head. Just one more push and we'll be welcoming your baby into the world," Dr. Sneed informed Tina as he placed his gloves on. "Now all you have to do is relax and take deep breaths. In a few minutes this will be all over."

Tina held the two iron bars located at the sides of her hospital bed tightly. *Relax??* She thought annoyed. *Easy for you to say, you're not lying here with your legs spread open with a baby's head sticking out.* She was sweating profusely. She had never been so exhausted in her life. She had been pushing for almost a half hour. Joshua's birth was a breeze compared to this.

She began having cramps since yesterday but figured it was just false contractions since she was not due for another month. The next morning she found blood in her underwear. Bryan panicked and quickly rushed her to the hospital. He was a mess. He yelled at everyone and told them they were being incompetent because she wasn't placed in a room fast enough. He was driving her insane. The first couple of hours were very painful. She was in labor for twenty-four hours. For some reason she was dilating slowly.

"I can't do this," she cried. "I'm so tired."

"Come on baby, just one more push and it's over," Bryan coaxed her as he wiped some sweat off her forehead. He held her hand tight. "You can do it, honey. I love you, baby." It was déjà vu all over again but only this time the circumstances were different. She was giving birth again but only this time it was Bryan by her side not Monica. She found out about her pregnancy two weeks after he proposed. Her pregnancy was perfect. He treated her like a queen. Not letting her do anything strenuous and making late night stops for butter pecan ice cream and pickles.

"Bryan, please," she groaned. "I feel like I'm going to pass out."

He kissed her forehead again. "You're a strong woman, Tina. You can do anything you want once you put your mind to it. You got me didn't you?"

She laughed a little. "You're too much," she huffed.

"Okay, Mrs. Henderson. It's now or never," Dr. Sneed told her. "Now when I tell you to push, you need to give it all you've got."

She nodded and braced herself. "I know the drill."

"Alright, *push*," her doctor yelled.

With all her might she pushed and squealed at the same time. A moment later her cries were drowned out by another. Suddenly there were cheers in the room. "It's a girl," her doctor laughed. "Gorgeous with a head full of hair," he exclaimed.

The next couple of seconds was a blur to her. All she caught was a glimpse of her baby as Dr. Sneed held her up for a moment. Tina laughed tearfully. She was beautiful. Dr. Sneed asked Bryan if he wanted to cut the umbilical cord. She closed her eyes and rested for a moment. Her baby continued to cry. "Is she okay?" she asked Bryan as she felt his hands entwine with hers.

He stroked her hair. "She's fine," he assured her.

"Ten fingers and ten toes," she asked again.

"Ten fingers and ten toes."

"I want to hold her. What are they doing to her?"

"They're making sure everything is okay."

"Are you still okay with her name?" she asked a moment later.

"Of course, it's a beautiful name. Shauna Simone Henderson."

She nodded then closed her eyes to rest once more. She missed her friend terribly. Giving her baby Shauna's name meant so much to her. Suddenly, her baby's crying stopped and beeping sounds were heard. She heard a nurse shout, "Code blue, code blue." Tina's eyes fluttered open. Two other nurses burst into her room quickly with a machine following behind them. Her heart dropped. She grabbed onto Bryan whose expression changed to alarm. "What the hell is happening," she cried.

"S-she's..." his voice trailed.

With all her strength, she used the railings to pull herself up slowly. She burst into tears as she watched her tiny little baby lay limp on the table. There were so many people around her. An oxygen mask was placed on her tiny nose and mouth. Her eyes were closed. "Oh God, no," she sobbed trying to get out of bed.

"Baby no," Bryan yelled pulling her back. He held her tight as she continued to bawl on his chest.

"She's stable," someone shouted a moment later.

"Get her to the NICU stat," Dr. Sneed bellowed. Tina turned around as her baby was placed in an incubator and rushed out of her room.

"Doctor, what's wrong with her?" she asked as the room began to empty.

He came towards them, his face looked grim. "She was in distress while coming through the birth canal," he answered. He made his way towards the door. "I can't tell you anymore until we do further testing. I'm sorry but I will be back as soon as I can."

"Is she going to be okay?" Bryan asked before he could leave. Tina glanced at him as he hugged her shoulders. There was a look of fear in his eyes.

Dr. Sneed turned around and gave them a faint smile. "Don't worry she's in good hands," he told them confidently. "We'll give her the best care possible."

"It's my fault," Tina declared tearfully as he left out the door. "I should've gone straight to the hospital when I first felt those cramps."

He pulled her to look at him and wiped her tears away. "Don't you dare say that," he scolded her. "She will be okay. She's strong just like her mother."

She sniffled. "And what if she's not? What if we lose her? I can't go through something like this again," she cried. "I just can't."

Bryan didn't know what else to say. She was right. They had no idea what the outcome would be until tests were run. All he could do right then was hold his wife and pray that everything will be all right.

*   *   *

Pete sat in his car parked in front of Mimi's café contemplating whether or not he should enter. It was almost a year ago when everyone heard the horrifying news that Shauna had been shot. She died at the scene before the ambulance could get to her. It was shocking to everyone that Keith turned out to be the gunman. The police found him dead in his home that same night with a single gunshot to the head. His death was ruled to be a suicide. The news of Shauna's death devastated both Monica and Tina but Pete took it the hardest. The woman he loved died in his arms. Everyday he blamed himself for her death.

Her funeral was filled with family and friends. The service was held at the same church her parents attended and buried at the same cemetery. He remained numb throughout the sermon. After the service family and friends were asked to come forward and pay their last respects. His heart raced as he walked towards the front. Tears became visible as he caught a glimpse of her beautiful face. He stared at her as she lay in her casket. She looked so peaceful. It took all his strength to keep himself from holding her. He finally laid a trinket bracelet he had brought for her on top of her folded hands. Tears began to fall quickly.

It was at the cemetery where he finally broke down. As her casket was being lowered into the ground, he began to sob and call out her name. Three men had to hold him down to keep from reaching out for her. After her funeral, he left town. He went to visit his parents in Seattle and stayed there for a while. He returned home a month later feeling more at ease.

As he walked into his house, he found his table surrounded with mail. He had asked a friend to check on his house periodically and retrieve his mail while he was away. Most were bills and junk mail but one particular envelope caught his eye. Shauna's name was displayed on the front. His hands began to tremble as he picked it up. He swallowed hard and tore it open.

My Dearest Pete,

It's my wedding day and it should be the happiest day of my life but it's not. I can't stop thinking about you. I can't lie to you anymore. You asked me before how I felt about you and I told you I had no feelings, but I lied. I love you, Pete. I love you so much it hurts. Seeing you again has made me so happy in so many ways yet sad in another. I want to be with you but can't. I've made a commitment to a man who loves me with all his heart and I have to stand by it. I can't break another man's heart again.

I want you to know that I never forgot the night we made love. I never wanted you to stay away from me, but it's just that being around you is so hard. Please try to understand and don't hate me. I know it feels like I'm leaving you again but I'm not. My love for you will never change. You will forever be in my heart

I Love You
Always and forever
Shauna.

P.S. I got accepted to Feldman University. I got in because you believed in me. Thank you

He held that same letter in his hand almost a year later as he walked into the café. He needed closure and being able to go to the café again was the first step. His heart pounded wildly as he stood in front of the counter. He was already having flashbacks of her smiles and laughter. "Um, sir can I help you? I have other customers waiting."

He finally looked at the girl behind the counter. "Sorry," he mumbled. "I'll have a coffee please."

He abruptly decided it was all too much for him. He placed money on the counter as the clerk handed him his coffee. As he turned to leave, he couldn't help but glance quickly at the booth where he first saw her again. His breath caught in his throat as he stared at who he saw before him. For a moment he couldn't move. It was her, sitting at their booth alive and as beautiful as the day he first laid eyes on her.

She was staring out the window. Her face looked sad. He closed his eyes for a moment figuring his eyes were playing tricks on him. He opened them slowly. She was still there. There were distinct changes in her features but he didn't care. The love of his life had come back to him. All he wanted to do is hold her in his arms forever. He headed towards her table in a slow pace. He let out a deep breath as he approached her booth.

"Shauna…baby is that you? Have you come back to me?"

The woman looked towards him. She was taken aback for a moment but then her expression turned into remorse when she saw a hopeful look in his eyes. "I'm sorry," she answered. "I'm not Shauna. I'm her sister Ciara.

*   *   *

"Baby, if you don't get out of bed right now, you're going to be late for work," Sean murmured while caressing Monica's back softly.

Monica turned towards him and smiled. "Can't we just stay in this bed forever? I wish you can come with me."

He smiled in return. "Now you know I'm off for two weeks."

She pouted and snuggled closer to him. "I know, I know. I'm going to miss you so much. I wish you didn't have to go to Jersey."

He grinned then stroked her cheek tenderly. "I'm going to miss you too but you know I have to go see my family. There are some things I have to deal with." He had received a disturbing phone call from his mother last week. His youngest brother is acting out in school and causing fights. She was at her wits end. She wanted him to come home and knock some sense into him and that was what he promised to do.

Monica nodded. "I understand. You do what you need to do baby. Just hurry up and come back. I'll be right here keeping our bed warm."

He grinned then kissed her lightly on her lips. "Now that's an offer I can't refuse. Hopefully the next time I go back there, I'll have you by my side."

Suddenly she felt a twinge of nervousness. She pushed it to the side quickly. "Sounds like a plan to me."

"Good because I've been telling her all about you. She can't wait to meet you."

She flashed him a smile then hastily got out of bed. "Can't wait to meet her too," she told him but doubted his mother would be actually excited to see her. The age difference would definitely make her think otherwise.

He caught her arm softly. "Hey, where are you going?" he murmured huskily.

She laughed. "Just like you said. If I don't get ready, I'm going to be late. With this new position I really need to set an example."

It was now his turn to pout. "I guess you're right," he sighed. "I'll just stay here in this comfortable bed all alone."

She crawled back into bed and slipped out of her nightgown. "Okay, what can I get for fifteen minutes?"

He cupped her breast softly, "How about something quick and hard?"

She moved close. She gazed into his eyes lovingly. "Hmmm, exactly what I was thinking," she giggled as he grabbed her and placed her under him.

When she arrived to work Jackie informed her that the owner of the company had stopped by. She winced. *Maybe I shouldn't have had that last quickie,* she thought. She nodded and walked into her new office formerly known as Mr. Dykes's office.

A couple of months ago rumors began circulating that he was laundering money from clients. Within a month he had purchased a new Mercedes Benz, took a trip to Hawaii and lavished on expensive restaurants. He was finally investigated and within one week he kindly stepped down from his position. When Monica was offered the position she was ecstatic. Her hard work had finally paid off. The new income was more than she ever expected but it came with a price. Last month at a monthly meeting, she was informed the company would have to begin downsizing its employees. It was the last thing she wanted to be involved in yet had no choice.

She exhaled loudly as she closed the door to her office quietly. "Having a bad morning?" a deep voice asked behind her.

She gasped and turned around quickly. There in her chair staring back at her, was a dark-skinned handsome man. His dark chocolate skin was smooth and his face clean shaven. He sized her up slowly. Monica could feel his eyes on every part of her body. She blushed profusely. "Excuse me, how did you get in here?" she asked finally.

"I asked you a question first."

His voice gave her goose bumps. "Who are you?"

"You still haven't answered my question."

She marched towards her desk and reached for her phone. "I'm calling security."

He chuckled. She frowned at his response. "Oh, so you think this is funny?"

He shrugged. "A little"

She began dialing. "Well you won't think it's funny once security drags you out of here."

He placed his hand on top of her dialing finger. "I don't think they will be of assistance."

She stared at his large hand that completely covered hers, "And why not?"

"They're not allowed to throw out the owner of the company."

Her jaw dropped. Her cheeks burned again. "Oh, um, I'm sorry. Mr. uh."

"Meyers," he supplied with a raised eyebrow. "So are you still going to call security?"

She quickly pulled her hand away then placed the receiver back in its place. "Um, no sir, I apologize. I didn't know...I mean I've never seen you in person before."

"Well, no time better than the present."

"Yes, I agree," she smiled embarrassed. She always assumed the owners were Caucasian. She was now able to take a closer look at him. His hair was neatly trimmed and his dark brown eyes were captivating. She quickly cleared her throat and placed her briefcase on her desk. Her palms began to sweat. "So, what brings you to the office Mr. Meyers?"

"Do you normally come into the office this late?" he countered looking at his watch.

She quickly shook her head. "Uh, no sir, I was stuck in traffic," she lied.

"I see." He pulled out an envelope from the inside of his jacket. "I came by to give you the list."

"The list?"

"Were you not present at the meeting?"

"Yes. I was there."

"Then I'm sure you were told about the downsizing process. It will begin this week."

"This week?" she repeated suddenly short of breath. "Wow, it's that time already?"

"Yes," he answered. He finally stood up and came around her desk. He stood in front of her. He was over six feet tall. His expensive cologne engulfed her nostrils. He was so close. He handed her the list. "Is this going to be a problem?" he asked firmly.

She took the envelope from his hand. She took a step back. "No sir. I will work on it right away."

He smiled finally revealing pearly white teeth. "Good. I'm glad we have an understanding. There will be a lot of changes in the upcoming weeks. My partner and I will now be present at every monthly meeting. I will also be spending more time around the office to make sure things run smoothly. After that money laundering scandal, I need to make sure nothing like that will ever happen again." He held out his hand. "It was a pleasure meeting you, Ms. Stevens."

She shook his hand. It was strong and firm. "Same here."

She walked him to the door then let out a deep sigh of relief as she closed it behind him. She stared at the envelope in her hand as she walked back to her desk. Slowly she tore it open. She skimmed through the names praying she didn't know anyone on there. Her breath caught in her throat as she read the last name on the page. Her hand began to tremble as she read it once more.

Sean Madison